Paper Dolls

Robert Tucker

Paper Dolls is the memoir of a girl who becomes a young woman in a passionate search for an enduring friendship. Deprived of her older sister, Tess Vanderveer, by the neediness of an Irish ghetto girl, Dove Delaney, Gwen also loses the friendship of Millie Dietz, the beautiful daughter of the family cook and housekeeper, Gladys. Gwen's mother takes Millie away to the high society of New York City in the 1930s and 1940s.

Born into the wealth and privilege of a Boston Beacon Hill family, Gwen and Tess Vanderveer do not value their status. Their father ignores them and their mother doesn't care to raise them. She leaves that chore to Gladys Dietz, who becomes a second mother to Gwen

Upon Tess's graduation from Wellesley College, she and her secret childhood friend from the Irish ghetto disappear.

World War II begins and changes Gwen's life with her marriage to Eddie Gebhardt, a reckless fighter pilot.

Years later, during the 1950s, Gwen learns what became of her rebel sister and how that affects her own conflicts as a wife and mother and as a journalist seeking personal meaning and truth through the social and cultural changes of feminism.

"We need to be long-distance runners to make a real social revolution. And you can't be a long-distance runner unless you have some inner strength. . . . Many institutions are designed to undermine our self-authority in order to get us to obey their authority."
(Gloria Steinem)

Table pf Contents

Prologue

Even though we lived in the same three-story house, my sister Tess and I rarely saw our parents. They seemed to exist elsewhere like strangers coming and going among the large rooms and vast hallways. Or through a window, we would see them depart to lead their separate lives, Mother in a chauffeured limousine, and father in his sporty red roadster.

My sister's defense was to react with sarcasm. She called them phantoms. We were among the objects they owned and ignored, like the paintings and sculptures and vases and wood and brocade furniture, and mother's jewelry, furs, and gowns. We were obligatory decorations that attested to our parents' status in their privileged *de rigeur* social circle. Mother's fixation on dressing us with fashionable wardrobes reflected her own impeccable taste.

Chapter 1
The Thief

What I most resented about Dove Delany was that she stole my sister from me. I became aware that this was happening when Tess was thirteen and I had just turned ten. I would have to say that Dove's parents had misnamed her. Glowing pink skin and snapping blue eyes gave her a natural beauty that I found disconcerting.

She wasn't anything at all like a soft gentle dove, quite the opposite, more like a dark falcon, to my way of thinking. People were prey to her. When I was around her, I always felt like she was sizing me up for her next meal. Even though she didn't have bird's claws and her chewed fingernails were stubby and dirty, I imagined she could swoop down and lift me off clutched in her darting hands and drop me in the Atlantic Ocean whose waves pounded our shore less than a mile away.

She had a quick mind and was fast about everything she did. She could even run faster than Tess, who could outrun most boys our age.

I was never sure how they became friends in the first place, because Tess and I weren't supposed to associate with "the riff raff" down the hill, as our mother called them. But since she almost never paid attention to us, we mingled anyway. Tess said "Mother didn't tell us we couldn't mingle. So we're not associating. We're mingling."

Although I didn't understand the difference, Tess explained that associating meant going to parties, like Mother did. Mingling meant doing things with friends of our own choosing.

Tess and I sympathized with children less-privileged than we, meaning they came from poor families. We didn't think of ourselves as being rich and privileged, but our parents were, which benefited us. We lived in a free-standing Greek-style mansion on Pinckney Street in Beacon Hill, a Boston suburb. Of course, they did things rich parents do. They made us wear expensive clothes and attend social affairs like rich kids did, even if we didn't care for them.

Tess's haughty strawberry-blonde halo towered over me by three inches. Her long legs and arms and slender torso gave her a naturally athletic body as opposed to my childhood chunkiness. I thought it unfair that she had inherited our mother's perfectly etched nose and imperious wide brown eyes. I had brown eyes and thick dark brows, but my expression was friendly and accommodating, not imperious.

I tended to look more like our father, whose tall, powerful physique dominated any room he entered. Tess's athletic ability came from him. Although my facial features were a soft gentle version of his craggy blonde Dutch origin, I didn't match the poster image of a cute, rosy-cheeked Dutch girl wearing a blue frock and wooden shoes and carrying a basket of tulips.

I felt fearful the first time Tess and I sneaked out of the house and ventured down from Beacon Hill onto the narrow cobbled streets of the Roxbury ghetto. Our housekeeper nanny, Gladys Dietz, would have stopped us had she known what we were doing, but we gave her the slip.

Many of the Irish men and women worked in our father's Tipton Textile Mills. From his and mother's disparaging remarks about its poverty, breeding, drinking, brawling, gambling, corruption, and gang violence, Roxbury was to be shunned and avoided.

Tess refused to hold my hand and I had to race to keep up with her as she walked quickly along, dodging freight and fruit and vegetable-laden trucks, past red and brown brick row houses, and storefronts, and avoiding men smoking and lounging at the open doors of saloons leaking the sour vapor of beer into the streets.

We might never have gone to where Dove Delaney lived had we not accidentally met her in a public park at the base of Beacon Hill. She was

5

sitting alone on one of the park swings and watched us walking toward the playground area. Her shabby dress and scuffed high-top shoes conveyed she was one of the poor kids. Tess sat on the swing next to her and framed her with an unwavering sidewise glance to let the tough-looking girl with the mean expression know she was not intimidated.

Although I wanted to swing, I remained standing away from them in case their unspoken antagonism suddenly erupted into a fight. They were about the same size and age, thirteen. I had never seen my older sister fight anyone, except a boy once who pulled her pigtail and she gave him a bloody nose. I had also noticed how combative and aggressive she was playing field hockey at a private college preparatory school for girls where I was also a student.

The strange girl spoke, "You live up on the hill, don't cha?"

"Yeah," said Tess.

"Thought so. You wearin' fancy clothes and all that."

"Doesn't matter."

"I've got two dresses," said Dove. "This one ain't my best."

"I don't care about dresses," said Tess lightly.

"Why? How many you got?"

"It doesn't matter," said Tess. "I don't care about them. You live around here?"

"Roxbury. Betcha don't dare come there."

"Why not? It's a free country."

"You could get the snot beat outta you, Miss Fancy Pants."

"No one's gonna beat the snot outta me."

"Not free. I can't come up the hill and walk around your neighborhood."

"Says who?" Tess retorted.

"I tried once and some high class dame told me to get my ass back to where I belonged."

"What did you do," asked Tess, "try to steal something?"

6

"Nothin'. That's all you think about us Irish down here, that we want to steal yer shit."

"Well, did you?"

"I wanted to snatch her purse, but there was a policeman standin' nearby."

"You should go anywhere you want," said Tess adamantly.

"That's what you think. We ain't the same, girly."

"If you call me girly or miss fancy pants again, I'll punch you in the mouth."

"Oh, tough Jane, 're ya."

"What's a Jane?" asked Tess.

"A Jane's a girl. Street talk."

"Okay, big deal. My name's Tess. What's yours?"

"Dove Delaney. My brother's the leader of the Delaney gang."

"He has a gang named after him?"

"Yeah."

"That must make him famous."

"He's famous where we live."

"Maybe I can come by and see you sometime," said Tess. "Like I said. It's a free country."

"Not likely."

"Why not?"

"It's a tough neighborhood."

"Doesn't scare me," said Tess. "Just tell me how to find your house."

Dove smirked. "Don't have a house."

"Where do you live?"

"A flat."

"Okay then, a flat."

"If you come and see me, can I come and see you and not told to scat like some alley cat?" Dove demanded.

"Yeah, I can meet you and bring you to the house. Only we have to do it when my mother's not there."

"Why's that? She don't like Irish? A lot of people don't."

"She won't let us bring friends to the house," said Tess.

Dove's feral grin unnerved me. I sensed she could get us into trouble. She shoved a foot against the ground and put her swing in motion. Tess immediately copied her and within a minute, they were pumping themselves into high swooping arcs, legs straight and feet pointed at the leafy treetops as though they would be catapulted into flight.

On another day, Tess finally found the formidable side street teeming with children, playing hopscotch, skipping rope, shooting marbles, shouting at each other like girls did on our playground at school. Only here, boys mixed in with the girls and their voices were louder.

Three girls Dove's age gathered around us and demanded to know, "Who is she?"

"My new friend, Tess," Dove crowed.

"Tess what?"

"Vanderveer," said Tess.

"You ain't Irish."

"No, I'm Dutch."

"She lives on the hill," said Dove with a smirk of superiority. I saw her smirk a lot when she was with Tess. The smirk was her mask.

"So, what's a high hat like her doin' here?" A girl with sullen eyes and a flinty face asked.

"She wants to see where I live," said Dove boastfully.

"You mean she's lookin' down her nose at us. Hoi Poloi Jane is all she is."

"She gonna stake you so you don't have to work in no can house, Delaney? That's where yer gonna be in a couple years," a voice taunted.

8

"Shut yer rotten mouth, Flynn," Dove stepped up to the tall older girl with ratty dark hair. "That's all you got ahead fer you, you and yer boobs."

"She take you to see her house?" asked another, this one with sprung red curls and teasing blue eyes.

Dove looked at Tess for an answer.

"She gets to come to my house," said Tess.

"Bet it's a grand house," said the third girl whose features looked slightly misshapen like someone's hand had pushed them in.

They all wore the same kind of tawdry dresses and shoes like Dove and gazed enviously at Tess's clothes.

"You live in one a them mansions. I seen them once," said the first girl.

Tess shrugged as though where she lived wasn't important.

"Wanna play Kerbs?" Dove asked.

"Kerbs?"

"Yeah," Dove snatched the soccer ball the first girl was holding and kicked it out onto the open street, dashed to pick it up, leaped to the other side, turned, and hurled the ball. As it bounced off the opposite curb, she retrieved it at the middle of the street, and threw it again for extra points.

"Come on, Tess," she shouted. "You can be on my team."

A few children stared at me once, then, when I didn't say anything, went back to their games. Standing alone against a dirty brick tenement wall, I was ignored as though I wasn't even there. No one invited me to come and play hopscotch or skip rope. I was good at both at my school. So I just watched the circus activities going on before me, especially the cheering camaraderie between my sister and Dove Delaney. Despite insults and accusations of cheating from boys across the street on the other curb, they were unbeatable.

When they were finally done, Dove tossed the ball to the boys. As she and Tess walked over to me, Dove asked, "You got jack for ice cream?"

9

"Jack?"

"Money. You hang around with me and you'll learn to talk Irish."

Tess reached into her coat pocket. She always carried money. "Where do they sell ice cream?"

"Corner store. You can see my house first."

"Where is it?"

"Yer lookin' at it." Dove led her to the door of one of the wall to wall row houses. "Ma and Dah ain't home. I ain't the oldest, but I have to look out for my little brothers and sisters. My older sister, Keira, works with 'em at the mill. That's where I have to go in a couple years."

"What's a can house? That girl, Flynn, said you can work in a can house."

"A brothel, a whore house where prostitutes live."

"What's that?"

"Where men pay to do it to girls."

"Do it?"

"You sure don't know much for a high hat. That thing between yer legs where you piss, men stick their dick in there, or they want you to suck 'em off." The corners of her eyes crinkled at Tess's blank expression. "You know, like a lollipop." Her tongue flicked out in a lascivious swipe across her upper lip.

"Who told you this?"

"Colum, my big brother. He's sixteen. He knows everything. That's why he's a gang leader."

"Show me your house," said Tess, wanting to change the subject I could see was distasteful to her.

As Dove pushed open the front door, I followed closely behind Tess into a dank, dark kitchen with a coal-burning stove and a living room furnished with a worn, sagging couch, a stuffed armchair, and three wooden side chairs.

"Ma and me keep it up nice. Bedrooms upstairs is just bedrooms. Ain't nothin' to brag about. We have to share beds. Ma cooks on Sundays after church when she ain't workin'. What church you go to?"

"Emmanuel."

"That's Episcopalian. You know yer goin' to hell, 'cause you ain't Catholic."

"I'm a good person. I'm not going to hell. I don't believe in it."

"Then you don't stand a chance to make it to heaven."

"I don't believe in heaven either," said Tess.

Dove's eyes widened. "You're nuts. You're crazy. You don't believe in heaven, yer goin' to hell."

"Nope, they aren't real places. They only exist in your mind."

"I've seen pictures," Dove retorted. "They're real. I go to St. Josephs, so I ain't goin' to hell."

"Good for you. I saw your house. Let's go buy ice cream." Tess nearly stumbled over me as she turned to leave.

Just casually walking along the street, hoping to catch Dove by surprise, Tess suddenly bolted into a sprint, but she couldn't out-distance her new friend. Moments later, laughing fiendishly, Dove caught up to her and passed her, which angered Tess in a good-humored way.

They seemed to be a perfect match for one another, both rakish daredevils, nothing ladylike about them. Although Tess projected an arrogant elegant beauty, Dove encouraged and brought out her worst habits. She had never spit on the sidewalk until she saw Dove do it.

The first time, Dove gave her a competitive sidewise glance, expecting Tess to follow her example. And, of course, Tess did. Unaccustomed to spitting, her effort amounted to no more than a weak dribble from the side of her lips, which sent Dove into paroxysms of laughter. "You have to work up a gob," she screeched. Then she showed Tess how to hack and work up a gob. This while we were on our way to buy ice cream cones.

She approved Tess's second effort with a punch to her shoulder. Except for Dove, I had never seen girls punch shoulders like the Irish boys. Spitting was the early indication of Dove's influence and control over my sister.

I had to run to keep up with them to the drug store soda fountain three blocks away. I thought they were trying to lose me, especially when they turned a corner and I couldn't see where they went. When I reached the corner, they were gone. To my relief, at the end of the block, I came to the drug store and saw them inside at the counter through the front window. Wiping at tears with the back of my hand, I pushed open the door and entered.

Mingled aromas of tobacco, medicines, and sweet confections wafted from stacked shelves behind the counter. Tess and Dove were ordering their ice cream cone flavors from the middle-aged clerk dipping a metal scoop into a small rectangular freezer with the top removed. Elbow deep, he cocked his semi-bald head back over his shoulder and asked, "One or two?"

"Two, chocolate," Dove responded, taking the initiative to order first.

The clerk's gray mustache twitched back and forth as he handed the hard-packed cone to Dove with a brown-eyed twinkle. "There ye go." He turned to Tess. "And what about you lass?"

"A double strawberry."

"Double strawberry, just like yer hair." He turned back to the horizontal freezer, grabbed a wafer cone, rinsed the scoop in a bowl of water, then jammed it down into the next tub of ice cream.

"I want vanilla," I spoke up, as the clerk presented Tess with her selection.

"Lick it fast around the edges," instructed Dove. "It's already melting."

"You paying for her?" the clerk nodded at me and toweled off the scoop with a corner of his stained white apron.

Tess barely paused as her pink tongue took rapid swipes of her ice cream which reminded me of the image Dove had described to us about the can house. "Yeah."

I received my ice cream cone with both hands like it was a holy grail. I gingerly licked the tangy sweet strawberry crown, not wanting to risk any of it toppling off onto the dirty linoleum floor.

Dove paid the clerk fifteen cents for the three cones and we marched out.

As we left the drugstore and continued along the street, Dove suddenly said, "Uh-oh, just ignore them manky micks. The big one is my brother, Colum. He used to be a fine thing, but he got his nose broke in a fight. Says it makes girls want him even more."

I could see where the broken nose gave Colum's ruddy Celtic features a fierce debonair countenance. Slouched like rumpled thugs smoking cigarettes in a pool hall doorway, his two friends were thin and sallow by comparison, as though attached to him for social sustenance.

As we approached, Colum whistled at the distinct difference between Tess's and Dove's clothes. I was half-hidden walking behind them. "Look what the cat dragged in. Where'd you find the strays?"

"Beacon Hill. Tess is my new friend."

"Little far from home, ain't they?"

"Don't matter. She's my friend. She come down the hill to see me special."

"What about the chiseler?"

"Little sister. She just tags along."

"So, they adopt you or somethin'? You goin' home with 'em?" asked Colum with a sneer.

"No, I'm showin' 'em how to go back so they don't get lost and run in to the likes of you."

"How come you're eatin' ice cream cones and me and my pals ain't got any?"

13

"My friend."

"She paid?"

"I ain't givin' you a lick," said Dove.

Colum's head motioned his buddies to step over in front of us and block our way. "Well, maybe you want to get yer pretty little friends home, she should buy us an ice cream."

"Stop actin' the maggot, Colum. Yer blockin' the road."

"It's okay," said Tess, reaching into her coat pocket. She handed Callum three nickels.

"I like yer friend, little sister. She's smarter 'n you and better lookin'. Too bad she ain't as old as me. I got somethin' she like to lick."

"Shut yer dirty rotten mouth," Dove shouted.

Laughing, Colum and his pals circumvented us and ran down the street back in the direction of the drug store.

"It's getting late," said Tess. "We need to get home or Gladys will call the police. She must know by now we're gone."

"She your ma?"

"No, our cook and housekeeper. And she's our nanny."

Dove burst out laughing. "You have a cook and housekeeper? How much you pay her? I'll come and cook and keep house fer you. I'll be yer nanny. I do it here for free."

"I'll have you over sometime when my mother's gone."

Dove asked. "You know how to get back?"

"I can figure it out," said Tess.

"You want, I can walk you to the hill. What street you live on?"

"Pinckney."

"Which mansion is yours?"

"Third one on the right as you go up the hill."

"Gettin' dark soon," said Dove. "You don't wanna be down here after dark."

"You don't have to protect me," said Tess.

"Hey, yer my friend. What're friends for?"

Walking quickly along the ghetto streets, they glanced at one another in an unspoken competition of licking their ice cream cones to see who would finish first.

I, on the other hand, took my time and actually enjoyed mine, even though some of the ice cream dripped down the side of the wafer cone onto my sleeve.

At the bottom of Beacon Hill, we stopped and Dove asked Tess, "When we gonna see each other again?"

"After school tomorrow. We can meet at the park."

"You gonna show up?"

"I always do what I say I'm going to do," Tess snapped.

"Just codding ya. It's a good thing, 'cause I always do what I say I'm gonna do." Dove spit into the palm of her right hand and held it out.

To my disgust, Tess spit into the palm of her right hand and met Dove's hand with a wet smeary smack and a single hearty shake. She didn't wipe her hand off on her coat afterwards either.

Dove turned with a triumphant grin and sauntered away into the tenements.

Chapter 2

Scavenger

Tess started up the hill ahead of me. Whether walking or running, I was always out of breath chasing after her. Even though she waited for me to catch up, wherever we went, she willfully left me behind as an unspoken message of her dominance. My chest heaving to take in air, I arrived moments later. Her gladiator eyes looked at me, not with scorn but sympathy that made me feel diminished. Then we walked on.

As we approached the pretentious mansion we called our house, the stark difference between where we lived and Dove Delaney's neighborhood registered in my mind. At the time, given my lack of maturity, I didn't know whether to feel grateful or ashamed.

In retrospect, considering what ultimately happened between them, I wondered if Tess's friendship with Dove was a compensation for guilt over her station in life with privileges that she never appreciated.

We walked around the driveway to the servant's entrance because Tess said she didn't like to pound the brass knocker at the front door and have to wait for Gladys or one of the two servants to answer.

Harmon and Ivo Nevens were usually prompt and I had no complaints. They were always formal and overly polite to Tess and me. They didn't relate to us but acted like surrogate automatons for our parents. If they weren't asked to do something, we avoided them and they avoided us. We were just part of their job. Us and them. Them and us.

When Gladys, our German cook and housekeeper opened the door, she immediately scolded us. "*Gott im himmel*, I was sick to death *mit* worry about you two. If you're going to run off, at least tell me where. Where did you go?"

"Roxbury," said Tess. "I have a new friend."

16

"*Danke* be to *Gott* your *mutter* zu *haus nicht.*"

"You won't tell her," said Tess.

"Nein, nein, she blame me and den I lose my job."

"We don't want you to go," I said. "We love you, Gladys."

"I love you like *meine* own *Tochter*. Now, *komen sie* in quickly, *schnell, schnell.*"

If mother and father required our presence at the dinner table, wearing white gloves and tuxedo tails, Harmon and Ivo waited on us. They were both intense-eyed Dutchmen with slick black hair, straight noses, and trim jaws that seemed to have sprung from the same mold. They weren't twins but could not be mistaken for being brothers. Tess and I never bothered to ask. Sometimes, we heard them talking in Dutch to our father.

We knew that on their days off, they liked to go fishing from a pier at Boston harbor. Tess and I had seen them carrying fishing poles and a large bucket as they trudged down the hill. They always came back with the bucket filled with smelly fish that Gladys cleaned and cooked.

We also knew they liked to go swimming during the summer and would take the trolley to the beach. Tess once asked if we could go with them, but they said our parents would have to grant permission. When we asked Mother, she said no. "Harmon and Ivo are entitled to a day to themselves without you tagging along. Besides, I'm not comfortable with you going to the beach without your father. The ocean is too dangerous for you anyway."

"But he never goes to the beach to swim," said Tess. "He just likes to sail his boat."

"It's called a yacht, dear, not a boat."

"A yacht then." On rare occasions, Father would take Tess and me on his yacht out into the bay, but never beyond into the ocean. He said the waves and currents were too rough. We had to wear yellow life jackets and just sit on the bench. We weren't big enough or strong enough to help with the rigging and he wouldn't let us steer. Tess complained that "sailing is boring when we can't do anything but sit and watch the seagulls."

"I will speak with your father," said Mother, "but he has the final word."

A week went by and we thought Mother had forgotten about us, but the final word was "No," without any further explanation.

Our parents' other employee was George Oswell. The gray uniformed English chauffeur drove us to and brought us home from school. I wondered why he wore black calf-skin leather gloves, polished riding boots and jodhpurs. Driving a Rolls Royce limousine was nothing like riding a horse. Polite and mannerly, he spoke in a formal clipped way like he was biting off words as they scuttled out from under his gray mustache, and he ended almost every sentence with the word "what?"

"So how are you young ladies this morning? You're both looking chipper." We didn't know why he complimented us. We wore the same uniform every day, tan skirt, dark blue sweater over a white blouse, red and white striped tie, and dark blue knee socks. "Ready for another bracing day of exercising your brains, what?"

His formality irritated Tess. She thought he was pretentious, but other than a tight smirk, she never let on. I just thought he was comical, bowing as he held the door open for us, as though we were royalty. He felt compelled to fill the silence while he drove and shared the news of the day he had read in the morning paper, as though we could understand what he was talking about, mostly politics and finance and what foreign powers were doing. They were topics he shared when driving our Father and probably figured that because we were his children, we would be interested too. Nothing could have been farther from the truth. But we listened politely while he chattered on "what?"

He walked with a slight limp he told us was from a war wound. He had been a British officer during the First World War. He also smoked cigarettes while waiting for us to come out of the school. Tess told me smoking cigarettes was a habit British officers had. The odor of smoke clinging to his uniform made my eyes water.

He and Harmon and Ivo lived in servants' quarters further down the hall from Gladys's apartment. Their daily lives were regulated to the needs and requirements of our Mother and Father, which were quite different.

Because of Mother's sleeping habits and morning routine, she and Father rarely saw each other until dinnertime and often not at all for several days because of demands at the mill and Mother's social agenda. To us, they lead different lives.

She would rise at mid-morning and Gladys would bring her breakfast of juice, coffee, fresh fruit, a soft-boiled egg and toast. Gladys would give her one hour to enjoy her "morning repast" as she called it, then return to the room to remove the breakfast tray.

Mother would see to her "toilette" as she called it, which included Gladys running a hot bath for her and leaving her to soak in privacy for another hour.

Mother used to have a personal maid who ran her bath and helped her dress but had dismissed her when the maid became pregnant. Mother had then decided she didn't need an attendant, since she spent most of her time living at her New York apartment where she had a French cook and housekeeper, a servant and a chauffeur.

Since he slept in a different bedroom than Mother, so as not to disturb her, Father would rise early, eat a quick breakfast of eggs, and rolls and sausage, and have George drive him to the mill. George would return for Tess and me and drop us off at school. He would be at Mother's beck and call for the rest of the day and often into the evening. On such occasions, Father would drive his silver Jaguar Roadster to work and

Gladys would come for us on the trolley at the end of the daily school session.

Tess and I preferred riding the trolley to being chauffeured in the limousine. We could actually talk to Gladys about our teachers and other girls in our classes. With George, we couldn't get a word in edgewise. Since we were a captive audience, he preferred to pontificate. Other than the servants, Harmon and Ivo, he didn't appear to have any friends. But our parents didn't give him much time to himself, except an occasional day off. He never told us where he went and Tess and I didn't think we should pry. I felt a little sorry for him until we learned from Gladys he met with old British Army chums at a pub in town.

Our Mother's married name, Astrid Vanderveer, was listed in the New York social register as a true member of high society with wealth and an appropriate and acceptable family history.

She spent her days in New York shopping for the latest fashions, going to luncheons and playing bridge with a select circle of women, attending the theater or an opera, late night dining in the finest restaurants where Father occasionally joined her, and living at their lavish beach home at Newport for the summer social calendar.

We had never been interested in Father's world and what went on at the mill until Dove came into our lives. Her description of the work her parents performed gave us a new perspective, particularly Tess, who actively sought opportunities to justify her resistance to Mother and Father and how we lived.

Dove came to our house to escape from the squalid conditions of the tenements. After seeing the large white porcelain bathtub Tess and I shared, she wanted to take a bath almost every time she came to visit. Tess filled the voluminous claw-foot porcelain tub with hot soapy water. We watched her soak in the rising steam and listened to her chatter about her dreams and wishes.

"Someday, I'll have a bathroom and a tub like this. I'll take a bath every day with bubbles and I'll smell sweet and clean."

She would always use the toilet when she arrived and before she left to go home. She would flush several times.

"And I won't have to shit in a pot no more."

After she finished, dirt and soot rimmed the tub. Tess didn't want Gladys to see it, so she told Dove she had to clean it herself. Dove hummed a tune and enthusiastically scrubbed away the evidence.

Another time, I saw a crazy look in Dove's eyes and she said our house was like a dream world to her. She even tried on some of Tess's clothes and wore a dress home with her old one rolled up and tucked under her arm.

"When Mah caught me wearin' it, she thought I stole it," said Dove. "I told her no, that a friend gave it to me. She didn't believe me and screamed that she didn't raise me to be a thief. I told her I wasn't no thief," Dove related.

Mah raised her hand about to slap me. "Tell me the truth. Where did you get that dress?"

"I told you a friend gave it to me."

"Friend? What kind 'a friend has the money to give you a nice dress like that? It must be worth ten dollars. You workin' fer a pimp? You a can girl now?"

"Is that all you ken ever think of me? I ain't a low life. I ain't no whore."

"Who is yer friend?"

"Her name's Tess Vanderveer. Lives on Beacon Hill."

"Beacon Hill? What th' hell you doin' up there? You broke in and stole that dress, didn't you?"

"She asked me to her house. She's my friend."

"Vanderveer – Is that the same Vanderveer who owns the mill?"

"I don't know. She didn't say nothin' 'bout her dah."

21

"How'd you get to know her anway?"

"She come up to me in the park. We started the gab. We was just havin' craic is all."

On a Sunday morning, she unexpectedly showed up at the servants' entrance. Gladys admitted her and told her to wait in the kitchen. She called us to come down from upstairs.

"Aren't you supposed to be in church," asked Tess.

"Didn't feel like it. Priest bores me stiff," said Dove. "All the stuff he says puts me to sleep."

"Does that mean you're going to hell?" Tess laughed.

"Not me. Not a chance. Just don't gi' me no more dresses," said Dove. "I can't take 'em home. She'll be like to kill me or take the dress away and sell it on the street. She tells me I need to stop goin' to school and work in the mill soon. Don't want to," her shrieking wail prickled my skin. "Don't want to become like them. They look like they goin' die any day. Life has gone out of 'em. Look like death. Dah drinks away half what he earns at the pub. Mah hates 'im fer it. She don't get to drink, 'cept takes a whiskey to calm her shakes and help her sleep.

"They come home coughin' up gobs from the dust and their bodies shakin' like they got the palsy after workin' sixteen hours every day in the weavin' room. Mah is a weaver and Dah's an inspector. Been at it fer years, but still, all they get paid is thirteen dollars a week. Can hardly feed our family on thirteen dollars a week, even when it's both of 'em bringin' home thirteen dollars. The mill is hell," she said. "Workin' there, yer in hell without even dyin' first."

We were sitting on the floor in Tess's room watching Dove sketch drawings of us, and our dresses and shoes taken from the closet, and objects on the window ledge. When I looked at the drawings of Tess and me, the likeness surprised me. She was actually quite good and she had never had drawing lessons.

After Dove's tirade, Tess wanted to see the mill for herself. She asked George to drive her and Dove out there. He said, "I think we should ask your father first. He may not appreciate you coming there without permission and I don't need a tongue lashing."

"We don't have to go inside," said Tess. "I just want to see what it looks like."

"I can tell ye what it looks like and I even been inside it," said Dove. "Never want to go back. Never."

"You get to ride in a limousine," said Tess.

Dove's eyes narrowed. "You tryin' to trick me into goin'?"

"You know we have a limousine. You've seen it parked out in the courtyard."

"I didn't think you rode in it."

"We go to school in it. Our chauffeur drives. You ever been in one?" Tess needled her.

"You know I ain't. When would that ever happen?"

"It can happen as soon as I get permission. I just have to ask George to take us out there," said Tess. "But it has to be on a non-school day."

George told our Father that Tess and I had expressed an interest in seeing the mill and had requested that he drive us. When Father asked us why, Tess had given the excuse she was writing about the textile industry mills for a school history project. I found the subject just as interesting as she did, but for a different reason that later influenced me as a writer.

Tess did not resist my demand to go along. Although she and Dove raced ahead, George waited for me to catch up.

The deep sea-blue gloss of the limousine stunned Dove. Tess had to nudge her along to the door held open by George. Dove gulped and gingerly climbed inside after Tess and slid across the tan leather seat. The luxury of the Rolls Royce Phantom that we took for granted overwhelmed her. The purr of the engine and soft cushioned ride on the large tires created the sensation of floating along the streets and roads bordered by pastel-colored row houses and brown brick buildings lined up like sentinels watching us pass.

Black and gray smoke belched from the Tipton Mill stacks and invaded the sky. The four story brown brick factory occupied several hundred yards of the Charles riverbank.

An armed guard waved us through the iron gate integrated with the burnished copper letter 'T' like a coat-of-arms. George parked at the front entrance and held the passenger door open for us.

When Dove didn't follow us, George looked in and asked, "Miss, are you coming?"

With a stubborn pout, she slouched down in the seat. "I'll stay here," she insisted. "I don't want to go in. I've seen it before."

"You said you wanted to see it," said Tess.

"I just wanted to ride in the limousine. You said you wanted to see it."

"Never mind." Tess looked at George. "She can wait for us."

He closed the car door and escorted us into the building. A steady mechanical roar reverberated behind the walls. George raised a gloved hand to a second guard, who pointed to adjacent stairs leading to the upper floors. We walked down a long hall and stopped at a door with a gold letter stenciled sign on the glass that read Andreas Vanderveer, President.

A slender, severely dressed woman with dark hair pulled back into a tight bun to accentuate her high, wide forehead and accusing eyes, rose from her desk to greet us, but Father entered from his inner office with another man wearing a leather apron, a floor supervisor, who gave us a nod and hurried out.

Other than occasional sailing rides on his yacht, our visit to the mill was the first time he seemed to take a genuine interest in us, likely because we took an interest in him. I think he would have preferred that at least one of us had been a boy. He could have taught a son how to sail and play polo and socialize with other sons born into wealth and privilege.

24

He could have brought him into the family business, whereas Tess and I were meant to become wives of men like himself.

He motioned us to come into his office where an expansive window allowed us to look down over the factory floor. What caught my eye were shuttles shooting back and forth across the beds of hundreds of looms like darting fish weaving thread into cloth.

"So that's what a mill looks like. Impressive isn't it?" he said.

Tess and I nodded.

Most of the workers were women. From her reading research, Tess told me that women originally had come from farms to work in the mills, but because of low pay, long grueling hours, and being treated like prisoners, they would leave and Irish immigrants replaced them, needing the jobs to survive, and enduring the same conditions.

"Over there on the right you can see workers bringing up cotton fiber from the basement," Father directed our attention. "When the cotton bales are brought in, they're broken up and pickers clean twigs and dirt from the cotton. We do that down there because the dust can cause a fire. The next machines with the metal teeth card and stretch the cotton into ropes that are spooled on those spinning frames onto bobbins. The yarn is made into balls that go to all those looms you see in the weave room. That's where the cloth is made. Amazing, isn't it?"

Again, we nodded in unison.

"Any questions?"

I feared asking about the working conditions Dove had mentioned might anger him and Tess just shook her head. But I was curious about several young girls who kept dodging in and out from under the looms. I worked up the nerve to ask, "What are those girls doing?"

"They're called scavengers. They pick up the cotton scraps that fall under the loom. The cotton is still good and can be reused."

I noticed that the weavers had their hair tied back with bandanas, to avoid getting caught in a loom. "The force could break someone's neck," said Father. They also had cotton stuffed into their ears.

"I'd take you down on the floor, but it's too dangerous with all those moving parts and the noise is deafening." The sound vibrated against the glass.

After a few minutes, he said, "Have you seen enough? I have work to do."

Tess nodded. "Thank you." She touched my arm. "It's time to go."

We moved to the door and heard Father say behind us, "Thank you for bringing them, George."

"My pleasure. Have a nice day, sir."

I didn't know how driving us there could be a pleasure for him, but I didn't worry about it. I just wondered if we'd get Dove out of the limousine. She acted like she wanted to live in there.

As we got into the limousine, Dove asked Tess, "So, you gonna go work there?" and laughed.

"You're right," said Tess. "You don't want to work there."

"What was it like?"

"Loud. You said you've been there."

"I was for one week, as a scavenger. I had to work under the machines picking up cotton that fell off. If I wasn't quick enough and didn't get out in time, the machine could crush me. They had four and five and six year old kids doing that. I said I quit. The boss told me I could be a piecer instead, since I was eight at the time. I told 'im no and never went back, even though Dah beat the hell outta me with his belt. He and Ma said I had to make money to help buy food. Colum worked at a warehouse and drove a delivery truck. They told me if I didn't work at the mill, I had to go work at the fish cannery. I tried, but they didn't have any jobs fer me. Just as well, it stank to high heaven. So I look after my kid brother and little sister. They said if I don't pull my weight, they'll kick me out." Her sly expression did not escape Tess. "Then I'll have to come live with you permanent."

Chapter 3

Envy

I had always been jealous of Dove Delaney, because she monopolized Tess and excluded me, which hurt my feelings. I was rescued from my loneliness when Gladys Dietz, our German cook and housekeeper, brought her daughter, Millie, to live with us.

Gladys's husband, Ekkehardt, was a ship mechanic in the merchant marines and was gone for months at a time on freighters bound for foreign lands. She said being married to him was almost like not having a husband at all. When he was home for short periods, he stayed at a rough boarding house for merchant seamen at the wharf. Mother and Father wouldn't allow him to stay at our house when he was in port. As much as Gladys hated having to pay "conjugal visits" to the boarding house, she said she was being "a dutiful wife."

From time to time, she would take their daughter, Millie, from a foster home and paid room and board for her to see her father.

Gladys's generous smile, buxom body, and thick strong arms ensnared Tess and me with warm hugs, which we sought often, since our mother never hugged us. She only presented her face for a peck on the cheek and occasionally touched us at arms' length as her manner of embrace, as though we might contaminate her with some kind of disease. With Gladys, I buried my nose in her white apron and inhaled the aromas of freshly baked bread and savory seasonings embedded in her clothes.

She did housework with a steady clumping energy. Errant wisps of brown hair escaped from under her bandana as she moved through the rooms on sturdy, low-heeled shoes.

One day, I overheard the conversation Gladys had with my mother about letting her daughter, Millie, come and live with us.

"She's my only child," said Gladys, "and she's separated from seeing me and my husband. It would be a kindness for her to come and stay with me. She and Gwen could be friends."

"You are hired help, Gladys," said Mother, "and you do a good job. But to suggest your daughter can be a friend of my daughter is inconceivable."

"I don't mean to impose," said Gladys, "I'm just thinking of my daughter's welfare."

"We are not a welfare house," Gladys. "You have your nerve even asking me. We pay you a good wage and you have an exceptionally comfortable room."

"For which I'm truly grateful, Mrs. Vanderveer."

"These are bad times, Gladys. You're lucky you're not out begging on the streets."

"I am grateful to be here," said Gladys. "All I'm doing is asking. My daughter is not fortunate like your girls."

"That is none of my concern."

I felt like shouting something when I heard Mother say that, but hoping she would change her mind I kept quiet. Gladys was treading on eggs with my Mother and I didn't want to break them.

Even though at first, Mother didn't like the idea of Millie coming to live with us, she gave her approval on the condition that Millie be confined to her mother's quarters.

Meeting Millie for the first time was like encountering a shy diaphanous fairy who had just stepped out of one of my picture books. Her long hair was so blonde it was ghostly white. Her arms and legs as thin as sticks looked made for levitation. Downcast milky blue eyes drifted away with only a brief glance. My enthusiasm raised only a compressed smile. I could barely discern her soft-spoken words and, later, often had to ask her to repeat what she had just said.

29

When Gladys first brought her to the house, Millie stared transfixed at the glistening gold and glass chandelier suspended from the domed ceiling over the foyer.

Gladys introduced me. "Gwen, my daughter, Millie. Millie, this is Gwen Vanderveer, the little girl I told you about. She's ten years old, just like you."

Millie quickly glanced at me, then down at her scuffed shoes. She said nothing.

"Hi, Millie," I said. "It's nice to meet you."

At that moment, Tess and Dove came clattering down the sweeping white marble staircase behind us as though flying in from heaven. Millie looked up at the noise of their approach.

"Who's this?" demanded Tess.

"Millie, my daughter," said Gladys. "She's going to live here with me. I have your mother's approval. My husband's in the merchant marine. He's gone most of the time. Millie, this is Tess Vanderveer and her friend, Dove Delaney."

Dove gave Millie a once-over and was unimpressed. "Okay, we met her." Tess and Dove turned and raced back up the stairs to Tess's bedroom where they endlessly played checkers and dominoes and card games and Dove taught Tess how to gamble using toothpicks for money.

A flush of embarrassment crept up Millie's neck and spread across her pale face.

Happy at the prospect I would have Millie to myself as a friend, I asked Gladys, "Can we play?"

She picked up the small suitcase she had set down. "After I show Millie where our room is."

"Okay, can I come along?"

"If you'd like."

I fell in beside Millie as we followed Gladys through the Georgian furnished dining room, through tall, hand-carved doors into a sitting room, along a dim hallway to a spacious kitchen festooned with hanging polished copper pots and glassware in windowed cupboards, to another of the myriad halls that led to Gladys's apartment.

"We can go to my room and play," I said.

I became aware of how Millie viewed the world when she opened her suitcase and brought out her folder book and a pair of blunt scissors. "I'll bring my paper doll cut-outs," she said in a quiet voice.

"Why don't I make you lunch first," said Gladys. "Millie was too excited about coming here this morning to eat breakfast."

"All right," I said. "I'm always hungry. I never miss a meal, especially if you make it."

We sat down at the table and waited impatiently while Gladys tucked thin slices of roast beef and cheddar cheese between buttered rye bread. She placed a pickle on the plate with each sandwich and poured us glasses of milk. I kept up with Millie's hungry chomping. Certain we were done eating, Gladys excused us and we clattered out of the kitchen.

Millie protectively clutched the book to her chest with both arms as though it were a priceless treasure. The rich-burgundy draped mosaic windows and painted wainscoted walls and intricately carved, dark-stained crown molding ceilings drew her attention from following me and she lagged behind as we passed from room to room.

Interspersed with New England boating scenes, paintings by Cezanne, Van Gogh, Monet, and Degas my mother had collected during her European travels adorned the dark green walls along with old tintype ancestral photographs of my immigrant paternal grandparents and great grandparents who had migrated from the Netherlands during the late 1800s.

Further along the wall, later photographs of my mother as a debutant and a generational portrait of her family posed at the front entrance of a British country home. Her father wore the white Naval uniform of a sea captain and had inherited a shipping company.

My great grandfather had established one of the first textile mills that became the origin of my parents' wealth and importance in society. Over time, given the demand for cloth, the mill operation had expanded to include six more mills along the Charles River.

The interior of our mansion that Tess and I took for granted and ignored was a grandiose fantasy to Millie. She hesitated in the ballroom to stare at the chandelier reflected in the polished tan wooden floor. She paused to examine the Chinese floral painting on a large porcelain urn standing in a corner, then stopped to look into the sounding board of a sable grand piano with hand-carved legs.

"Do you play this?" she asked timidly.

"No, my sister, Tess, has lessons. Otherwise, it only gets played when my Mother has parties or there's a ball with an orchestra."

She pressed one of the keys. The resounding note echoed throughout the room.

"It sounds nice," she said.

"Tess is pretty good," I said.

"Could I hear her some time?"

"You'll have to ask her. She'll probably say no. She gets grumpy when she plays. She says she doesn't like people listening to her, especially when Mother wants to show her off to friends."

She looked wistfully at the keyboard. "If I could play, I would want people to hear me. Can we go to your room now? I'll show you my paper dolls."

We left the ballroom and walked through the adjacent dining room and living room to the foyer and went up the sweeping staircase to my bedroom on the second level. Once inside, Millie knelt down, opened her book and spread three male and three female paper doll templates on the carpet and scattered an array of men's and women's clothing cutout patterns around her.

"This is how you do it," she said, taking up the pattern for a woman's dress.

I watched the scissors rounded ends as she carefully cut along the pattern lines.

"Then you take the dress and hold it against the lady and press the tabs to keep it in place. This is Sally. She's my favorite. I always put bright colored dresses on her because I want to be like her. People like bright colors and she's the most beautiful of my dolls. Here," she handed me the scissors. "You can do one. Pick a dress for Anne," she patted the floor indicating I should get down on my knees next to her.

I placed Anne on my lap and selected a purple evening gown pattern with matching high-heels, similar to what my Mother would wear. She also had a purse hung on a gold chain from one shoulder.

"That's nice," said Millie. "Anne is very pretty and likes to dress up and go to parties." She suddenly looked at me in a straightforward manner. "Do you have parties?"

"On our birthdays and Christmas." I wondered why she was asking.

"I've never been to one. Do you dress up?"

"We wear new shoes and dresses. Mother makes us."

"But don't you want to dress up?"

"Sometimes. I don't mind it so much, but Tess puts up a fuss."

"Because I live here now, could I come to your parties?"

"Sure, I don't see why not."

"Will your mother let me?"

"She let you come and stay here," I reminded.

"Yes, but Mother told me I'm supposed to stay in my room unless your mother's gone. I'm afraid of your mother. I'm afraid she might make me leave if I do something wrong."

"Tess and I do things wrong all the time."

Secretly defying Mother's ultimatums filled our childhood days. Not that we were naughty or difficult, we just didn't agree with her in many ways.

I didn't know why what we did or refused to do bothered her so much. We didn't think she and Father loved us anyway, since we rarely saw them, which was why we depended on Gladys.

"But you're her daughters," said Millie. "I'm a stranger. And I don't have nice clothes."

"The next time there's a party, I'll tell Mother you're my friend and I'm inviting you."

"But what about nice clothes?"

"You can wear one of my dresses. I have a closet full of them. Most of them I don't even wear anymore."

"Can I see them?"

I stood and she jumped up and followed me to my closet. As I pulled open the door to display a row of twenty dresses hanging from a horizontal rod, Millie's wide-eyed admiration raised a ripple of guilt in my mind, rather than pride. I wasn't showing off for her and didn't want her to think that, but I needn't have worried.

"Aren't you thankful?" she asked.

"For the dresses?"

"For everything you have. I'm thankful to be here."

I gave her a big smile. "I'm thankful you're here. Tess doesn't want to have much to do with me and I don't have any friends."

"I'll be your friend."

"You are my friend."

"Can I pick a dress to wear to your party?"

"My birthday isn't for three months. You can then."

After a last loving glance at the dresses, she returned to the paper dolls. I followed her and we resumed our places on the floor.

"Here," she said. "You do John. There are more parts to his uniform." She handed me John's template. The men cutouts had masculine costumes, a soldier, John, a businessman, Albert, wearing a fedora and holding a briefcase, Albert wearing a golf outfit with plus fours and yellow socks.

"It's Betty's turn." She picked up the third female template. "Betty and Albert are married." She dressed Betty, then pulled the templates of a boy and of a girl from the folder. "These are their children, Ben and Alice. I have clothes for them too."

I watched her match outfits to Ben and Alice.

"Betty and Albert are a good mother and father. Ben and Alice live with them in the same house. John is their uncle and comes to visit them when he's not away at war."

I was thinking that maybe John was more like her own father being gone and coming home.

Having the run of the house, Tess and I could go play with Millie. But when Mother was away shopping or socializing, "associating," we brought Millie to our rooms. At those times, Tess sneaked Dove Delaney into the house but ordered Millie and me to stay away from them. Tess explained to Dove that Gladys shared our secret, but we had to be careful that Dove didn't get caught. The real reason was that Dove just wanted Tess to herself.

Given our mother's frequent absences, Gladys took care of us most of the time. We looked to her for advice on what things to do and how to do them and she gave us permission to secretly do what Mother would not allow, like going down the hill to play with Irish kids in the tenements or at the park.

One day while we were playing a board game in my room, Millie looked up and said, "Listen. Do you hear that?"

"It's only Tess practicing the piano," I said.

"I want to listen." She quickly rose from the floor. We spent a lot of time doing activities on the floor. I followed her to the door. "Hurry," she said, "before she stops."

She raced ahead of me along the hall and down the staircase, then slowed and quietly and unperceptively entered the ballroom. We stopped upon seeing Dove seated next to Tess on the piano bench. Their backs faced us. Not wanting to disturb them, we seated ourselves on chairs near the door.

Tess was aggressively playing a passage from a Beethoven sonata in a minor key with explosive power chords that expressed her personality.

At the conclusion of the piece, Millie clapped and Tess and Dove whirled around on the bench. "What are you doing here?" Tess's shout echoed from the gold leaf covered walls.

"Millie wanted to hear you play," I said.

"No one gets to listen to me practice, but Dove. That's my rule."

"I'm sorry," said Millie. "I love to hear you play."

"I don't care," said Tess. "You can't stay."

"Come on, Millie," I nudged her arm. "We better go before she has a temper tantrum."

"And close the door on your way out," shouted Tess.

As Millie and I left the ballroom, I apologized to her. "I'm sorry about Tess. She gets strange sometimes."

"At least I heard one song."

I had difficulty persuading Millie to go outside with me. She was reluctant to leave the house. She wanted to stay in, as though being separated from her delusions about the mansion would not allow her to return. She seemed to forget that her mother lived and worked there and that she wouldn't be locked out.

My Mother was the one whom she admired, mainly because Mother took an interest in her. She even arranged for Millie to go to our school, enrolling her as a family niece, and buying her the school uniform. Wearing the blue sweater, tan skirt, red and white striped tie, knee socks and saddle shoes, she looked the same as all the other girls. Amazing to me, she seemed to interact with them so easily using the pretext of being a Vanderveer relative.

Our school wasn't Catholic, so we didn't have nuns for teachers. We had smart young women who had college degrees in education and specialized in certain subjects. Even though they were strict and demanding, their enthusiasm for us to learn and succeed was undeniable.

Sometimes, sitting in the bleachers, Millie and I would watch Tess and the older girls in her grade level play field hockey in after school games. Tess alternately played forward and midfield and was always in the middle of the fray, dribbling over the green turf or fighting for the ball with her curved hockey stick. Her special shoes gave her great speed and shin guards didn't slow her down. Her flaming hair streamed as she raced and whirled like a possessed creature, a goddess from a classical myth.

Academically she was at the top of her class. Even though she was beautiful and drew the attention and adoration of her classmates, she privately disdained popularity, but she played the social maneuvers and one-upmanship with a sense of superiority.

"I could never be like her," Millie said.

"No one could be like her," I said.

Millie and I were in the same class. I excelled in all the subjects, math, English, history, civics, except for music, drama, and dance. The teacher said Millie had a natural gift for the performing arts. She was a little slow in the other subjects. So I helped her with homework, which should have made her feel thankful and indebted to me. But she wasn't. She acted like she was entitled to have me tutor her.

Paper Dolls

At first, I wasn't certain why Mother devoted so much attention to Millie; but over time, I saw how Millie observed her and sought her advice about decorum and manners. In addition, Millie's petite beauty caught my Mother's eye. In lieu of Tess and me, except for Tess's piano playing, she made Millie her project, her third daughter.

Millie already spoke German and Mother began teaching her French and how to play bridge. I was never asked and I felt left out, but I didn't beg. I wasn't at all interested in playing bridge. I much more enjoyed Dove's gambling card games, when she and Tess would let me play, because they needed a third person to make the games more interesting, and they could easily cheat me.

She even took her shopping in downtown Boston. By the time Millie was a teenager, Mother occasionally even took her to New York where they went to the theater and shopped in upscale stores. She never asked me, but I wouldn't go if she did. She introduced Millie to friends as her niece.

Before long, Millie's closet was as filled with dresses as mine. Gladys had to move half of her own clothes to make room.

When Millie said she wanted to learn how to play the piano, Mother arranged for her to have lessons. Because Millie was my friend, I sat and watched and listened during her lessons with Mr. Spence on Saturday mornings. He was a soft-spoken, kindly man who wore brown tweed suits that matched the hair fringed over his ears.

Millie also practiced two hours every day. That was more than Tess did. I didn't sit around and listen to Millie play boring exercises. I went into Father's library and read books. I loved reading all kinds of books on different subjects. As a consequence, I developed superior writing skills. Ten years later, along with my parents' wealth and influence, my skills would make for an easy transition from a private school for girls into Wellesley College.

Although Millie's vacillating friendship discouraged me and I witnessed Dove's growing attachment to Tess, they were mostly desirous of and wanting what they did not have. They nibbled at our lives.

Chapter 4

Bigotry

The first time I became aware of the growing war in Europe, I was going downstairs to see Millie and paused at the open door to the library. Gladys and George were listening to news on the wooden radio.

"Chancellor Adolf Hitler has annexed Austria. The Nazi regime calls it *Anschluss*," said the announcer's voice. "The German army has marched across the border. Hitler was greeted by cheering crowds in Vienna and acknowledged the support of its citizens for an all-German *Reich*."

As an eleven year old in 1935, I didn't know who the Nazis were and the meaning of military aggression and why countries warred against each other in the first place.

Gladys read the stories of Nazi atrocities against German Jews when she cleaned up newspapers that my father left scattered in the library.

I had recently noticed a change in her. The daily broadcast news of events in Europe cast a pall over her that deflated her customary cheerful outlook. Visible worry and sadness haunted her eyes and her step was less energetic. I wondered if she might be ill. I mentioned my observation to Millie. Given the attention she received from my Mother, she seemed not to share my concern.

Our chauffeur, George Oswell, spoke up, "I fought the Huns in the last war and now they're coming back like a pestilence."

"Not all Germans are like them. My husband and I have family in Germany, brothers and sisters and their families. We aren't Nazis. What will become of them?"

"I apologize, Gladys," said George. "I didn't mean you."

"I know, but I'm thinking others will only see me and Ekkehardt like the Nazis. We are good Germans. We don't like war. We don't hate Jewish people."

Largely because of the daily news, when Gladys and Millie were alone and talking in German, they would suddenly grow quiet when I entered the room.

I asked Millie to teach me some German words, but she said she wasn't allowed, as though she were ashamed and had something to hide. I didn't understand the stigma that clung to them and would affect us for the rest of our lives.

Gladys and her husband had come to America fifteen years ago in 1926. Gladys had told Tess and me about their lives in the small seaport town of Warnemunde on the Baltic coast of Northern Germany.

She was the second youngest in a family of four brothers and three sisters. They lived next to the harbor where the red and blue painted fishing boats docked. She woke each morning to the screaming flocks of gulls that swarmed over the masts and the steep gray tiled rooftops of timbered houses that lined the access channel to the open sea.

Her father had been a fisherman. His eldest son, Jurgen, handled the nets on their trawler when they went out with the fleet. Gladys described the hold filled with fish they brought back shad, cod, flounder, and perch. Her father demanded that her younger brothers help clean the catch and sold most of it off the boat and at the daily open market in the town square.

The family had always had plenty to eat until the outbreak of World War I, in 1914, when her father and Jurgen were conscripted into Kaiser Wilhelm's army.

She and Ekkehardt had been childhood friends. He had apprenticed as a boat builder. His skills had not kept him from carrying a gun and being sent to the front where he had been assigned as a motor pool mechanic maintaining trucks and tanks.

Gladys had worked with her mother and sisters in the family bakery.

"The war was all we knew," she said. "Meine Fater und Brudder had to join the army. We no longer had fish to eat and flour to make bread. We made bread with potatoes turned into flour. When potatoes were gone to feed the soldiers, we had to eat turnips and made turnips into bread. We did not like turnips, but it was all we had to eat to survive. We were starving along with others. We were skin and bones. Many people grew sick and died. We were all tired of war. Fater and Jurgen did not come back. They were killed fighting in France.

Following their wedding, Gladys and Ekkehardt decided to leave the postwar conditions of Germany and seek a new life in America. Ekkehardt hired on as a merchant marine engine mechanic for a shipping line out of Boston.

After working in a local bakery, Gladys had been referred by a relative who knew the former Vanderveer housekeeper who had become pregnant. At her interview with my mother, she did not divulge that she had a daughter. She and Ekkehardt had placed Melissa in a foster care home so they could maintain their jobs.

Now, in 1938, by association, Gladys felt the pattern of war in Europe had reemerged and erupted like a nagging nightmare. The same countries were pitting their armies against German forces. The difference was the ethnic purge against the Jews whom the Nazis falsely blamed for economic inequalities in German society.

Hitler's master plan for world domination was the mass deportation, decimation, and genocide of races they believed were inferior and the colonization of their countries by the German Aryan master race. Hitler's goal of world domination was called *Lebensraum*, in which his racially superior society would claim the conquered living space.

Gladys told us she and Ekkehardt despised Hitler and felt only disgust for him as a vile monster.

Although the European conflict would not directly pull us into the war for eight more years, it began to reach out to us through Father's company and the demand for textiles and the competition it engendered.

Nylon made from Japanese silk had come into vogue during the 1930s and influenced the fashion industry for women's hosiery. Textile mills knitted and sold the hosiery to department stores.

Nylon's strength, light weight, elasticity, and mildew resistance also leant itself to wartime production for parachutes and aircraft tires, which soon exhausted the supply for hosiery. Women took to wearing socks or painting seams on their legs to give the appearance of silk stockings.

Turning fourteen became an ill-fated year for Tess. The Tipton mill was the source of Vanderveer wealth. Although textile production provided a livelihood for a few thousand employees, it became the origin of a rift between Tess and our parents involving Dove Delaney.

Dove trudged through knee deep snow up the south side of Beacon Hill past the Acorn Street sign, to Pinckney Street. Ragged clouds from the week-long storm parted, exposing a brilliant blue sky and sunlight that glistened off the pristine white cityscape with such intensity that pedestrians had to squint and shade their eyes.

Adorned with red ribbons, Christmas garland spiraled around the lamp posts. Woven wreaths nestled with yellow pears and clusters of red berries decorated the inviting front doors behind berms of snow thrust up by the early morning plow and eclipsed the bleakness of soot-streaked snow that blanketed the tenement streets below in cold hard silence.

The frosty air prickled her nasal hairs. She rubbed her red nose with a mittened hand and snugged her plum wool ski cap over her ears. Since she did not have boots, her socks and shoes were soaked. A pocket of her navy blue pea coat bulged with the orange it contained. The orange and a striped candy cane were the only Christmas present her parents could afford for each of their five children.

Their mother had served a fruit cake for breakfast, along with a bowl of buttered porridge sprinkled with brown sugar. Afterward, she had marched them to St. Joseph's church to hear the Christmas mass. Their father had remained at home to sleep for the rest of the morning. Not even the white-robed hallelujah choir put Dove in a holiday spirit. Not until she departed alone and approached Beacon Hill did anticipation and excitement pulse through her.

She protected the gift carried rolled up in newspaper under her arm. The pen and ink drawing captured the image of Tess Vanderveer in laborious detail from the studied memory imprinted on Dove's mind. She was certain her friend would appreciate her adulation conveyed by the artistic rendering. It honored the strength of their bond.

Following Tess's instruction to always go to the back door kitchen entrance, Dove's reception was not what she expected.

Releasing a cloud of savory herbs, cinnamon, and nutmeg aromas, Gladys opened the door at her knock.

"Merry Christmas, Gladys. I came to see Tess. I have a present for her."

"Oh, I'm sorry to tell you, Dove. Tess cannot see you today. She is with her family having Christmas morning."

"I brought her a present. Can't she come to the door?"

"They are having breakfast. I can't interrupt them."

"What about Melissa?"

"She is with them."

"She's not family. How come she gets to be with them and I'm not allowed?"

"Tess has told you about her mother."

"I know. I know." A frown distorted Dove's mouth. "But this is Christmas. It's different. I should be able to be with Tess."

"Come back tomorrow, in the afternoon. Mr. and Mrs. Vanderveer will be gone visiting with friends."

"Tomorrow? Are you joking? Today is Christmas and I have a present."

"You can leave it with me and I will give it to her," Gladys glanced back into the kitchen. She had an apple and a cherry pie in the oven that needed her attention.

"That's not the idea. It's my special present for her. I want to give it to her. I walked all the way up here in the snow. I'm freezing. Can I at least come inside and warm up?"

Gladys hesitated. "For only a few minutes. I'm very busy with much to do. Guests are coming for an evening dinner."

"A few minutes is all I need. Then I can leave the drawing I made for Tess." Dove gestured to the rolled package tucked under her arm.

"A drawing?"

"Yes, it's a drawing of Tess. I'm an artist."

Harmon, the serving butler suddenly entered the kitchen through the connecting dining room door. "Gladys, Mrs. Vanderveer would like to speak with you about the dinner tonight. And I need more croissants."

"I will be right there. Croissants are in the warming oven." Harmon placed four croissants from the warming oven on a plate and returned to the dining room. Gladys looked back at Dove. "You can come in for only a few minutes to get warm. Put your drawing on the table, then leave. You do not want to be seen here."

"A few minutes." Dove stepped through the doorway and watched Gladys clump across the kitchen and out into the dining room. As soon as Gladys was gone, Dove snatched a cold croissant from the table and rushed out through the other kitchen door into the hall. Looking back and forth to ensure no one would see her, she walked quickly along the hall to the main entry foyer which was hidden from the dining room. She charged as noiselessly as she could up the staircase and dashed to Tess's bedroom, entered, and closed the door.

With a sigh of relief, she stepped to the bed and unrolled the drawing. She weighted two sides with books to keep the drawing from rolling in on itself. Then she shrugged off her coat, sat in Tess's easy chair, removed her wet socks and shoes, and wriggled her toes in Tess's soft, fluffy white carpet. She ate the croissant and waited, knowing Tess would eventually come to her room.

Gladys returned to the kitchen. Distracted with last minute orders from Mrs. Vanderveer, she noticed that Dove Delaney was gone and must have taken the drawing with her. Gladys assumed Dove had shown better sense and would come back tomorrow.

Tess quickly finished her helping of ham and eggs and a croissant, then watched the butler's white-gloved hand serve a Christmas pudding.

Melissa and I sat next to each other across from Tess, with our parents at either end of the long table festooned with candles and red and green seasonal decorations on a white lace tablecloth.

Dominating a corner of the adjoining living room, wrapped presents surrounded the base of a ten foot pine hung with colorful balls and twinkling lights.

We were suitably attired in nice dresses and Mary Jane shoes according to Mother's requirements. She did not allow us to come downstairs wearing our robes, pajamas, and slippers for a casual gift exchange around the tree.

Tess and I never bought anything for Mother and Father. They bought for each other and attached little gift cards to a few meant to come from us. Tess didn't know why they even bothered with the charade, but the majority of the presents were for her and me and now, Millie. Gladys, the butlers, Harmon and Ivo, and George, the chauffeur, were also called in and each given presents, which they graciously accepted with feigned acts of gratitude and politeness.

Mother gave us mostly dresses and sports clothes, along with a few baubles we would wear only during parties or attending a concert or an opera in New York City. Oddly, she seemed to recognize my proclivity for literature and always included a book among my gifts. The last few years included Anne of Green Gables, Little Women, and the latest Nancy Drew mystery.

Following the breakfast ritual, I curled up on the couch with my book. Millie carried her new dress and a few smaller gifts to the apartment she and Gladys shared. Tess left her gift boxes in a pile and went upstairs to use the bathroom.

Upon entering her room and seeing Dove, she stopped in shock.

"Surprise! Merry Christmas!" said Dove.

Tess stepped inside and firmly shut the door. "What are you doing here? You know my mother's home. Did Gladys let you in?"

"She let me into the kitchen to get warm, then I kind of let myself in the rest of the way when she wasn't looking."

"If my mother sees you, you're going to get us both in trouble, and Gladys."

Dove rose from the chair. "I brought you a present." Her grand gesture directed Tess's attention to the bed.

"It's beautiful," said Tess. "It's really beautiful, but you could have given it to me at another time. It's not safe for you to be here."

"It's okay. I'm safe. Your mother doesn't know I'm here. Gladys doesn't know. All we have to do is keep quiet."

"That's not all we have to do. I have to go back downstairs. I can't just leave you here alone."

"Why not?"

"There's no place for you to hide."

"Why do I have to hide?" Dove asked.

"You don't know my Mother. I've told you about her. You don't want to know my Mother. I'm not allowed to have friends here."

"You mean friends like me."

"I explained to you before about her."

"Just because I live in Roxbury doesn't mean I'm not as good as you."

"I know that, but she doesn't and she doesn't care. Put your shoes and socks back on and your coat. I have to get you out of here before you're caught."

"Why don't you just tell her about me and let her meet me? You like me. We like each other."

"If I did that, you would never be able to come here again. And Gladys might get fired for not telling her."

"Do you have a present for me?"

"Not today. I'll have to bring it to you later."

"But you do have one."

"Yes, I have one, but not now. Put on your socks and shoes."

Tess watched and waited impatiently while Dove complied.

Dove looked up. "Okay, but you really like the drawing."

"Yes, I really like it. Now, get on your coat." Tess maneuvered her to the door. "Wait. Let me check in the hall to make sure it's clear. Okay, we have to hurry. Follow me."

As Tess and Dove were sneaking down the stairs, Mother saw them from the living room. Her eyes narrowed in a critical squint and she called out, "Tess, who is that with you?"

Tess and Dove froze near the bottom of the staircase. Mother strode quickly across the foyer to them. "Come down here!"

I could see them from the living room couch. Tess and Dove completed their descent. Neither bowed their heads nor looked away from Mother's imperious glare.

"Who is this?"

"Dove Delaney," said Tess. "She's my friend."

Mother shouted at Gladys. "Gladys, come out here!"

Her face taut as a drum, Gladys hurried down the hall from the kitchen.

48

"I put you in charge of looking after my girls and what do you do? How long has this been going on? How dare you let Tess bring riff-raff like this into our home?"

"I'm not riff-raff!" Dove retorted. "I'm as good as Tess or anybody! I'm even an artist!"

"I can hardly believe that. Where do you live?"

"Roxbury."

"I knew it," sneered Mother. "I can tell just by looking at you and hear it in your voice. You're just like the Irish who work in my husband's mill."

"My Ma and Dah work in his mill!"

"And that's where you should be, certainly not in my house and pretending to be my daughter's friend."

"I'm not pretending, Mrs. Vanderveer. Tess and me are friends."

"That's going to end right now. You are not welcome here and Tess is forbidden to have anything to do with you." She pointed to the front entrance. "There's the door. Get on home to your own kind."

Deeply hurt, blinded by tears, Dove ran out of the house. Stumbling and falling on the ice and snow, she staggered down Pinckney Street and disappeared into the ghetto.

Mother wasn't finished with Tess. The mesmerizing cold brutality of her voice stabbed Tess in such a way that she would do anything to contradict and challenge her from that moment on.

"Had I known what was going on behind my back, I would have placed you in a residential private school. And that's what I'm going to do, young lady." She turned to Gladys. "And as for you, if I weren't hosting a dinner party tonight and I didn't care about your daughter, I would send you packing now."

At an early age, I recognized my mother's indifference and insensitivity to others, especially to Tess and me, but witnessing her act of cruelty toward Dove brought tears to my eyes followed by anger and a

49

sense of helplessness that we were victims. But my feelings didn't begin to approach my sister's rage and desire for revenge that lasted all her life.

Not wanting to endure more of Mother's tirade, Tess turned and stumbled up the stairs to her room. The resounding slam of her door echoed down the hall. Mother stared after her as though she wanted to pursue Tess with her diatribe, then thought better of it and returned to the living room. I looked down at my book to avoid her glance, in case she decided I needed to be reprimanded, but there was no escape for me.

"Did you know about that Irish girl?" she asked.

I decided that lying to my Mother would not get me anywhere, so I said, "Yes, but I didn't do anything with them. They wouldn't let me."

"Well, that's encouraging. At least you have Millie to play with. She's much more acceptable, especially with my influence."

I didn't tell her that Millie wasn't available all that much because of her.

Up in her bedroom, Tess paced the floor, stared at Dove's drawing on her bed, then paced the floor again. She returned to the drawing, carefully rolled it up and tucked it away in her closet. She lifted an awkwardly shaped Christmas wrapped gift from the top shelf, held it for a few moments, and returned it to the shelf.

She went to the window over-looking the street. Dove was no longer in sight.

After Tess's first three knocks, Dove opened the door, releasing the smell of corn beef, cabbage and beans cooking on the stove. "What're you doin' here?"

"I'm your friend. I hate my mother." She handed her the cheerfully wrapped package. "Merry Christmas, Dove. This is for you."

"What do I want with your damn present?"

Dove's vicious response set Tess back and altered her attempt at reconciliation.

"We ain't friends," said Dove. "Why don't you just throw it in the snow or give it away to someone else?" she sneered. "Take it over to a can house. That's all it means to me."

"I'm sorry what my mother said to you. I am not her and you know that. So please, take the gift."

"It's kind of big and has an odd shape," Dove commented on the flat oblong oval configuration of the three foot package.

"Go ahead. Open it."

"Not here, standing in the doorway."

"Can I come in?"

"No, you cannot come in. You are not allowed in my house. My mother doesn't approve of you. She might not even let me keep this present."

"Is she home?"

"No, but you still can't come in."

"Come on, Dove. I apologized to you. I brought you this present. I want to be your friend."

"I'm not sure we can be friends anymore."

"Why not?"

"You know why not. I'm not your kind."

"That's stupid."

"How can you say that after what your mother did."

"Forget about her. I told you I'm not her. How about you let me come in. I'm freezing out here."

"How can you be freezing? You've got that heavy coat and cap and mittens and you're even wearing galoshes. I didn't wear galoshes when I came to your house. I don't even have 'em. My socks and shoes were soaking wet. And you made me put them back on and leave before they dried out. My toes could have been frostbit. What if I had to have my toes cut off because of you?"

"Well, then, you have to open your present without me."

"I don't need you to help. It's just wrapping paper."

"I'm not talking about the paper. Once you see the gift, you'll need my help."

"What is that supposed to mean?"

"If you let me come in and open the present, you'll see what I mean."

"All right, you can come in, but only to warm up," Dove stepped aside and Tess entered, stomping the snow off her boots.

"Yer messin' up the floor," Dove took the package.

"Open it," said Tess, "since you're only giving me a minute."

Dove placed the package on the bare kitchen table. Her two bundled younger sisters looked up from where they were warming themselves at the coal-burning stove.

"What you got?" asked one.

"None a yer business." Dove began tearing off the wrapping and ribbon.

"We want to see." The two girls jumped up from the wooden crates on which they were sitting.

Despite herself, the sight of an artist's pallet, tubes of oil paint, two brushes, and a pallet knife caused Dove to suppress an impulse to cry. "You know these won't do me no good without canvases and an easel. I'll need canvases and an easel. You're right. I do need your help, Missy Deep Pockets. I don't have no money to buy those things."

"I've got money. I'll buy them for you. We can buy them together."

"Well, I can't bring 'em home. I can't keep 'em here. I can't paint here. My Ma and Dah will kill me. They'll think I stole all this stuff."

"We can find someplace you can store them. Maybe the man at the art store downtown will let you. At the same place you buy your pen and ink. I showed him some of your drawings when I bought the pallet."

"You showed him?"

"Yes, I showed him. He's an artist too, you know. He has a studio in the back of the store."

"Why would he do that for me?"

"Let's ask him and find out. He said you have talent."

"He said that?"

"Yes, he said that. The art store is also a place we can meet without worrying about my mother catching us."

A softness crept into Dove's condemning eyes. "Why you doin' this for me?"

"The same you drew that picture of me. Because I'm your friend."

"I don't have no place to hide these."

"Get your coat and hat on. We can go to the art store today. You can keep them there."

"Now? You want to go now."

"I'm here, aren't I? My Mother went to New York. She'll be gone all week."

"Then I can come to yer place."

"Gladys won't let us. She'd have to tell my Mother or she'd lose her job. And even if we did, Mother would send me away to a private school somewhere and we wouldn't be able to see each other again, ever."

"I hate your mother, too."

"Let's go. We have to take the trolley."

Tess snatched her pea coat off a wall hook, stuffed the brushes, pallet knife, and paint tubes into her pockets, and rewrapped the easel. "Okay, let's go."

"Shall we tell Ma?" asked one of the girls.

"Don't tell her anything," Dove warned and herded Tess out the door.

Fortunately, our Mother didn't immediately follow through with her threat to send Tess to a private residential girls' school. Not this time.

Although she made Tess promise not to see Dove again, Tess lied and continued to secretly meet her at the art store in downtown Boston.

Chapter 5

Distortions

Since a thick wall separated our bedrooms, I kept my door open and listened to Tess rummaging around in her room. With Mother out of town on weekends, Tess had secretly been going to see Dove. I knew about the art store. Tess had told me that now Dove was a real artist and had a studio.

"Where is it?" I had asked.

"At the art store downtown. Don't you dare say anything about it to Mother."

"I won't. Can I go with you sometime?"

Tess said, "No, the art store is only for Dove and me. Besides, Dove doesn't like you. She won't want you there."

"But I'm your sister."

"What has that got to do with anything?"

"You can't keep me from going."

"I'll lose you if you try to follow me."

"We used to be friends. Why don't you like me?"

"I don't need you tagging along. I have my own life. You have yours. You have Millie."

"No, I don't. Mother has Millie. She's turning Millie into a snob, just like her. She doesn't want to do anything. Because she's Mother's favorite, she thinks she's better than me." I couldn't understand how Millie's relationship to my mother had turned out to be so different than with Tess and Me. Later, it occurred to me that Mother needed to be admired and so did Millie. They mutually admired each other. Mother became her mentor. I was the one left with nobody.

Since Millie was in New York with Mother, I spent most of my time in the kitchen with Gladys learning how to cook. We shopped for groceries together and went on daily walks. She understood that my spending time with her took my mind off my sadness at being rebuffed.

To fill my lonely hours, I thought maybe I should have a hobby. Tess played the piano. Dove drew and painted pictures. Millie graduated from cutting out paper dolls to modeling her growing accumulation of clothes and striking poses in front of my full length mirror when she wasn't out with Mother. Applying eye shadow and makeup also preoccupied her. I didn't understand why she felt compelled to improve her face, which didn't need any improvement. She already possessed a pristine beauty. The makeup made her look cheap and slatternly.

I grew tired and disgusted with watching and listening to her. The sound of her incessantly practicing the piano echoed through the house. Even closing my door, I couldn't escape the distant tinkling of scales and arpeggios, etudes, nocturnes, waltzes, marches, mazurkas, impromptus, and sonatas.

I didn't understand why everybody shut me out, except Gladys.

At some point, I realized everything wasn't about me. In fact, nothing was about me, which led to a curiosity and interest in how other people lived. Given the events and activities I observed and read and heard about from adults and listening to the radio with Gladys, I jotted down my thoughts in a diary.

As a young teenager, I decided that on non-school days, I was old enough to venture out alone into the city.

I always let Gladys know when and where I was going. She wanted to send Ivo along with me to protect me.

"I don't need protection," I said. "Tess goes out by herself."

"Tess is different. She's older and more independent."

"I can be independent."

"I worry about you, *liebchen*, going alone. You used to go with Tess."

"She won't let me. I'll be just fine."

"Ivo will go with you," said Gladys.

"I don't need anyone to go with me."

"Your *mutter* will not approve."

"She doesn't care and you don't have to tell her."

"I care. You are like my own child. I don't want you to be harmed."

"What harm? I'm just going to walk around in the city and look at things."

"The city is not a safe place for a young girl."

"What could happen to me? What?"

"You have to be careful of strangers. There are men with evil thoughts. Also, since your *fatter* has wealth, you could be abducted and held for ransom."

"I won't dress like this. I'll change how I look. I'll wear clothes like Dove."

"Ivo must go with you."

"What will people think if I have a butler following me around?"

"He will not wear his butler clothes. He will dress like an ordinary person."

"What if he says no, he doesn't want to go with me? He and Harmon would never take Tess and me to the beach. I don't even think they like us."

"They like you. They treat you with respect. That is their job. That is who they are. Ivo and Harmon will do what I ask. They know how important you are to your *mutter* and *fatter*. When they are gone, I am in charge of you. Taking care is my job, just like cooking and cleaning."

"We're not just like cooking and cleaning. I know you like us. I know you like me."

"I care about you and your sister."

"Tell Ivo I want to go somewhere today."

"Where?"

"Into the city, downtown."

"Wait until tomorrow. There is snow on the ground. I will find you some old clothes, an old coat."

"My coat will cover my dress and I'll wear galoshes over my shoes."

At first, the clash and clang of trolleys, the rumble of trucks and cars, and the aggressive rush of people intimidated me. Although I resented needing a chaperon, having Ivo at my side gave me a sense of security. He smiled and chatted and didn't act in a formal manner. He talked about his and Harmon's boyhood in Holland and about his first job working in a brewery. "Holland is famous for making beer," he said. "Beer and diamonds. Harmon worked as a diamond cutter and polisher before we came to America fifteen years ago."

"How did you become butlers?" I asked.

"We worked as servers at the Waldorf Astoria Hotel in New York City. Your mother and father stayed there often. They liked our professional service and being Dutch. They offered us jobs.

His street clothes and jaunty slouch hat transformed him. He seemed to enjoy being with me. He even asked me what I wanted to see and what I was writing in my notebook.

The first place I wanted to visit was the art store. We rode the trolley into downtown Boston. At Hanover and Union Streets, we got off and forged our way along sidewalks crowded with destitute men and women with forlorn faces and other businessmen wearing suits and fedoras. We skirted bootblack boys polishing shoes on a corner. Passing a man carrying a sandwich board advertising a cafeteria, we found the brick gallery tucked among canopied tobacco, shoemaker, clothing shops, and taverns. Red painted closed signs hung in display windows and doorways of many. I wondered how the art store could stay in business. Who could afford paintings and art supplies when most people did not have jobs and barely enough money to buy food?

I noticed a new poster in the front window featuring the logo drawing of an eagle side by side with a white and red striped artist's pallet with a brush inserted in the hole. A bell jingled over the door as we entered the store. A bespectacled man seated behind a glass display counter containing assorted paints and brushes looked up at us. He said nothing until he noticed us staring at drawings and paintings hung on the walls. Some were impressionist ocean scapes and street scenes, portraits, and several bizarre, distorted shapes of people and of modern art that left me feeling uncomfortable.

"Can I help you?" he asked without standing.

I turned to face him. "Does Dove Delaney come here?"

"She's one of my students."

"Student?"

"She's learning how to paint."

"Does my sister, Tess Vanderveer come with her?"

"They're friends, but your sister doesn't draw or paint."

"She told me you have a place for Dove to work."

"I have a studio at the back of the store."

"Do they come here often?"

"Once or twice a week. Dove comes more alone to work. She has talent."

"Are any of them hers?" I gestured to the paintings on the walls.

He put aside his book and limped from behind the counter. "I'm Peter," he said and shook hands with Ivo. I noticed he wore one brown leather shoe with a thicker heel than the other. "That one," he pointed to the medium-size canvas of a few faceless women and children on a tenement street.

"That's her street," I said. "I've been there. Why don't the people have faces?"

"That's her way of saying they don't have value and no identity."

"Why are those other paintings like scraps of paper?"

The man's thin face wrinkled into a bemused grin. "It's an expression of how the artist feels about what he sees, about life."

"It looks all scattered and messed up. That one looks like different body parts."

"That's an accurate perception. An artist sees what he wants to see. We create a different perception of reality to see beyond the surface of things. It's called surrealism. The distortions are expressionism. You seem interested."

"In my home country, Van Gogh and Mondrian made paintings like those," said Ivo.

"They influence my work and other artists today," said Peter.

"I was just wondering." At the time, I didn't know how anyone could do that. I just saw what I saw. I didn't know how to take it apart until many years later.

"That's what the artist intended, to make people wonder."

"Are you the artist?"

"Some of the paintings are mine."

I pointed to a small canvas of a man with tousled brown hair and deep brown eyes staring back at me through his glasses. "That one looks like you, but it isn't really you."

"It's a self-portrait."

"Oh. Can I see where Dove paints?"

He nodded. Ivo and I followed him through a drab curtain into a back room. Two paint-stained smocks hung on wall hooks. Dust motes swirled in shafts of sunlight from a high window bathing the room in a milky haze. Three half-finished canvases rested upright on A-frame easels. Two pallets surrounded by brushes, scrappers, and piles of wrinkled paint tubes filled the surface of a work bench.

"Okay," I said, after a few minutes. "We can go now."

The man held the curtain aside so Ivo and I could pass through. Ivo shook his hand and thanked him. My nondescript smile may have conveyed nothing or everything about me at that moment. He grinned at me. The bell on the door tinkled cheerily as Ivo and I walked out onto the street.

"Interesting place," said Ivo. "What do you think?"

"I don't know, but some of those paintings remind me of Tess. She always goes against the way things are."

"I noticed that about her too, as she is growing up. She questions things."

Ivo's comment jarred me. I never thought he and Harmon noticed anything about us other than that we were privileged children of wealthy parents.

Maneuvering through pedestrians and traffic, we followed a main street that led inevitably to the waterfront and the keening screams of gulls rising and swooping over the harbor.

We walked past a forest of masts of trawlers snugged bow to stern along the India Wharf. Fishermen spilled haddock, redfish, and hake onto the decks where they were transferred to men gutting fish on wooden benches and tossing them into metal tubs. We watched lobstermen packing freshly caught lobsters into barrels. The dense odor of fish replaced the air we breathed.

"It's time for lunch," said Ivo. "Are you hungry?"

I nodded.

"I'll take you where Harmon and I like to eat."

A greenish skein clung to a gray sculpted metal bell tucked within an anchor hanging above the heavy oak door of the Bell and Anchor Tavern. Ivo grabbed the wrought iron handle and pulled opened the door, releasing a wave of deep-fried fish, chowder, yeasty ale, and swirling tobacco smoke. A few heads turned as he ushered me into the harsh din of polyglot voices, Italian, German, Polish, Irish rumbling from bearded men wearing seamen's caps, rubber boots and leather coverall aprons stained with fish blood.

Hearing these men speaking their own foreign languages reinforced a growing awareness that I lived in a place surrounded by people unlike myself. Just as the distorted paintings hanging on the walls of the art store portrayed a different view of the world, the human behavior I observed, dissected, and analyzed and the ethnic, social and psychological differences I encountered throughout my life became my literary equivalent.

Ivo shouted to be heard and guided me to a rough-hewn wooden table being vacated by two fishermen. We sat and waited for a blousy, dark-haired barmaid with curly red hair and stern eyes that flashed with her saucy ripostes to coarse remarks from customers. She quickly cleared the table of chowder bowls and empty ale mugs and returned to take our order. Several minutes later, she returned with bowls of steaming fish chowder, sourdough bread, a side of fish and chips, an ale for Ivo, and a mug of apple cider for me.

I lifted a spoonful of the chowder to my lips and inhaled the aroma of seasoned cod, clams, and potatoes in thick white gravy. Ivo watched me savor my first bite. His eyes gleamed at my expression of delight.

My outing with Ivo awoke a curiosity in me that had lain dormant all my childhood years until that turning point in the Bell and Anchor Tavern. I determined I would have more of such experiences.

Chapter 6

Defiance

Instead of dwelling on myself all the time, I took notice and became aware of random comments I heard between my parents.

The conflict between Tess and our parents began building to a head when we overheard Father talking to Mother about market competition and problems at the mill.

"The mill is no longer competitive given the cost of labor," he said. "I'm looking into relocating. North Carolina has operating costs and low cost labor advantages. Other mills are moving operations there."

"You're only talking about the mill, aren't you?" Mother's vituperative voice put a damper on the dinner conversation. "I will never move to the South. You know what I think of those people, those Southerners. They're lazy white trash. And all those Negroes. I won't live in the middle of all those Negroes. I don't understand why they keep coming up here. They're crowding into the city. With the Irish and Italians, how many more ghettoes do we have to have?"

"I'm not asking you to move down there. I'll have to establish a residence and make frequent trips. My mill manager said he'll go."

"Well, of course, he'd be a fool to walk away from his job."

"There's union trouble brewing anyway."

"What kind of trouble? Those drunkards aren't going to strike, are they?"

"There's talk."

"Despicable. Absolutely despicable, the lot of them. They should be thanking us. They're lucky to have jobs at all."

Dove Delaney's mother and father were union members. I wondered what would happen to Dove if they joined the strike. I also wondered what would happen if my father moved the mill to North Carolina.

I listened to the radio news with Gladys on the radio about local and world events. I even started reading the daily newspaper that Father left in his study. That was where I read an article about President Franklin Delano Roosevelt and the Works Progress Administration. The story was the first time I saw in print the name of Congressman Harold Gebhardt, who was managing the Federally funded program for the state of Massachusetts. Some years later, his name would become much more familiar than a passing reference in a news article.

The President's goal was to stimulate the economy by providing paid employment to over three million men, women, and young people living in poverty during the Great Depression. To rise from being on relief, they received hourly wages for working on public construction projects for highways, roads, bridges, dams, airports, water systems, and sanitation plants.

After school one afternoon, Tess, Millie, and I crowded into the kitchen to enjoy our daily snack of cookies and milk that Gladys put out for us. She had left the local newspaper she had been reading open on the table. The front page headline caught Tess's eye. She stopped in mid-bite crunching a sweet chocolate chip cookie still warm from the oven.

"It's happening!"

"What?" I mumbled through a mouthful of crumbs.

"The mill workers are on strike. That means Dove's mother and father."

"What are they striking for?

Tess squinted and scanned the article. "It says they want better pay and better hours. The working conditions are hazardous and unhealthy, just like that time we went to see the mill. Look." She pointed to the large black and white photograph of men and women carrying signs. "They even have children marching on the picket line. I wonder if Dove is there. I'm going to find out."

Gladys looked up from stirring baking ingredients in a bowl with a wooden spoon. "You should not go. Your father will be angry."

"I don't care. What he's doing to his workers is not right. Don't any of you say anything to him." Her threatening gaze stayed on me. "I know they told you to snitch. You snitch and you'll be sorry."

I chewed vigorously and shook my head.

"Gladys, that means you and Millie." Without finishing her snack, Tess ran out of the kitchen and dashed up the stairs to her room.

I leaned over the table to better see the news story. Beyond what Tess had read to us, the sub-headline and column expanded on the position of the union leaders and the action being taken against my father. He was quoted as saying he would not and could not meet their demands, which would bankrupt the company. He threatened that if they did not end the strike, he would shut down the mill and move the operation to North Carolina.

Tess changed her school clothes for black tights, a sports skirt, and a blue sweater over a white blouse. She rushed through the kitchen and out through the back door to avoid Mother seeing her leave the house.

She made the short run down the hill in record time and jumped on just as the trolley pulled away from its stop. She paid the fare and squeezed in among standing passengers waiting for a seat to be vacated further along the line. Staggering against other bodies, she grabbed and hung on to a suspended leather loop.

The overhead electrical connectors popped and fizzled as the swaying coach lurched through mid-town street intersections. Stopping to drop and pick up passengers, the ride smoothed over tracks stretching out into the countryside toward the mill stacks spewing black smoke in the distance. Through the front window, Tess discerned the disheveled crowd moving back and forth past the closed gate like a disconsolate beast seeking access. The picketers were surprisingly silent letting their raised painted and printed signs and placards speak for them.

She stepped off the trolley. In search of Dove, she walked the line extending along the high chain link fence boundary of the mill. Dove spotted her first and called and waved to her. Tess smiled and waved and joined the odorous column of unwashed bodies in musty clothes trudging shoulder to shoulder.

"What are you doing here?" asked Dove.

"I support your cause," said Tess.

"But your Dah owns the mill."

"All the more reason."

"Won't you get into trouble?"

"He doesn't' know I'm here."

"Why do this? Why bother?"

"It gives us a chance to be together, to see each other."

"Yeah, I miss coming to your place."

"You been painting?"

"Yeah, at the art store. Peter lets me use his studio."

"That's great. I liked him when I met him."

"He's helping me with my technique. I'm getting better."

"I always thought you were the best."

Dove's face crinkled into a smile. "I'm glad we're still friends."

"We didn't stop being friends because of what happened."

"I know. You're not yer mah."

"That's fer sure. I'm not my mah." They giggled. "By the way, your mah and dah here somewhere?"

"They're standing at the gate. Dah is a union officer."

"Could I meet them finally? You never introduced me."

"They warn't home when you used to come see me."

"We're all here now."

"I never told 'em about the pallet and paints you gave me. They don't believe anyone would gi' me anything, like the coat. Mah thought I stole it, but she did let me keep it."

"Did you ever tell them about me?"

"I told 'em I had a friend and ya lived on the Hill."

"They didn't believe you?"

"Naw, I tried to get my brother, Colum, to tell 'em it was true, but he wouldn't do it. Said I was lyin', even though he saw you and you gave him jack for ice cream."

"Not very nice."

"That's how brothers are."

"I don't know anything about brothers. There's just Gwen and me at home."

"Don't forget Millie."

"She's not my sister."

"Good as could be."

"I don't have anything to do with her. She's my mother's pet."

"What are your parents' names?"

"Desmond and Maeve."

"That's them, my Mah and Dah." Dove pointed to a tall, emaciated man and a petite woman whose head came to his shoulder. A cloche hat concealed half of her thin face. She turned when Dove poked her arm and Tess instantly saw the resemblance of mother and daughter, except for the mother's weary expression and hard vacant stare.

"Mah, Dah, this is my friend I told you about, Tess Vanderveer."

Their eyes flicked over Tess like indiscriminate rain.

"It's nice to meet you, Mr. and Mrs. Delaney."

Desmond's rolled up sleeves exposed sinewy dark-haired arms. "Ya the same Vanderveer what owns the mill?"

"Her dah is the one," said Dove.

"He send you out here to spy on us?" asked Maeve.

"I'm not a spy," said Tess. "My father doesn't know I'm here. I came so I could be with Dove."

"Yeah, she told us how yer mah treated her, what she said. Dove cried her eyes out."

"I was so sorry," said Tess. "My mother is not a kind woman."

"We was thinkin' Dove shouldn't hobnob with you either," said Maeve. "Some of yer hoi polio was rubbin' off on her and she ain't hoi polio."

"I'm not either," said Tess.

A guffaw coughed from Desmond's mouth. "Yer family's rich. Ye got Jack. The rest of us are gut-suckin' poor. That's the difference."

"I'm not like my mother and father."

"And we don't care for the likes of you takin' pity on us," said Maeve. "We don't need no favors. In our family, we stand on our own two feet."

Tess nodded in agreement. "Dove is a friend I want to share with. It's not pity."

"She don't need yer hand-me-downs," said Maeve.

"They aren't hand-me-downs. They're gifts from me to her."

"You and Dove ain't the same kind of people."

"That's what my mother says, but it's not true."

"Don't talk back to me, Missy. We don't need you here. You ain't welcome here to be with us."

"I can talk to my father."

"You think you hold any sway o'er yer dah?" said Desmond. "He ain't gonna listen to you. He ain't gonna listen to us. That's why we're striking. We don't mean shit to 'im except he don't have nothin' to sell without we make it for 'im."

She glanced away through the heavy iron bars of the entrance gate and saw her father's figure in the large window overlooking the loading yard and the pandemonium of the strike. She wondered if he could see her in the crowd but thought he might be too far away.

"I'm sorry," she said. "I'm not like him."

"You ain't no politician. 'Less you can change the law, you sayin' yer sorry ain't worth a shit."

Tess turned to Dove. "I'll stay a while longer. Then I have to go back. Mainly I came to see you."

"I know and I'm glad you did." She led Tess away from her parents and into the crowd.

"I'll try to see you once in a while," said Tess. "We just need a time and place to meet."

Dove hooked her arm in the crook of Tess's elbow as they walked along.

Tess had talked to Gladys and me about politics when we were all listening to Father Charles Coughlin's broadcast on the radio. Andreas Vanderveer hated and despised the radio priest and Catholics because of Coughlin's anti-capitalist diatribes to millions of listeners. Coughlin wanted the redistribution of wealth by taxing the wealthy. He advocated Federal protection for union workers. He accused President Roosevelt of favoritism for Wall Street banks and how a small group of financiers were creating money at the expense of public welfare.

At nightfall, the city lights flashed by the trolley windows as Tess rode with Dove back into the city. They said their goodbyes at the bottom of Beacon Hill and went their separate ways. Tired and hungry, not suspecting what awaited her, Tess trudged up Pinckney Street to the mansion and entered by the back door. Gladys was cleaning up in the kitchen after the evening meal.

"Is my father here?"

"Yeah, he is very mad at you. He shouted at all of us, even your mother. He is waiting for you in the living room."

"Let him wait. I'm hungry. What do we have to eat?"

"Some leftovers, cheese and noodles."

"Can you fix me a plate?"

"I will, but I don't want him to yell at me."

"Don't worry, Gladys. I'll eat fast."

Gladys removed the food from the icebox and was about to spoon it into a pot on the stove.

Tess interrupted her. "I'll eat it cold."

"Kalt?"

"Yes, cold. And I'll have a glass of milk."

Her father suddenly appeared at the kitchen entrance. Startled by his lethal tone, Tess whirled to face him.

"I was expecting you to come through the front door," he said. "But then I remembered what a sneak you are and might come in the back way. And I was right. Come to the living room. Your mother and I have something to say to you."

"I'm going to eat something first. I'm hungry."

"Missing supper was your choice. Don't give her anything, Gladys." Tess's resentful fearless expression angered him further. "Come with me, now!"

She roughly brushed past him and stomped down the hall ahead of him into the living room. Seeing Mother seated on the couch, she perched on the edge of an armchair with a coffee table between them. Father sat at the opposite end of the couch from Mother. Tess's rigid posture and defiant stare did not waver.

"We think there is something wrong with you, Tess," said Mother. "You have chosen to disobey us over and over again."

What I want to know," said Father, "is how you found out about what is happening at the mill."

"I read about the strike in the newspaper."

"You had no business joining it. You had no business being there."

"My friend's mother and father work at the mill."

71

"You mean that Irish girl you were told to stop seeing?" asked Mother.

"Dove Delaney is my best friend. I will never stop seeing her."

"Oh, you will stop. You can be sure of that, young lady."

"She's a person, Mother, a human being, just like me."

"Don't get smart with me, Tess. Your father and I will decide who you see and what you do."

"So you're treating me like a prisoner instead of a daughter."

"We are providing you with a life and opportunities that are in your best interests."

"You mean your best interests."

"That's it, Tess. We've reached a breaking point."

"Well, why don't you just break and let me live my own life."

Father rose from the couch, walked over and hit her with a ringing slap. Tess's eyes teared, but she did not cry. Her hand touched the growing red bruise on her cheek.

"There will be no dinner for you tonight," he said. "Go up to your room and pack and be ready to leave early in the morning."

"Leave where? You're sending me away?"

"We think you'd be better off in a residential school," said Father.

"What residential school?"

"Kragen," said Father.

"Kragen!"

"Yes, Kragen, it's only a half day's drive."

"You know what kind of school that is?"

"Yes, it should suit you perfectly," said Mother.

Tess rose and headed for the stairs before Father could slap her again. "I guess I should count myself lucky I won't be living here anymore."

"George will drive you," said Father. "Be ready to leave by six a.m. Gladys will pack a breakfast for you."

"I just check myself in?"

"The arrangements have already been made."

I rushed down the hall and up the back stairs to the second floor just in time to hear Tess's bedroom door slam shut. My discreet knock met with Tess's outraged shout, "Stay away! Just stay the hell away!"

"Tess, it's me. Can I come in? We have to talk."

"No, I don't want to talk to you or anybody!"

" I have a plan," I said. "I want to help."

"There's nothing you can do! Mother and Father are cruel! They're dictators! They're evil!"

"Please, Tess, let me come in. At least hear what I have to say."

Tess suddenly pulled the door open. "What!"

"Not out here in the hall. Let me come in."

Tess stepped aside and I entered. She closed the door.

"What could you possibly do that would make a difference?"

"I can carry letters between you and Dove."

"What are you talking about?"

"You can send me letters without a return address. Harmon and Ivo bring in the mail. They can give me your letters addressed to me before Mother and Father see them. I can take them to Dove and she can give me letters to send back to you."

"They couldn't have gotten me farther away from Boston than if they sent me to Canada."

"I am so sorry for you."

"Don't be. Kragen has a reputation, but I'll be fine. It can't be any worse than living here under the Vanderveer regime." Tess heaved her suitcase onto the bed.

"I'll come downstairs with you to say goodbye tomorrow."

"You don't have to."

"I want to. You're my sister."

"You're a nice person. I hope some good things happen for you."

"You want some help?"

"No, I just want to be alone."

I walked toward her to give her a hug. She held out a stiff arm and shook her head. I quietly turned and left the room.

Chapter 7

The Go-Between

The Kragen Academy For Girls sits nestled among the wooded foothills of the White Mountains, the northernmost chain of the Appalachians between Maine and New Hampshire. Tess lived in exile at the residential school for the next three years and refused to come home, even during holidays. Her absence did not perturb Mother and Father, which saddened and infuriated me.

Despite her insistence that I not bother, I woke early the next morning to say a somber goodbye. Tess dozed for much of the long ride with our chauffeur, George Oswell.

As the limousine passed under the wrought iron arch bearing the Kragen name, Tess could see uniformed girls walking in sporadic small groups from an adjacent three story dormitory and dining hall to the main gray stone building housing the school office and classrooms on the second and third floors. On the other side, a gymnasium stood next to an athletic field where a dozen older girls wearing black tights and sports skirts maintained a steady jog around the cinder track.

George parked the limousine at the entrance and Tess held the heavy wooden door open for him to carry in her luggage. A sign prominently displayed the name, Margaret Kragen, Head Mistress, at a front corner of the vacant desk.

"Should I wait?" George asked.

"No need," said Tess. "Thank you for driving me."

"Gladys and Harmon and Ivo and I will miss you."

"I'll make the best of it here."

"Until next time."

"Maybe."

"Goodbye."

Tess remained silent. George started back to the door, then paused as a tall, elegant women with long flaxen hair entered from a side hall.

"Hello, you must be Tess Vanderveer. I'm Margaret Kragen. Your father said you would be arriving today."

A plain gray skirt and white shirtwaist blouse did not detract from her commanding beauty. Tess noticed a slight Polish accent, unlike the clipped New England twang she was accustomed to hearing.

"Are you her chauffeur?" she asked George.

"Yes, ma'am."

"Would you inform Mr. and Mrs. Vanderveer their daughter has been safely delivered."

What did she think I was, said Tess in a letter, *a package?*

"Yes, ma'am, as soon as I return."

"Thank you."

"You're welcome, ma'am."

"Please have a seat," said Margaret as soon as George was gone.

Tess took the center of the three chairs primly positioned before her desk. Margaret seated herself. Tess discerned a compressed smile that made her uncomfortable, as Margaret studied her. "Do you feel nervous?"

"No, why do you ask?"

"You look tense. Most students when they arrive are nervous. They don't know what to expect. Kragen has a fearsome reputation as a school for troubled girls. Perhaps you've heard."

"I have a school friend who was here for one year. I'm sure I'll do fine," said Tess.

"Did your parents tell you why they enrolled you?"

"I disobeyed them. They think I'm difficult."

"Many of the girls here have a streak of independence. Have you thought of yourself as having an independent nature?"

"I've never thought otherwise."

"That's to your credit."

"What do you mean?"

"In two years, you'll be going out into the world. You won't be an impressionable young girl anymore. You'll have to compete. That's what we prepare you for, the competition. Are you competitive?"

"In track and field hockey."

"We encourage competitiveness in sports, but also in academic achievement. How have you done in your other school?"

"I'm not the best, but I'm among the top of my class."

"Good, we expect a lot from you, but we provide you with the intellectual and academic tools to succeed. What college are you planning to attend after you graduate?"

"Wellesley, my mother insists."

"Wellesley is a good school, one of the best. Whatever your mother's reasons; we're not grooming you to find a husband."

"That's refreshing."

"Times are changing and they'll change even more in the coming years. Our mission is to make you a part of those changes."

"Does my mother know that? She wouldn't approve."

"Let's make that our little secret."

After two months, letters began arriving addressed to me from Tess with no return address on the envelope. Most of what happened to her, I gleaned from the letters. At the end of each one, she asked me to deliver it to Dove, making me an accomplice in her deception. She was forbidden to have any contact with Dove.

Suspecting the letters might be from Tess, Ivo gave them to Gladys to give to me when I got home from school with Millie and went to the kitchen for milk and cookies. I stuck each letter in among my books, quickly devoured my snack, then raced upstairs to my room and closed the door. I opened the letter carefully, but with great anticipation. Even though she started with *"Dear, Dove,"* I felt Tess was also talking directly to me.

I'm sure Gwen found a way to tell you by now that I have been exiled to a residential private school in New Hampshire. Let me not mince words. At first, I thought the Kragen School For Girls would be nothing more than a prison.

Since the day I arrived and was given an orientation, what I thought was a depressing start turned out not to be so. Sure, they have rules. What school doesn't? But if you break one here, more happens than going to sit in the principal's office. The principal, Margaret Kragen, calls them consequences for our actions.

Her husband, Paul, is the athletic coach and runs the sports programs, which I don't mind at all. All students have to call them Mr. or Mrs. Kragen although Mr. Kragen told us we can call him coach. Between the two of them, I like him better. Margaret is two-faced. She pretends to be cold with a streak of sadism but is actually polite and cordial. I think her contempt is an act. After all, she is the dramatic arts teacher.

My roommate adores her. Lydia Tyson, aspires to become a stage and movie actress. She isn't what I would call beautiful, but her springy dark curls and blistering blue eyes give her an engaging charm. She could probably play comedy roles.

She constantly reads character parts out loud from play scripts and wants me to read the parts of other characters. She said I'm actually good and should try out for the plays directed by Margaret. I can't say I'm interested. I prefer being on the track and basketball and field hockey teams. Mr. Kragen, Paul, although we're not supposed to call him that, coaches all the sports. He's sort of like a father to us and we call him coach.

He's a rough-looking handsome man, a head taller than Margaret. He's rock solid and played professional football in Poland. He has a broken nose to prove how violent that sport is. His nose does not disfigure his face. His unruly dark hair, blue eyes, and hard weathered features make him look dashing. But he has a surprisingly gentle manner and never raises his voice and shouts at us. He calls us over from the field or off the court and talks to us and gives us advice and we listen and try to do our best for him and for our team. He stresses how important it is to think of ourselves as a team. Such things had never occurred to me before.

I ran the high hurdles, one-hundred yard dash, the half-mile relay, and the high jump. I ran the best times and have set the school record for the high jump.

The school population is only 120 girls from early to late teens. My English and composition and French teacher is Constance Bennet. Paul Kragen is the math teacher and coach. Margaret Kragen teaches history and civics classes and music and dramatic arts. A raised stage at one end of the gym is used for school presentations and theater productions.

I sing in the school choir just like at Providence. Margaret told me I am a well-modulated mezzo soprano. I'm afraid my singing voice is the only thing well-modulated about me. When she found out I play the piano and can sight read, she made me the chief accompanist.

All the girls have to fix their beds each morning, which is something I've never done my whole life. Once a week, a housekeeper washes our sheets and towels, but we have to wash and iron our own clothes, also something I've never done before.

The dining hall cafeteria serves three meals a day, not at all like the food Gladys made for us. Mostly we get soups and stews, fried chicken, canned vegetables, and sausage and noodle dishes. There is always freshly baked bread and cookies, cakes, and pies. I think I am putting on weight but shed the pounds running on the track team.

The cook is a stout, gray-haired polish woman helped by two other younger Polish women. The scarves and dresses they wear give them the appearance of European peasants. They are very chatty and smiling as the girls slide their trays along the line. The food is surprisingly good. We have hearty appetites. No one complains.

I noticed an upbeat tone of satisfaction and contentment in Tess's letters. At home, she had always been surly and confrontational, except when she was with Dove and blatantly excluded me. I was thinking that life at Kragen Academy was probably good for her.

Believing Dove would be anxious about Tess, I ventured down the hill into the tenements the next day to deliver the letter. I was surprised that she told me to wait while she read.

She seemed glad to see me, since I provided a connection to Tess. Dove apologized for her past behavior and acted like she was my friend.

"As soon as you get a letter, bring it to me," she said.

"I will. That's why I'm here."

"You promise?"

"I promise. I promised Tess."

"How far away is the school?"

"Up north in New Hampshire."

"I wonder if there's any way I could go visit her."

"I don't know."

"I want to write her, but I ain't good at words and spelling. Could you write what I tell you and send it to her?"

"Yes. I can write your letter. I'll explain to Tess. Do you have a pencil and paper?"

Dove tore a sheet of lined paper from her school tablet and handed it to me along with a pencil. "Thanks for doin' this. I wasn't sure if you liked me."

"Even if we aren't friends, you're Tess's friend. I care about her. That's why I'm here."

"I don't know anyone else like her. She's special. She's means more to me than a friend."

I wasn't sure what Dove meant by that, but I didn't ask. "So, what do you want to say?"

"Dear, Tess, It sounds like the school's okay, but I wish it wasn't so far away or I'd come and see ya. Yer Dah closed down the mill. My mah and dah don't have jobs, 'cept dah might get work with the WPA."

"I know," I said sympathetically. "My father moved the mill operations to North Carolina."

"I thought he shut down 'cause of the strike."

"I don't know all the reasons why. It had to do with money."

"I know," said Dove. "We all know. He didn't want to pay the workers what they deserve."

In 1938, with the demand for nylon, Father had made a gradual transition of the mill location to benefit from the market, not only for women's girdles and stockings, but for parachute silk and the production of tents and tires that withstood mildew during military operations. Phasing out the New England mill had allowed him to increase its profitability by employing low cost labor in the South.

The letters I wrote for Dove were a hodgepodge of unconnected thoughts about her artwork and her family. My Father closing down the mill was a traumatic time for them. She told me how her parents reacted to losing their jobs.

"They went crazy," she said. "Dah got drunk at the pub. Mah got work sewing at a sweat shop. Colum worked loading and unloading ships at the dock. After he sobered up, Dah applied to the WPA and got work on a street repair crew. I quit school."

"Quit school? Why?"

"I'm workin' fer Peter now. The WPA pays him. He pays me six dollars a week to help paint murals in government buildings. Won't make me rich, but now I'm a professional."

"That's great, Dove. I'll put that in your letter to Tess. I saw one of your paintings at the art store. I met Peter. He said you're very talented. I just wondered why you didn't give the people's faces eyes and a nose, and mouth."

"It says something about the people, about us and who we are, where we live. Peter said the painting tells us no one sees us Irish as people. He says the painting tells us we don't exist for others who look at us. We have names, but we don't have identities. We're just Irish poor."

Since she had read Tess's letter, Dove was talkative and upbeat. She asked, "You want to go with me sometime?"

"Go where?"

"The art store. I'll show you how I paint. I've done lots of canvases. I can also show you the mural Peter and me are workin' on. There are three other artists workin' with us."

"Okay, I suppose so."

Once we were on the street and on the trolley, I could see from Dove's expression that her thoughts were elsewhere, maybe about Tess and maybe about her painting or both. From time to time, she glanced at me to confirm I was actually with her as a physical connection to Tess.

When we arrived at the art store, I noticed a new poster in the front window featuring the logo drawing of an eagle side by side with a white and red striped artist's pallet and a brush inserted in the hole.

Dove introduced me to Peter, who said we had met. When I asked about the WPA poster in the window, he explained that the store was now funded by the Federal Art Project to encourage and support local artists. He showed me a news article he had posted on the wall featuring a black and white photograph of Senator Harold Gebhardt, who oversaw Federal funding for the state of Massachusetts. This was the first, but not the last time I would see his name.

Paper Dolls

The Federal Art Project was the visual arts segment of the Great Depression-era Works Progress Administration, a Federal One program. Funded under the Emergency Relief Appropriation Act of 1935, it employs artists and artisans for the creation of murals, paintings, sculpture, graphic art, posters, and photography.

The Project was operated by community art centers throughout the country for craft workers and artists to exhibit their work and educate others.

The Federal Art Project employed out-of-work artists and provided art for public buildings, libraries, and hospitals. Artists earned $23.60 a week for art production, art instruction and art research. The art-research group was compiling an Index of American Design, a comprehensive study of American material culture.

After Dove showed me a growing collection of her paintings and drawings, she took me on a tour of three mural projects on which she was working with Peter and other artists. Her work was my first glimpse of a career and notorious reputation that lured Tess into a counter-cultural underworld and severed her from her family origin.

Chapter 8

In Retrospect

When I was a child, I was more of an observer than a doer. I took my cues from my older sister and tried to copy and emulate her through our growing years into young adulthood. Her directions and advice often contradicted what and whom our mother tried to mold us to become, a fashionable society woman like herself. As our lives unfolded, we seemed to have a gift to socially embarrass her.

How she lived held no appeal for us. Our preferences and disobedience resulted in angry confrontations, especially over our choice of friends. To be blunt, Mother was a snob.

Tess was always a competitive, sarcastic, moody sort. She embraced any physical and academic challenge presented to her. I wondered why she seemed uncharacteristically chipper the day she graduated from Wellesley. Under duress from our parents and true to her nature, she had initially refused to attend any of the upscale Ivy League sister schools. To get away from Mother harassing her, she had agreed on Wellesley, a highly regarded women's college.

In some way, the competitive social challenges suited her. She had been more than a match for the snobbiest girls who didn't understand why she scorned their elitist claims. She also made enemies.

Lacking her exemplary fortitude, I was a sophomore at Wellesley, two years behind her and not nearly as smart. The summer of 1941, she graduated with honors at the top of her class.

A week later, she went missing. There was no reason or evidence as to why.

The commencement took place at Founders Hall. Tess was one of twenty-five graduating seniors. Enrollments and the small number of graduates had declined during The Depression. Only daughters of affluent families who had not lost their wealth attended Wellesley and other Ivy League schools.

Supported by the mission and culture of the college administration, Tess was outspoken against male dogma that sports made women less feminine and that they were too fragile to participate in strenuous activities that would harm their reproductive organs. She went beyond wearing leggings and was the first in her class to appear on the track field wearing shorts, eliciting audible gasps from the bleacher crowd.

Photographs of her athletic performance and sports commentaries populated newspapers and magazines with always an emphasis on her beauty and sexuality.

Since I volunteered as a writer for the Wellesley campus newspaper, I covered women's sporting and social events, the sorority teas, theatrical productions by the dramatic arts club and visiting performers, authors and famous speakers, and the war bond drive. I wrote an editorial encouraging student cooperation and announcements of the choir presenting Sunday vesper services, society program meetings held by Phi Sigma, Tau Zeta Epsilon, and Alpha Kappa Chi. I also wrote articles on swing dancing and reviews of concerts by the Boston Symphony.

In the midst of all the campus activities, I made time to study diligently.

With the closing encouraging words of the college President's inspirational speech ringing in my head, I joined Mother and Father in a small congratulatory enclave around my sister, Tess, who acknowledged praises from our parents, several fellow students, and professors and instructors circulating among the crowd.

Knowing Tess, I wondered if President McAffee's motivational and patriotic message had in some way influenced her to just cast aside all expectations and disappear on behalf of the war effort. McAffee herself was a U.S. Navy Lieutenant Commander of the WAVES (Women Accepted For Volunteer Emergency Service).

Without disparaging the fathers in the audience and acknowledging the value and importance of wives and mothers, the Dean Signaled the academic achievements of the young women and encouraged them to realize their individual potential to excel in their chosen fields and not settle for a life of only self-indulgence and domestic responsibility.

I noticed my mother bristle at that comment. She had never had to work a day of her life and considered attending college was a ritual to finding a husband.

More than a year ago, mother had unsuccessfully tried to advise Tess on the importance of landing a suitable male from one of the Ivy League universities as though he were a trophy fish. Mother knew many families in her social set whose sons would qualify in her opinion. Tess ignored her at the mere mention of any of them.

As Tess and I were growing up, where Tess fought against our Mother, I tried to understand why she was the way she was. Her personality wasn't just a matter of being born into the New England aristocracy. Societal influences of class elitism reinforced and shaped her.

My first and only encounter with a cotillion was my mother's doing. Tess refused to cooperate and be involved. She held stronger opinions than Mother about such events. I tended to succumb to Mother's dominating personality. Millie, on the other hand, bought in to the ritual lock, stock, and barrel.

The Vanderveer family possessed what was called hereditary nobility. As a young woman came of age, she had to establish her identity of wealth in the costly ritual of a cotillion. The debutante was put on a pedestal as the symbol of social success by cultural divine right.

The social status of a debutant recalled a fantasy of the past that masked the massive poverty, joblessness and hunger that surrounded us by the artifice of aristocracy.

When Tess didn't return, I went to the campus to help her pack and move out of her dorm. Her roommate was gone. Tess's diploma, cap, and gown lay where she had haphazardly flung them onto her unmade bed.

I checked the closet and discovered half of her clothes were still hanging. Her suitcase was gone.

I went downstairs to the first floor and asked the housemother, Miss Lampson, to describe briefly, if she had seen Tess. Miss Lampson said she thought Tess had gone home the day after the ceremony. She hadn't seen or talked with her since.

That's when I began to worry.

"Tess told me she was going to the beach with a friend," I said. "But I don't know which one."

If I were to hazard a guess, her best friend, Dove Delaney, would have something to do with it. Dove had been stalking my sister for years. She even turned up as a waitress working in a local restaurant near the campus and insinuated herself into Tess's social life in a way that discouraged college men who tried to date her. Her relationship with Dove became the subject of slanderous gossip.

One ugly incident occurred at The Well following a track meet. Drawn to her athletic prowess, Hank Stacker, a Harvard business major, was fixated on Tess. I knew who he was. I noticed he attended every sports event in which she participated and sat in the first row bleacher seats.

He was the privileged son of a Wall Street banker and considered himself a lady's man. His narcissism and toxic masculinity were legend. With his slick dark hair and narcissistic blue-eyed movie star looks, he didn't believe any woman could say no to him.

He had come into the tavern with four of his buddies and had taken over a table when he noticed Tess and me sitting at a booth. They palavered with each other and guffawed at some crude joke. Then Hank rose from his chair and strode over to us. Thrusting out his muscular chest to emphasize his tall physique and university sweater, he beamed a gloating toothy smile down at Tess.

"Congratulations on the meet. You are one amazing girl to watch. You could compete in the Olympics."

Tess glanced at him, then back at me, but did not respond.

"I hear you're modest, but that's okay. I'm Hank Stacker, captain of the rowing team and the wrestling team at Harvard. You might have heard of me. I'd like to go out with you. I know we'd hit it off."

Wearing her blue waitress uniform, Dove suddenly appeared at his side. "She doesn't date guys from Harvard."

His brow wrinkled. "Who the hell are you? Was I talking to you?"

"Why don't you go back to your table so I can take your order."

"You know this bitch?" he asked Tess.

"She's my best friend."

"She go to Wellesley?"

"No," said Dove, "I work here."

"You're not a student?"

"I'm an artist."

"Artist of what, flipping burgers and slinging hash?"

"Tess, you were about to give me yours and Gwen's orders when Mr. America showed up. What'll it be?"

"Hey, cupcake," Hank sneered, "I'm talking to her. You have to wait your turn."

"You have to go back to your table, Stacker." Tess's voice was polite, but low and menacing.

"You two ganging up on me? That sounds like fun. We could do a threesome."

"You're disgusting," Tess's disapproving stare modified his expression. He stepped back with a defensive sneer, then sauntered away to his table.

"What would you like?" Dove asked Tess.

"I've kind of lost my appetite but I'll have a cheeseburger medium well and fries and a beer."

"Sounds good." Dove jotted the order on her pad and turned to me. "Gwen?"

"I'll have the same."

"Got it." Dove went to the kitchen counter, tore the chit off her pad and handed it to one of the two cooks.

"I can do more for you than she can with her tongue!" Hank shouted across the room. He and his cronies snickered and ogled Dove as she came over to take their orders.

She raised her pad and pencil. "Okay, little boys," she said, "what'll it be?"

Hank's lips curled in a lascivious smile. "Why don't you lift your skirt, drop your panties, and bend over the table."

Dove slowly and deliberately turned away and walked to the bar. She asked the bartender to fill a pitcher of beer from the tap. Carrying the pitcher, she walked back to the table and poured the contents onto Hank's lap. "Looks like you wet your pants, little boy."

Hank shot up out of his chair with a snarl. His open hand swung at her in a roundhouse arc that connected with her face. Her head snapped back and she fell crashing onto a neighboring table scattering its four occupants.

Encouraged by the shouts of his friends, he dragged her off the table with a hard fall to the floor and kicked her in the ribs. A moment later, he was staring at the jagged teeth of a broken beer bottle brandished by Tess.

"You have a nice face, Hank, but not nice enough."

The bottle flashed at him like a striking snake opening his left cheek with a bloody gash. He shrieked and staggered back.

"You touch her again; I'll do the other side of your face."

As his supporters jumped up and moved toward her, Tess menaced them with the bottle. Howling at the blood streaming down his neck staining his crimson sweater, Hank rushed out of the tavern with his friends crowding after him.

"I'll kill you for this!" he shouted. "I'll kill you, you bitch!"

I ran over to help Tess lift Dove to her feet. We sat her on a bar stool. The bartender handed her ice wrapped in a towel to hold against her swollen cheek.

"I called the cops," he said. "They'll be here any minute."

"We don't need the cops," said Dove. "I'll be all right."

"Well, you have witnesses. It was self-defense. You need to take the rest of the day off? I can call Alice to cover for you."

"No, I need the tips."

"I can take you over to the infirmary," said Tess. "He kicked you in the ribs."

"It's okay. I'm tough."

The police siren died in the parking lot.

Surprisingly, Hank Stacker did not press charges. I assumed the publicity of a trial and the police report of the incident would have proven embarrassing. We did learn that the gash required sixteen stitches and left his once beautiful face with a permanent scar that he flaunted as a badge of honor.

Hank did not come to any more track meets and he and his friends never appeared again at The Well.

The disappearance of Tess was a turning point in my life. My attempts to find her put me on a personal exploratory path of who I would become and what I would do with my own life.

Chapter 9

As For Me

Justine Vogel became my closest friend. I first met her when we were assigned to share a dormitory room at Wellesley. I was moving in my personal belongings when she appeared at the open door. Her disarming smile and friendly manner impressed me. As we exchanged introductions, I felt an instant kinship at the first thing she shared about herself.

"I can tell you everything you want to know about anatomy and how your organs function. My dad started me reading his medical books when I was ten years old. He wanted me to go to Harvard and become a doctor, but I'd rather analyze literature and human behavior than dissect cadavers."

"Do you plan to teach?"

"After I get my Masters in five years, I'll be looking for a job in New York publishing."

"Have you decided on a thesis?"

"I read a lot, all the books I can get my hands on. The one thing among the many that has caught my attention is how women are depicted. My emphasis will be the roles of women in literature."

"I never thought about graduate school," I said sheepishly.

"Plenty of time for that." She opened a large suitcase and began hanging its contents in our shared closet.

"Where's your home?"

"I grew up in New York, Manhattan. My dad's a surgeon at Bellevue Hospital."

"I'm from Boston."

"You're close to home. You ever visit New York?"

"I've been there with my mother to shop and see Broadway shows."

Energy and excitement clung to Justine like an urban aura. She carried her slender body with a sophistication and purpose I did not possess. A brunette crown of coiffed marcel curls rippled over her head and merged with a long wave descending to broad shoulders. The uplifted tip of her solid brave nose conveyed a sense of intelligence and superiority without condescension balanced by gentle brown eyes. A fashionable dress hovered and swirled over shapely legs. Her high heels clicked with dance-like precision across the wooden floor. My Mother would love her.

Justine was a patrician, but with a significant difference. She was not snobbish or pretentious. I noticed how she listened to others with genuine interest in them and what they were saying. She asked questions and encouraged them and they came away liking her. Her popularity at teas, club meetings, and social events was unquestionable.

Numerous friends of hers I didn't know waved and called out greetings when we walked across the campus together. Girls stopped by our room to see her and tended to ignore me. I would leave and go to the library to study.

But when we were alone, particularly after an English literature or a world history class, or a concert or a play, we engaged in animated discussions expressing our perceptions and opinions. Her intellectual superiority tended to influence me. I came to see her as my mentor, as well as my roommate.

Given the resistance to and advent of a war with Germany, world affairs was among the preeminent topics in the campus newspaper that prompted lively debates. The bombing of London and the sinking of freighters by German U-Boat torpedoes brought the threat to our shores.

Justine would expound on how literature mirrored political and social mores and behavior. She was the first person I encountered who suggested that literature could do more to promote women's equality.

"Men are not superior to us. That has been the status quo for centuries because they subjugated women and limited them to roles of wives and mothers. Biblical law falsely ordains inequality because it was written by men."

"You think books are going to change that?"

"Definitely, what people read tells them how to live their lives. We have to change from men telling women what to think and do. Women have to learn to think and do for themselves. They have to resist and cause changes to happen."

"Don't you plan to get married and have children?" I asked.

"Very likely, but not under the love, cherish, and obey condition I have to be subservient to my husband. Women are not formless, soft-minded baby factories. I had a wonderful childhood although growing up without a brother or sister, my parents spoiled me. I have since distinguished between the advantages of privilege and the realities of existence. I think I gained my empathy for others because my mother is a teacher and my father is a doctor. In both fields, they had to care about people."

"My sister and I weren't brought up that way, but neither of us are like our parents."

"Tess, the track star?"

"Yeah, that's her."

"She's kind of aloof, isn't she? Not very approachable. I tried to introduce myself and she gave me the brush-off."

"Sounds like Tess. She's not the friendly type. More of a loner. Likes to keep to herself."

"Certainly doesn't fit the Wellesley woman model, at least not socially."

"She doesn't care about clubs and teas and social events. Just sports. She's her own person."

"She more like the kind of independent woman I'm talking about."

"She is independent. Our parents sent her off to a tough private school her last three years of high school. She refused to come home for the whole three years, not even for holidays."

"Sounds like a rebel."

"She is that and proud of it."

"You two get along?"

"She thought I was a drag on her when we were younger. She had a special friend, a poor Irish girl who lived in the ghetto. She was the cause of our parents sending Tess away to the residential school. I told you my parents were snobs. That was an example. They couldn't stand the thought of Tess associating with the Irish girl. Beneath her class."

"Does Tess talk to your parents?"

"Hardly, she does her best to avoid them."

"I went to public schools and never knew the difference. My best friend was Vicki Semple. She hated to be called Victoria. Her mother named her after Queen Victoria, who died forty years ago. Her mother said Victoria was an elegant name. Whenever I got mad at her, I'd call her Victoria and she'd walk around like she was putting on airs. Her acting snooty made me laugh. She was clumsy as a clown. She had four brothers, all older except for one. Her older brothers treated her horribly, teasing her and putting her down all the time because of her freckles and wild red hair. She had white skin too, alabaster white. They were a Scottish family. So red hair and freckles were common. She, in turn, was kind to her little brother, who adored her."

"Are you still friends? Do you see her?"

"She's studying to be a nurse. We see each other occasionally on holidays. Actually, she was more interested in my father's medical books than I was. She wanted to become a doctor, but medical schools don't accept women. She was told women were not meant to be doctors." Justine laughed. "We're told we're too emotional."

"Nurses work just as much with patients as doctors."

97

"Doctors claim to be smarter and make the decisions that nurses carry out."

"That's not what your dad told you, was it?"

"No, he's different. He depends on his nurses to make decisions, especially during surgery. They're trained to do their jobs. But he wouldn't be able to get me into medical school if I wanted to anyway."

Justine and I had attended dances and mixers on our campus and at Harvard. We had met some nice boys. I had my first kiss with an engineering major and even allowed him to put his hand under my blouse, but nothing more. I was sorry to disappoint him, but I just wasn't ready to go all the way.

My dating habits changed our junior year when Justine entered what she described as "a serious relationship" with a Harvard medical student. Justine would hate me for describing her like this, but she was gaga over him. I think he reminded her of her father.

They had met at a mixer I had not attended due to a heavy study load and a term paper I was writing on the role of the mother in modern literature, due in two days. The essay described how mothers were depicted as being submissive and nurturing but could also be aggressively punishing and domineering.

It would one day be incorporated into the book I would write.

Justine had come back to the dorm late from the dance and discovered I was still up rattling the keys of my Underwood typewriter.

"Gwen, oh, Gwen, I met him, the man of my dreams," she said.

"That doesn't sound like you, gushing about the man of your dreams. He must be something special."

"Oh, he is." Justine kicked off her shoes and flounced onto her bed. Her arms stretched luxuriously above her head. "Yes, he is. He's irresistible."

"So, what's his name?"

"Ronald Sarkozy. He's beginning his second year in medical school. I could tell from the look in his eyes that we hit it off right away. He has the most hypnotic chocolate brown eyes. I could drown in them."

"Sounds like you're in love."

"If I didn't know myself better, I would say yes."

"Don't deny it. You're both infatuated with each other."

"I think it's more than that. I've never felt like this about a man before. I can't describe it. He's tall, dark and handsome in a huggable kind of way. You can't imagine how I felt when we slow-danced."

"You're giving me a pretty good idea."

"He's Hungarian. He came to America with his parents when he was a little boy. He grew up in New Jersey with a brother and a sister. They're a very close family. He told me all about them. He has such enthusiasm about everything."

"Sounds like you. You should be suited for each other."

She ignored my comment. "We didn't stay 'til the end of the dance. We left early and went out for coffee. I drank two cups. I'm wired. I won't be able to fall asleep."

"That's good. Then my typing won't keep you awake."

"I couldn't sleep anyway."

"He derailed you."

"I guess that's a good way to put it."

"So, did you set a wedding date?"

"Don't be silly. Marriage is out of the question, at least for several years. I have a career to think about."

"Do you think he'll wait for several years?"

"He also has a career to think about. After med school, there's a four year residency."

"Do you think you can wait that long?"

"He's very reasonable about such things."

"He's also a man and you're a woman in love."

"Don't be obtuse, Gwen. We're not animals. We can control our impulses."

"But do you want to? Remember, you're a progressive woman."

"That doesn't mean I'm promiscuous."

"Aren't you full of contradictions. With the man you're going to marry someday, what does it matter?"

"I guess it does matter, if it turns out that we're serious."

"What if he offers you an engagement ring? Will you accept?"

"I would have to think about it."

"You could support him while he's doing his residency."

"Since when did you add matchmaker to your resume'?"

"When do I get to meet him?"

"The next time I go out with him. You're coming with me and you get to date his roommate."

"A double blind date?"

"That's what it's called, babe."

"Have you met him before?"

"No, but Ron says he's a looker and he has chutzpah."

"Chutzpah?"

"Ron says he's kind of forward, aggressive, rough around the edges, you know. Also very competitive. He'd have to be to set a two mile record. I'm winded after walking two city blocks."

"You need to exercise more."

"You mean like your sister? No thanks. I am not an athlete."

"Not like her. She's extreme. We could play golf. That's just hitting the ball and walking. Or how about tennis? We just have to hit the ball to each other so we don't have to chase after it."

"I played field hockey in high school and hated it. I'm meant for intellectual pursuits," said Justine.

"I can't say I've done much, but I do like to swim."

"Did you swim when you were a little girl?"

"Only a little. Ivo took Tess and me to the beach a few times. I was afraid of the waves, but I got over it. Tess was fearless like she is about everything. She's rough around the edges too."

"Who's Ivo?"

"Our butler. He and his brother are excellent swimmers."

"We didn't have a butler. We didn't have that kind of money. My parents wouldn't have hired a butler anyway. Mom liked to cook and I learned from her and how to clean the house."

"You'll make a good wife for Ron. You're already trained."

"Oh, please."

We had a cook and housekeeper, Gladys Dietz. Her daughter lived with us. She's quite beautiful. She became a model for a New York fashion house."

"Well, that's interesting. You never mentioned her before."

"No, she was supposed to be my friend, but my mother took a special interest in her instead of me."

"Did that make you angry?"

"Not angry, sad mostly. Hurt, but I got over it."

"Interesting how important our friends were when we were kids. It's still important, but in different ways. Either it's mutual admiration or we attach ourselves to others for the parts we don't have."

"Just promise me one thing," I said.

"What's that?"

"Promise me I'll be a bridesmaid at your wedding."

"Oh, you are incorrigible. It's a good thing we're friends."

We laughed.

Chapter 10

Meeting Eddie

Meeting Eddie began a rite of passage for me.

I don't know why I felt anxious about Ron Sarkozy's roommate, probably because I didn't handle rejection well. I was able to swallow my pride and not let it show. I could even shrug it off as though the relationship were unimportant to me. But being rejected left hidden scars, so I compensated by excelling in and being recognized for academic excellence. Also, writing for the Wellesley News put me in touch with a wide range of faculty and students who considered what I was doing was important and that perception attached itself to me. I was recognized and respected as an amateur journalist.

I always made deadlines, which was much appreciated by the editor, Susan Blanchard, a senior who would go on to work for the Cleveland News Sentinel after she graduated. I wondered if I might follow her career footsteps to some other news organization.

Panic seized me when the housemother called our room to let us know our dates had arrived and were downstairs in the lobby. I was doing some last-minute primping in the bathroom mirror. I heard Justine answer the phone and say, "Thanks, Emma, tell them we'll be right down." She hung up and said loudly, "Okay, Gwen, you look gorgeous. The boys are waiting. Time to go. "

I stomped out of the bathroom. "Don't make fun of me. I don't look gorgeous. Lana Turner and Lauren Bacall are gorgeous. Katharine Hepburn and Ava Gardner are gorgeous."

"We shouldn't compare ourselves to film goddesses," said Justine. "You're a different kind of gorgeous. You're attractive and you have a gorgeous personality."

"But I'm not beautiful. I know you're just being nice."

"Being beautiful is overrated. The proof's in the pudding. Who knows what the night will bring, except that it's freezing out."

"What is the night going to bring?"

"Ron didn't tell me where they're taking us."

"Sounds special. I do like surprises."

"You ready?"

"As ready as I'm gonna be."

"Grab your coat. Let's go."

I followed her out the door and along the hall. Not wanting to appear over-anxious and hoping for a glimpse of my blind date, I hesitated going down the stairs. He and Ron bounced up from the couch with expectant smiles. Ignoring Ron's intent to introduce us, my date barged ahead and met me at the foot of the stairs.

"I know you're not Justine," he said, "so you have got to be Gwen." He extended his right hand. "I'm Eddie Gebhardt, Ron's dorm mate."

"It's very nice to meet you, Eddie. Justine told me a little about you."

"All the good things, I hope."

"Only good things to tell," said Justine. "You can astound her with the details."

"Astound? You're setting up quite an expectation. I'll try my best to live up to it."

"Hello, darling," Justine greeted Ron with a brief kiss on the lips.

"Darling? Listen to that," said Eddie. "Already sound like an old married couple."

"It's only a kiss," said Justine. "Doesn't go any further than that."

"Not if Ron has anything to say about it. He's head over heels in love with you."

"Not necessary, chum. I don't need any help."

"It's okay to share all his secrets, Eddie," said Justine.

Ron chuckled. "It might be more fun for you to pry them out of me."

Eddie offered me his arm. "Shall we?" His dark good looks and swaggering charm left me feeling a little off-balance. His restless hazel eyes reflected an intense competitive spirit leaving me no doubt that he was in charge.

We went out the door and down the walk to a light green Pontiac Streamliner Coupe parked at the curb. Eddie held open the rear passenger door for me and Ron the front for Justine. When we were all settled into the luxury leather seats and Ron started the motor, Justine asked. "Can you tell us now?"

"Tell you what?" said Ron with a grin.

"Where you're taking us."

"Then it wouldn't be a surprise."

"So, Gwen, where you from?" Eddie asked.

"Right here in Boston."

"Beacon Hill, right?"

"How did you know?"

"I recognized the name Vanderveer. My mother mentioned your mother. They probably know each other, run in the same circles."

"Is your father the Congressman?"

"The very same. You see his name on a political flyer?"

"A news article about the WPA."

"Oh, yeah, he's a New Deal man, a big supporter of FDR."

Rob spoke over his shoulder. "Did Justine tell you Eddie's a track star at Harvard? He set and broke his own two mile record. Pretty amazing."

"I saw your sister at a Wellesley meet," said Eddie. "Hurdles and high jump. She's amazing."

"Maybe you two should get together," I said half-jokingly.

"What? No, you kidding? She's not for me. She's a thoroughbred, too high strung."

"What does that make me, a nag?" I grinned at his discomfort.

"Of course not."

104

"Come on, you two," said Justine. "Stop talking about us like we're horse flesh."

"We should go to the races at Aqueduct sometime," said Eddie. "My bookie has all the hot tips."

"You have a bookie?" I asked.

"Who doesn't? He's down the hill from where you grew up."

"Roxbury?"

"No, the North End, the Italian sector. Name's Vittorio Bellini. Can't say I've made a killing, but I have made enough coin to keep me in the game. I like to play the ponies."

"You like games period," said Ron.

"I like to win. I play to win. That's how my old man raised me. He ran for re-election six times so far and won every time."

"There's no such thing as a friendly game of poker with Eddie."

"Poker is serious business. But I don't play with the wops. Too dangerous. They play for keeps. I tried once and they accused me of cheating. I gave back all my winnings and never went there again. Just play the ponies."

"Not to change the subject," said Ron, "but Eddie and I received our draft notices two days ago."

Justine touched his arm. "What are you going to do?"

"Have to go through boot camp at Newport, then Naval officer training at Columbia University in New York."

"But you're studying to become a doctor."

"I'll be in the medical corps. Finish what I need there and come out with an MD."

"Does that mean you'll be sent to the front lines?"

"I could be on a ship somewhere in the South Pacific."

"What about you?" I asked Eddie.

"Fighter pilot. Basic at Camp Edwards here in Mass and ninety day wonder officer and pilot training at Camp Blanding in Miami. Have a

105

buddy down there who's training for aerial combat. Says the rush is nothing like he's ever known."

"But you'll be in such danger," I said.

"That's where the rush comes in. War is not for wimps. Being a fighter pilot is not a safe occupation. That's the beauty of it. With me in the cockpit, it's more dangerous for the other guy, the enemy. I'm gonna blow him out of the sky."

"Enough war talk, Eddie. We've got ladies with us."

"They're tough. They can handle it. Hell, even women are joining up or going to work in factories. They have to do men's jobs."

"What are you majoring in?"

"Business and law. I'm going to be a lawyer and go into politics like my old man. He can open doors for me."

"Gwen is a news writer," said Ron.

"Only for the college newspaper," I said. "I'm an English major, like Justine."

"You could do publicity and PR for me when I run for office," said Eddie with a laugh.

"Jumpin' the gun there a little, aren't you?"

"Just pullin' your leg, but you never know how things turn out."

"That's for sure," said Ron with a glancing grin at Justine.

We remained silent for the rest of the short drive into Boston. I recognized we were entering the Bay Village south of the Public Gardens. My guess was confirmed when we pulled up at the Cocoanut Grove night club.

"Here we are, girls," said Ron. "I'll let you and Eddie out and park wherever I can find a spot." He edged into the traffic jam.

We waited for Ron, then joined the growing crowd of off-duty sailors and army soldiers and their dates with a scattering of civilians entering the one-and-a-half story brick and concrete building. Inside they dispersed to various dining rooms with a tropical South Seas atmosphere created by decorative palm tree support columns, rattan and bamboo walls and dark blue satin canopies. The brassy swing sounds and syncopated pounding drum beat of an orchestra drew us into the main dining room.

We claimed a table next to couples jitterbugging on the dance floor and ordered pre-dinner cocktails. Justine and I had Manhattans and Ron and Eddie scotch and bourbon. Not being much of a drinker, the alcohol went right to my head. I succumbed to my giddiness and the toe-tapping woodwind riffs and trombone glides. Ron and Justine quickly finished their drinks and slipped into the mob of dancers.

Eddie grabbed me by the hand and maneuvered us to a space among the jumping, bouncing, twirling bodies. My practice at college mixers paid off in matching his rapid footwork and rhythmic twists and turns. "You know how to swing," he shouted. We were both sweating and breathing hard at the conclusion of the number and returned to the table.

Savory aromas floated past on hoisted trays stacked with gourmet concoctions.

"Just worked up an appetite," said Eddie. "How about you?"

"Starving."

"Another drink?"

"Need to eat first," I said.

"We'll have wine with dinner."

Ron and Justine emerged from the dancers scattering back to their tables. "Great band," said Ron, noticing we were reading our menus. "Looks like you want to order."

"You like seafood," Eddie asked me.

"Yes."

"Then I recommend the lobster thermidor. The chef makes it with cognac and melted gruyere cheese."

"I'm partial to lobster. Do you know the chef?"

"Sure, he's a personal friend of my old man."

Ron and Justine took their seats and scanned their menus.

When we were ready, Eddie signaled the waiter, who came over to take our orders. Ron ordered a bottle of champagne that chilled in a tableside sterling ice bucket. "To celebrate," he said. After the pouring, we raised our flutes of effervescent bubbles and Eddie proposed a toast. "To a beautiful evening with our beautiful gals."

Justine chimed in, "And to our handsome guys."

"Hear hear," said Ron.

We drank up, poured a second round while waiting to be served, and Ron ordered a chardonnay to go with our salads and seafood entrees. I was feeling tipsy by the end of the meal. Since we were going downstairs to the Melody Lounge in the basement for after dinner drinks, we declined coffee and dessert. Too stuffed.

We followed the flow of patrons to the dimly-lit Melody Lounge where a young pianist and singer under palm trees on a revolving stage was playing Broadway show tunes. The bar was packed, but we were able to squeeze the four of us around a table for two. A smiling harried waitress with blonde hair unraveling in wisps took our drink orders. The boys ordered cognac. Justine requested a black Russian and I selected a grasshopper for its minty flavor and to settle my stomach. Even with my childhood upbringing, rich cuisine did not always agree with me.

The noise decibel level was too high to be able to carry on a conversation without shouting at each other, so we just settled back and listened to the jazz stylings of the pianist.

A half hour later, the palm fronds suddenly burst into flames from an unknown source. The pianist abruptly stopped playing as someone shouted fire. The blaze tore across the false ceiling and exploded into an inferno on the upper floors. We heard women screaming in the main dining room. Showered with sparks and burning fabric, the crowd erupted in a pandemonium stampeding for the stairs. Like a live animal, flames licked at women's dresses and consumed their hair.

Eddie grabbed my hand and we wormed our way after Ron and Justine through the heaving shoving bodies and anguished faces. Toppled metal tables and chairs tripped my legs and feet. Eddie lunged to keep me from falling and being trampled.

Seeing where the piano player and the bartender and two waitresses had disappeared through a door at the rear of the lounge, we followed and discovered a stairway to the kitchen on the first floor. The white uniformed chef, sous chefs and waiters careened through spilled pots and pans and cookware and broke through a service window onto a loading area. We charged after them, climbed through the window, and ran down the street to get away from the choking smoke and conflagration devouring the building. Ron hesitated and started to go back at hearing the heart-rending screams of tightly-packed people trapped inside by locked doors that wouldn't open.

"It's too late," said Eddie. "It's too late."

We heard approaching sirens and watched the arrival of fire trucks and the crews deploy hoses arcing high-powered streams of water to the roof. Firefighters attacked the jammed revolving entrance door with axes and dragged out smoldering bodies spraying them with cold water in the freezing night.

My teeth chattered nonstop. Shivering without our coats, we stumbled around the trucks and through gawking onlookers to where Ron had parked his car. The windows steamed as we sat inside trying to cope with the tragedy. Ron held a sobbing Justine. Eddie's arms encircled me until my trembling subsided. Eventually, Ron started the car and drove us back to the campus.

We later learned that 492 people had died and hundreds were injured from burns and smoke inhalation.

The recent memory of burned bodies and, a month later, receiving a letter from Eddie describing his "adventures in basic training" at Camp

Edwards emphasized for me how precarious life was. Also, that Ron and Justine were getting married as soon as he finished his training at Columbia prompted me to encourage Eddie to propose.

Chapter 11

All About Eddie

I think looking back what attracted me to Eddie in the first place was his unabashed enthusiasm. He was incorrigible in many ways. He was self-centered, persistent, and insistent that everything in our relationship was all about him. He grabbed life by the horns and let nothing get in his way.

Until we met, I had always lacked confidence, intimidated and excluded by strong personalities like Tess and Dove Delaney. Eddie was different. He included me as the tolerant unconditional loving mother he lacked as a boy. He had been raised in private residential schools and admitted to being a bully.

"I was a trouble-maker when I was a kid. Got kicked out of three private schools."

We were tobogganing on fresh snow like two little kids wearing fur-lined parkas having the time of our lives and not a care in the world. Rosy cheeks and the exuberant sparkle in our eyes belied concerns of what lay ahead for us. Our laughter exhaled balloons of vapor in the frosty air.

After seven runs, we collapsed at the bottom of the barren hill we had been climbing. From the top, we could look out over 1300 military barracks that housed 30,000 soldiers, warehouses, hundreds of trucks and jeeps parked at the motor pool, aircraft hangars, tarmac, and antiaircraft gunnery ranges of the Camp Edwards Army Base and to the endless blue horizon of the Atlantic Ocean.

Huddled close to one another with our backs to the wind, we shared a flask of brandy.

I removed my mitten to reveal the diamond engagement ring he had given me two days ago when I had visited him on the base.

"I can't get over how beautiful it is. It's so big. Look how it sparkles and the setting is so unique. When did you ever have time to buy it?"

"I didn't. It belonged to my mother until she and my old man got divorced."

"You gave me your mother's wedding ring?"

"She gave it to me and told me to have better luck than she did."

"Better luck?"

"It's not just gonna be luck with you and me. I love you, Gwen. You're everything I ever wanted in a woman. That's a very expensive ring, worth ten thousand dollars."

"Ten thousand? Well, that does make me feel special." I leaned over and kissed him. The euphoric effect of the brandy displaced my initial reaction to learning I was wearing his mother's expensive ring. After all, it was only a ring, a symbol that held some significance for Eddie.

He confided in me that he and his mother had never been close. Her expression of affection had been superficial. "She bought me things but I never got to spend much time with her, because I was farmed out to boarding school when I was just a kid. I hated it. In the beginning, I was picked on, because I cried a lot. But I got over it and pretty soon, I was the one kicking ass."

I commiserated with him and shared how his experience reminded me of the empty relationship I had with my own mother and how Gladys, our housekeeper, had become my surrogate mother.

As we dragged the toboggan back to the base entrance gate, Eddie said, "We haven't really talked about the wedding. I'm not avoiding it, but I thought it was something the bride arranged. When I finish training, we could do it at the base chapel, if you want, nothing fancy."

"That suits me fine," I said. "My mother would probably want to make it an event for the society section. She would say a wedding on an army base is beneath her, but, you know, she doesn't even have to come. This is about the two of us."

"I think my mother would show up just to see who got her ring. But she might not if my old man is there. She really hates him."

"Whatever happened between them?"

"The usual. He was having an affair with a divorcee, who married him when he and my mother divorced."

"Why is that the usual?"

"I don't know. It just happens sometimes, especially in those social circles. My old man was a hard-ass to live with. He was a mean unsympathetic lawyer and became an even meaner politician. He always does the bidding of the money men. Doesn't much give a shit about the little guy, families, and the rest of the country."

"I saw his name in a news story about the WPA."

"That's just publicity to make him look like a good guy. He isn't. He hates President Roosevelt and the New Deal. The war is changing all that. He and his cronies are getting rich off the war, manufacturing planes, all those trucks and jeeps, weapons and supplies."

"The same with my father. He makes cloth for uniforms and he converted one of his mills from textiles to silk for parachutes."

"Maybe someday I'll have to use one. Actually, I will during jump training."

"When can I visit you again?"

"In about a month. I'll have another Sunday off. I'll call you. In the meantime, you can buy a wedding dress."

"I was thinking maybe I should just wear a nice suit. A wedding dress seems like I'm overdoing it."

"Whatever you'd like. I have to wear a uniform."

"I will have a bouquet."

"Absolutely."

"Will Ron be your best man?"

"No one better."

"Since I don't know what became of my sister, Justine will be my maid of honor. I won't have any bridesmaids."

"We'll go out to dinner afterwards."

"Not the Cocoanut Grove."

"Not the Cocoanut Grove, although with all the new fire regulations, it could be the safest place to eat in town."

Under the eye of the guard, we kissed goodbye at the kiosk.

"Stay warm," Eddie murmured.

"Hard to stay warm without you holding me."

"Only a few more weeks."

"I'll have a hard time concentrating on my studies."

"Pretty soon, you'll have a break."

"I'll have to wait 'til after you come back to graduate."

"It'll be worth the wait."

"You can say that again. I love you, Eddie."

"I love you. One more kiss, then I gotta go."

"One more."

After the one more, he picked up the toboggan and walked through the gate toward the headquarters building. He glanced back and raised his free hand in a final wave. I vigorously waved back until he passed from sight and I heard the guard say, "He's gone, ma'am. You can stop waving."

I slowly lowered my hand, then turned and walked away to the rail stop and waited for the arrival of the trolley. Despite the sensation of Eddie's kisses, the warmth of my parka, and the fading effect of the brandy, I shivered in the biting wind coming off the ocean.

I rode the trolley into downtown Boston, then switched to the Wellesley campus line. I tried to avoid standing face to face with anybody so other passengers wouldn't smell brandy on my breath and think I was a sot.

Trudging through the knee deep snow across the campus yard to the women's dorm, my thoughts about the wedding and the interruption of my studies blotted other concerns, like eating, until needle-like hunger pains drove me in the direction of the dining hall.

Upon entering the crowd of young women wearing brightly-colored snowflake pattern sweaters, I stowed my mittens in the deep pockets of my parka and unzipped it. I pushed a brown plastic tray along the cafeteria counter bars and selected a large helping of beef and vegetable stew over mashed potatoes, a chunk of French bread, three pieces of chocolate fudge cake, and a cup of coffee. I claimed an unoccupied table and hung my parka over the back of a chair. I ate voraciously, barely taking time to breathe between bites.

Bloated, warm, and sleepy, I walked to the dorm, stomped up the stairs in my snow encrusted boots, and blundered into my room. A pillow and a neatly folded blanket occupied Justine's empty bed. She had moved out to live with Ron in an apartment near the Columbia University campus in New York for the duration of his training.

We talked on the phone from time to time. She told me that when he graduated, he might be assigned medical duty on an aircraft carrier in the South Pacific. I wondered if it might be a carrier that Eddie would one day fly from. That would be a nice situation, two close buddies on the same ship.

I hung my parka in the closet, kicked off my boots, peeled down my leggings, and went to the bathroom. Then, fully clothed, I climbed into bed and pulled the blankets up to my chin. I was asleep as soon as my head hit the pillow.

I dreamt I was being dragged at the end of a rope by a black and white spotted horse while the pounding hooves of the herd thundered around me. I attributed the dream to my eating too much chocolate cake.

An ominous act added to my heightened anxiety about getting married at a time of war. Mother called to tell me that her housekeeper, Gladys, and Gladys' husband had been arrested by the FBI as enemy aliens, because of their German name and origin. No information as to what became of them was available.

Mother said she had lied to the agents who came pounding on the door that she was Millie's mother and had saved Millie from being handcuffed and taken.

Because Eddie's last name, Gebhardt, was a German surname, I began making some inquiries to find out the source of what was happening. His father, Harold, was not an immigrant, and being a congressman exempted him from coming under suspicion.

I knew Gladys and her husband could not possibly be spies.

I read in the newspapers about the internment of Japanese on the West Coast, but nothing about German American citizens. With only a month away from the wedding, I did a little investigating of my own to see if I could locate Gladys and her husband and have them freed. What I discovered and the secrecy of the persecution shocked me.

I took time away from studying for final exams to go to the local FBI office. When I walked into the open bay, I saw sixty or seventy armed agents wearing shoulder holsters, many with rifles and shotguns propped against their desks. Ringing phones and the steady clacking of typewriter keys filled the air with confusion. An officious young man with trimmed brown hair and wearing a pressed brown suit rose from behind his desk bearing the nameplate Cyrus McNab.

"I'm Special Agent Cyrus McNab. May I help you?"

"I certainly hope so. You have falsely arrested my mother's housekeeper, Gladys Dietz."

"You have no business being here." His hard dark eyes and menacing tone did not intimidate me.

"Gladys Dietz has been our housekeeper for twenty years. I've known her since I was a small child. She is a kind and decent person, not an enemy alien as you insinuate."

"We have reason to believe she might be in collusion with Nazi soldiers coming to our shores."

"Based on what? What proof do you have? That's a false accusation and you know it. She is innocent."

He thrust his square chin and hawk nose close to my face. The smell of spearmint gum and cigarettes on his breath nauseated me. "Before you go any farther, Miss, what did you say your name is?"

"Vanderveer, Gwen Vanderveer."

"Miss Vanderveer, you are interfering with an agent of the FBI. I can have you arrested and jailed."

"No, you can't. I know my rights."

"We are at war, Miss Vanderveer. Civil rights are preempted in the interest of national security."

"She's an American citizen. Can you at least tell me what you have done with her?"

"No, she is in custodial detention. that's classified information."

"A cook and housekeeper is classified information? Custodial detention? Does that mean you can hold her indefinitely without due process? You can't be serious."

"I'm very serious, Miss Vanderveer, and if you don't turn around and leave this office, I will arrest you and put you in jail and you will stand trial as a war criminal. And I'm not talking about custodial detention. I'm talking about arrest and indictment."

I suddenly couldn't help myself from laughing, but he abruptly cut me off.

"Ma'am, you just about pushed me too far." He held up his badge. "If you don't leave at once, I will arrest you and read you your rights and then lock you in jail."

"I thought you said I don't have any rights."

"As a citizen who is not under suspicion of collaboration with the enemy, you still have your constitutional rights."

"Isn't this what the Nazi gestapo do, railroad people?"

"Get out, Miss Vanderveer," he roared. "Get the hell out!" He grabbed my arm and roughed me to the door, opened it, and shoved me into the hall. The slam behind me rattled the glass.

I left the FBI office and rode the trolley home to Beacon Hill.

"Hello, Gwen," Ivo greeted me at the door. "It's very good to see you. Congratulations on your engagement. Your mother told us."

"Thank you, Ivo."

How is college? Your mother says you graduate this month. She and Millie are in New York. Mr. Vanderveer is at the mill in North Carolina."

"I went to the FBI office downtown to ask about Gladys. An agent wouldn't answer my questions and kicked me out."

"Did your mother call you?"

"Yes, I want to know what happened."

"Five FBI agents came into the house. They had a warrant for Gladys's arrest and to search her room. They took her radio and pictures of her family and letters from relatives in Germany."

"What about Millie? Was she here?"

"Mrs. Vanderveer told them that Millie was her daughter to keep her from being taken."

"The agent I spoke with said Gladys was placed in custodial detention. No charge was brought against her except that she's originally from Germany."

"Friends told me surprise arrests and house searches are being conducted in German households who have members of the Bund," said Ivo. "The FBI is looking for fifth column documents and communication. They're confiscating radios, explosives, and devices to signal invading U-boats coming ashore. A Federal ordinance requires that all residential and office building windows be blacked out at night so the silhouettes of

American ships, especially tankers and battleships cannot be detected against the cityscape by German submarines in coastal waters.

In talking to Harmon and Ivo, I learned that swarms of FBI agents had made a sweep through the Italian sector too and arrested (custodial detention) a large number of men who had been shipped to internment camps. I learned that a similar persecution of Japanese-American citizens was happening on the West Coast.

"There doesn't seem to be anything we can do."

Ivo shook his head. "Should I have George drive you back to school?"

"What about gas rationing?"

"With Mr. Vanderveer gone most of the time, George hasn't done much driving. Millie and your mother take the train into New York. Your mother buys a first class compartment, otherwise she wouldn't be able to get seats. Soldiers have priority."

"Well, okay, I have much to do."

George drove me back to the Wellesley campus. Enroute, we waited at a railroad crossing for a long passenger train with all the windows blacked out to pass. Knowing the chain of cars concealed innocent American citizens of German and Italian descent, I felt ashamed watching from a chauffeured limousine.

Because of my marriage to Eddie, I did not attend the graduation ceremony. My diploma would be mailed to me. I packed and moved out of the dorm back to Beacon Hill two days before the wedding.

Mother's excuse for not being there was that she no longer had a cook. She and Millie stayed in her New York apartment. Without her saying so, she considered a military wedding not up to her standards and beneath my dignity. I didn't even bother to ask her to attend. She did give me an expensive string of pearls which I wore with my Lilli Ann rayon crepe suit at the ceremony.

The wedding took place in a functional, nondenominational chapel. A benign, middle-aged chaplain, in uniform, conducted the ceremony. He prompted us through our vows in a desultory tone, more like he was reading us our last rites.

Ron and Justine joined us for a quiet dinner in an Italian restaurant. None of us were in a mood to celebrate. The toast offered by Ron had a forced hollow ring despite the congratulatory uplifting phrases.

Justine and Ron had moved into an apartment near the Columbia campus while he completed his training as a doctor and would enter the Navy medical corps.

Eddie and I stayed at a downtown Boston hotel for two nights before departing by train for Miami. Drinking and passionate sex became our way of blocking out the disagreeable realities of wartime, at least disagreeable to me. Eddie loved every minute of it.

Chapter 12

Army Wife

Traveling with a military spouse fell under the category of permissible travel by train with no guarantee you would have a seat. Many of the trains were designed to transport large numbers of tanks and jeeps on flatcars. Soldiers traveled on troop trains for military personnel in reconfigured Pullman sleeper cars. Even box cars with three tiers of bunks were used. I was able to have a seat only because Eddie's father pulled some strings with a general in Washington.

Shouts and cries from wives and mothers with small children filled the air as we joined the jostling soldiers waiting to board on the wooden station platform.

Arms and hands wildly waved goodbye when the faces of sons or a husband appeared at a passenger car window. Wind-driven clouds of black smoke chuffing from the coal-burning engine drifted back over the crowd.

Hefting my suitcase and Eddie his duffle bag, we clambered up the steps of the nearest car platform and stepped through the door into a bedlam of winter uniformed soldiers rapidly claiming empty seats.

"We're going to be left standing in the aisle," I shouted at Eddie.

"No, just keep walking. Follow me. We go to first class. My old man paid off a friend who works at the Pentagon. All it took was a phone call."

We bumped and shuffled along against a tide of soldiers until we reached a Pullman near the dining car. Eddie checked our tickets and said, "Here we are." He slid open a door and urged me into a private compartment. "We've got this all to ourselves. Commode's down at the end. I'll stow the luggage." He hefted his duffle and my suitcase up onto an overhead rack. "Okay, let's settle in. We've got two days ahead of us. I can't wait to take a swim when we get there. My buddy wrote that the white sand beaches are incredible and the clear blue ocean is so warm it feels like bath water. We'll be having a vacation."

The train headed southeast through Virginia farms and the rolling green landscape of Carolina cotton and tobacco plantations. Through the train window, I noticed the transition to the piney woods of Georgia and down through the palmetto swamps of Florida to Miami Beach, the central base of military operations.

We read books and played card games to stave off boredom. We left the compartment only for meals in the dining car and to use the commode. We had to step around soldiers engaged in loud games of dice in the aisle swirling with cigarette and cigar smoke.

At night, we modified our seats into a bed.

Eddie was among the first wave of soldiers matriculating through the OCS training center. Florida was as much of a new adventure for him as it would be for me.

We stepped off the train at the Miami station into a disembarking mob of soldiers being called into formation to board military trucks that would transport them to training barracks at Camp Blanding.

Miles of luxury hotels had been converted to living quarters for single officers undergoing training. They stayed in one of the hotel room barracks, ate in the dining room mess hall, took written exams in a movie theater testing center, learned life saving techniques in the hotel pool and ocean, practiced synchronized marching drills on golf course parade grounds, and received rifle training on an isolated beach not so far from hotel and residential areas that the distant popping of gunfire could be heard.

Eddie's friend had said we could find a room in the high rent, limited vacancy tourist section of town where there were no available rooms for low paid military personnel. He said the housing crisis left wives and children wanting to see their husbands and fathers, for what could be the last time, out in the streets.

Rent control did not ease the demand for the eighty thousand apartments leased to the Federal Government. Miami was a hive swarming with khaki uniformed men and women.

Tired and gritty with the stink of travel at close quarters, we spotted the USO sign posted high on a flat gray stucco single story building that had once been used to store freight and baggage. My suitcase thumped against my leg as we maneuvered through the crowd toward the service center.

Walking through the doorway, we encountered wall to wall soldiers and wives and children occupying all the available couches, tables and chairs or waiting in long lines to speak with military clerks and civilian hostesses. The rumble of voices and crying of babies filled the air.

We saw exhausted angry mothers with babies in carriages, with babies in their arms and with toddlers. Unable to find housing, they had been turned away to roam the streets, homeless, sleeping on park benches or in deserted automobiles and dependent on emergency breadlines set up by the Red Cross to distribute food.

I waited in a long line to use the women's restroom where I could at least wash my face. With no place to rest, I removed my shoes and leaned against a wall, then eventually sat on my suitcase.

Eddie returned from the men's restroom and grabbed a local newspaper from a stack at the reception desk. "I saw a restaurant down the street when we came in," he said. He grasped my hand as we maneuvered out the door and along the sidewalk congested with milling soldiers and civilians.

"It's so hot and humid here and so many people," I said.

"The Army and Navy have taken over all the hotels and apartments. We're lucky to have a room in an older house. My buddy said it's a nice place."

He held the door open for me to enter the Palmetto Café.

A cute freckle-faced waitress wearing a blue and white dress and a candy-striped apron seated us at a vacated table toward the rear of the restaurant. "I'll be back to take your order," she said. As we sat down and read the menu, we had to raise our voices to be heard above the chatter.

"Everything on here is fish," I said.

"It's a seafood restaurant. Seafood is mostly what they serve in Miami. There's a whole ocean full of it out there. At my briefing before we left Boston, they said meat is rationed unless you live in the hotel barracks. Civilians can buy only a pound and a half a week from a butcher anywhere."

"Do you know anything about these fish? I don't know what to order."

"I'm not familiar with all the different varieties, but I heard grouper is delicious . The menu says it's a grilled white fish. Comes with French fries and coleslaw."

"Okay, I'll try it."

"They had to stop serving sweet tea here because of the sugar ration," said Eddie. "Sweet tea is southern. We can have regular iced tea. You won't see sugar bowls on the tables. Can't get it for coffee either." He signaled to the waitress. We gave our orders, then he scanned the front page news articles.

After we left the restaurant, I was surprised at seeing a woman driving the city bus Eddie and I boarded on Flagler Avenue, the main street through Miami.

"Women are doing most of the jobs that men used to," Eddie explained. "Happening all over the country. There are even some training to be pilots. A lot of women are mechanics and building ships and airplanes in factories. There's a big push nation-wide to get food and equipment and supplies from farms and factories to where the fighting is happening on the front lines. Some women are on tree-cutting crews and even building houses. You won't see a milkman anymore. Women deliver the milk. Almost every able-bodied man is in the service. According to the *Signal News*, we're living in the era of the new woman."

"I guess that makes me a new woman," I laughed flippantly. I liked the sound of the phrase but didn't know how it applied to me.

The bus let us off at a neighborhood of two story Spanish style urban houses with red tile roofs.

"We're only a block from the bus stop here," said Eddie. "So it's easy to go into town."

"What about groceries?"

"There's a market within easy walking distance. You can shop with Mrs. Chelton. She's the landlady my friend told me about."

"Do we need anything for the room?"

"It comes furnished. We have to do our own towels and laundry. Mrs. Chelton has a washing machine. We're on the second floor. We have to share the bathroom with another couple when they arrive. Here we are."

The size and architecture and tropical foliage impressed me. "Mrs. Chelton must be rich to have a house like this," I said. "Do we have to pay rent?"

"No, I get a living allowance."

"That's nice."

"We'll be okay. We can live on my commission."

"What will I do? I'm not used to not working."

"Maybe you can volunteer at The Red Cross."

As we entered the house, Mrs. Chelton came through the back door into the kitchen and unloaded baskets of fruit and vegetables from her victory garden.

We dropped our luggage in the front room and waved to her through the connecting archway. "Hello, Mrs. Chelton," said Eddie. "We're your new tenants. I'm Lieutenant Eddie Gebhardt and this is my wife, Gwen."

126

"Oh, welcome, welcome. It's so nice to meet you. I didn't know what day you would arrive." Dressed in a simple print dress and wearing low-heeled laced black shoes, Mrs. Chelton reminded me a little of Gladys. They had similar weathered wrinkled European faces.

She came around the table. Ignoring my extended hand, she gave me a hug. "And call me Norma." Then she gave Eddie a hug. "It will be nice to have a young couple in the house. I'll show you to your room. Come with me."

On the way through the living room, Eddie snatched his duffle bag and I awkwardly bumped along with my suitcase as we followed her up the stairs.

"The bathroom's down at the end of the hall. I had extra towel racks installed. There are cups for toothbrushes and extra rolls of toilet paper in the storage cupboard."

She gestured at the open door to the second unoccupied bedroom. "The Wengers will be staying here. Bob Wenger signed a contract a week ago. He's bivouacked at the Biltmore Hotel until his wife arrives. And here's your room. I'll let you get settled. Come down when you're ready."

I inhaled the sweet floral scent of jasmine and orange blossoms wafting through the open windows and listened to the melodic trilling of a mockingbird.

"Nice, huh," said Eddie.

"Real nice. Like you said, a tropical paradise."

Early the next morning, Eddie reported to headquarters at the Biltmore Resort Hotel.

The savory aroma of bacon and fresh coffee lured me downstairs to the kitchen. Norma turned from the sizzling iron skillet on the stove. "Good morning, dear. Did you sleep well?"

"Like a baby. Those down pillows are like floating on a cloud."

"How do you like your eggs?"

"Scrambled."

"And toast?"

"Not burned."

"I bake my own bread and I never burn toast. I also put up my own blueberry preserves and strawberry jam. I see you're wearing regular socks and shoes. If you plan on going into town, you might want to buy a pair of sandals. They're much more comfortable."

"I'll do that. Can I help with anything?"

"Just take a seat. Would you like coffee and orange juice? It's fresh-squeezed. Oranges are right off my trees in the back. I'll show you my victory garden after breakfast. Grow most of my own fruit and vegetables. Always had a green thumb."

"We never had a garden when I was growing up, but I spent a lot of time in the kitchen with our cook and housekeeper, Gladys Dietz."

She placed a glass of orange juice in front of me and poured a mug of coffee. "Cream right there, but no sugar. It's rationed."

"I take it black."

"Did she teach you how to cook?"

"She let me help with simple things."

"Sounds like you enjoyed her company."

"Yes, I miss her very much. I wanted her to come to my wedding. She was more of a mother to me than my own mother."

"What happened to Gladys?"

"She and her husband were arrested by the FBI and sent to an internment camp just for being German. But they're U.S. citizens."

"My parents came from Germany back in 1875. Such a long time ago. They lived in New York. I was born there in 1883. My maiden name is Bergmann. They were bakers. That's how I learned to cook. I met Percy when I came to Florida on a holiday. He owned a citrus fruit company for many years before he died and left me with a large inheritance. I sold the company but most of the money was lost during the crash. The war has picked up the economy here like everywhere else. The Government pays me six dollars a month for each room I rent."

She served the bacon and scrambled eggs and placed the toast next to two jars of jam. "What you said about Gladys and her husband being German, there are German POWs incarcerated here at Camp Blanding."

"Here? Where the officers are training?"

"Not with the officers. They're kept in a prison on the base. Some of them are used for construction and road crews and farm labor, since our men have gone overseas to fight."

"I tried to find out what happened to Gladys, but the FBI wouldn't tell me."

"My Percy fought in the first world war. He had no love for the Germans. Now, here we are again. We don't live in a safe world. I didn't tell you about blackouts at night."

"I know about them. We had them in Boston."

"You can have your light on upstairs. Just be sure the blackout curtain is closed."

"These eggs are delicious."

"Thanks. I have four hens. I collect their eggs every couple of days."

"The orange juice is out of this world."

"Picked right off the tree this morning."

"Can't get any fresher than that."

I took the bus into town and browsed the stores on Flagler Avenue. After two hours, I came home with a pair of leather sandals, a swimsuit, two pairs of shorts and light summer tops, and two halter tops to let the suntan my chest and arms and shoulders. Eddie said my tan was sexy.

We ate dinner with Norma that evening. Afterwards, she showed us old photographs of her family. "Percy and I raised nine children, three girls and six boys. All the boys went in the Navy. Girls married with children of their own. Two moved out to California. My youngest daughter and her family live in Chicago. That's where her husband was sent for Navy training. Odd, you'd think. We have the Caribbean on one side and the Atlantic on the other right here. Anyhow, I don't see much of my grandchildren."

Chapter 13

Sand In Our Shoes

Bob and Mary Wenger arrived early in the evening one week later. I didn't realize at the time that Mary was among several women in my life who set me on the path of writing my book.

Norma and I had just come in from gardening and were spreading vegetables on the counter and storing perishables in the refrigerator. We heard the front door open and a strong male voice call out, "Hello, anybody home?"

Norma stepped to the kitchen archway and greeted them with her gracious smile. "We're here."

"Mrs. Chelton, my wife has finally arrived," the young lieutenant announced with an unabashed grin.

"Come on in. We're happy to see you. The Gebhardts moved in last week. I have a full house. Gwen is here with me. We were just out in the garden. Welcome, Dear." She gave Mary a hug. "Bob's told us about you. You are every bit as beautiful as he says. Hope you don't mind my dirty hands. Gwen and I have been digging in the garden."

Drying my hands on a towel, I joined Norma in the living room. The attractive couple appeared to have stepped out of a movie. Bob Wenger's smile beamed clear across the room. Brown eyes projected a gentle warmth, so different than Eddie's intense stare. The removal of his field cap revealed a flash of blonde hair that matched the shade of Mary's marcel waves that cascaded to thin shoulders. A plain A-line dress emphasized her slender build. Blue eyes, a small nose, high cheekbones, and rosy skin gave her the appearance of a shy Viennese princess.

"I'm Gwen Gebhardt." I put aside my hand towel, walked over and exchanged greetings.   "Pleased to meet you. We should celebrate your arrival. Tonight, our husbands can take us out on the town." My deep contralto laugh and forward manner startled Mary.

My hood of thick shoulder-length brunette hair must have seemed domineering to her. I saw Bob glance at the top portion of my tan cleavage looming from my tropical orange and lemon yellow skirt and halter. Mary gazed at my sun-bronzed bare feet exposed in wedge sandals. Garden dirt rimmed my toenails.

"Mary's pretty tired from the trip," said Bob. "I think the weekend will be better, and besides, Eddie and I have to report at the crack of dawn. Is he back from training yet?"

"Not yet. He's flying around in one of those buzz bombs out there," I spoke with the clipped enunciation, raised Rs and elongated vowels of a New England accent.

"We ate dinner downtown. Mary wants to soak in a tub and get some sleep."

"I know what you mean," I said. "I rode one of those trains. Bet you had lots of offers to sit on a lap."

Mary's lips compressed in a sheepish grin. "I turned them all down."

"You stood up the whole trip?"

"Two polite soldiers made room. It was snug, but okay."

"Eddie's father had some pull with the railroad. He's a congressman. So I got a seat."

"Tell Eddie I'll see him in the morning," said Bob.

"I know. Special night."

Mary's face flushed with embarrassment. She touched Bob's arm. He picked up her suitcase and they headed for the stairs.

"Good night, kids," Norma called after them.

"It's a great tub," I shouted. "Enjoy your bath."

Mary's flushed face briefly glanced back over her shoulder.

The next morning, Mary came down the stairs and hesitated in the kitchen archway.

"Good morning, Dear," Norma's cheery greeting and motioning her to enter dispelled any uncertainty that she might be intruding. "Did you sleep well?"

"Yes, it's a comfortable bed."

"Morning, Mary," I raised a glass pitcher. "Orange juice? Coffee? Both?" To appear less intimidating, I was wearing dark bell bottom slacks and a tan short sleeve shirt.

"I'll have both, thank you."

"I'll bet you're hungry," said Norma. "I was just making scrambled eggs and toast."

"I saw Eddie and Bob off," I said. "I'm in the habit of waking up early and going for a walk. I like the cool morning air before it gets hot and muggy."

"How do you like your toast?" asked Norma. "Light or dark."

"Sort of in between."

"Medium, I should have guessed. You're not an extreme person."

I poured her coffee. "Would you like to do something today?"

"I don't know. I hadn't thought about it. I have to wash some clothes. What did you have in mind?"

"I volunteer at The Red Cross. They can always use help. We can work a few hours, then hit the beach."

"Hit the beach?"

"Go to the beach. It's lovely. White sand, warm blue water."

"I don't have a bathing suit."

"We'll go shopping and buy you one."

"I don't know how to swim."

"You can wade in the surf. Get a suntan."

"I burn easily."

"I have lotion."

"How about tomorrow?"

"There's no time like the present. We're not here for that long." I noticed her sudden anxiety. "I didn't mean that like it sounds. We have kind of a respite here, a short vacation. Eddie and Bob will ship out overseas in a few months. We have a taste of Miami. We have sand in our shoes. Eddie says he wants to move here after the war. You know, you're right. You need a day to settle in. Let's make it tomorrow."

Norma glanced across the table at Mary "Your eggs okay?"

"They're delicious. I've never had them cooked like this before."

"It's my version of a seafood omelet. I sprinkle a little cheddar and green peppers on it. I keep some chickens out in back. They give me fresh eggs every morning."

"When I was a girl, my Dad tried raising chickens, but they all died."

"Did you live on a farm?"

"My Mum and Dad kept a garden. They grew our vegetables and we had fruit trees. We helped Mum with the canning."

"So you had good years growing up."

She nodded.

"Where were you born?"

"I beg pardon."

"Where were you born?"

"A small town in Pennsylvania. I consider Rockford, Illinois my home. It's a city."

"I lived in New York before meeting my husband here in Florida."

"Bob told me you had orchards and a fruit company," I said.

"We did and we did well. Raised nine children, three girls and six boys. All the boys went in the Navy. Girls married with children of their own. You remind me of my youngest girl, Midge. She was a shy one too."

Unsure how to respond to the implication, Mary looked down at her plate.

"It's okay to be shy. Cautious I call it. Don't just charge in. Figure things out. Look before you leap. You and Bob are going to have children, aren't you?"

"If he makes it back."

"Don't think like that. Plan for it. Have a child. Just believe he'll come back. You religious? You pray?"

"No, I'm not. I don't think praying helps."

"Then you're realistic."

"What do you mean?"

"You don't bury yourself in wishful thinking, hoping some miracle will happen."

"I do wish for things. My brother and sisters and I did wish for things growing up. We didn't have much."

"That small town life?"

"Yes, but we didn't stay."

"Now, you're out in the world."

"Somehow it doesn't seem real here," said Mary.

"It is and it isn't. Bob told me how you met in Rockford." Norma smiled. "Very romantic."

"It was romantic. We don't have much, but we do have each other."

"You have a positive outlook. That's what matters."

"The war isn't romantic," said Mary. "It's frightful."

"War isn't romantic. It's deadly. There are German U-boats off our coast and Japan has attacked us in California. Our men have to fight, just like any other warriors."

"I don't think of Bob as a warrior. He's very kind and gentle. I can't imagine him killing anybody."

"Actually, Dear, I can't either. Come. I'll show you the washing machine. There's a clothesline in the back yard to hang your things."

I finished my coffee and pushed back my chair. "Well, I'm off. You both have a swell day." My smile included Norma. She raised her hand. "See you later, Dear. Have a wonderful day."

The next morning, as the bus pulled to a stop near the Biltmore Hotel, Mary and I glimpsed several hundred shirtless men performing synchronized calisthenics on the beach. Caressed by warm sea breezes, we paused to watch for a few minutes.

"Our guys are out there somewhere," I said. "Shall we go?"

We continued along the sidewalk in the direction of The Red Cross headquarters adjacent to a wing of the hotel which had been converted to a hospital for returning wounded soldiers.

We looked up at the unaccustomed drone of P-51 Mustangs, Navy Hellcats, and PBM Avengers crossing the Florida skies from dawn to dusk. Eddie had schooled me on identifying military aircraft.

A hovering flotilla of massive air dirigibles used to spot German submarines in coastal waters patrolled the shorelines. Military police carrying bayoneted rifles patrolled the beaches crowded with civilian women and children and off-duty soldiers.

A few miles offshore, low-flying B18 "Bolo" bombers in squadron formation skimmed along fifty feet above the azure Atlantic surface in practice raids to avoid enemy radar detection.

The rattle of automatic gunfire and distant explosions of bombs offshore farther up the coast caused a sense of foreboding in the "tropical paradise." Out of sight, amphibious landing craft loaded with young infantry soldiers stormed isolated beaches. The military presence was everywhere we looked and listened, air, land, and sea.

"The entire city goes dark every night in compliance with a blackout regulation to prevent enemy U-boats from seeing Navy warships and commercial freighters against the Miami skyline."

"I didn't know they were that close," said Mary.

"They're out there all right. Eddie told me some Germans were captured and imprisoned at Camp Blanding.

A flurry of women volunteers rolling bandages and packaging medical supplies to be shipped to the front lines occupied The Red Cross center.

"Don't be put off by the number," I said. "They can always use another pair of hands."

After a brief introduction to the serious mannered middle-aged woman in charge, wearing a white arm band with a red cross, Mary joined me on the bandage rolling assembly line. The filmy gauze raised images in my mind of the bloody wounds it would be used to wrap.

Mary seemed to grow increasingly anxious as the morning progressed. The women along the line silently concentrated on their task. She was visibly relieved when she heard me say, "Time for lunch. I usually only work mornings. The afternoon is ours. After lunch, we'll get you a bathing suit."

"I don't have the money to spend."

"I'll buy one. My gift to you as a new bride."

"I can't accept that," said Mary, trailing after me out the door into brilliant afternoon sunshine and the swish and sizzle of waves crashing on the beach.

"Oh, sure you can. Eddie and I are flush. He made a killing at Hialeah last weekend. It's for me, for us to enjoy."

"What's Hialeah?"

"Racetrack. Horse racing. Eddie's a risk taker. He likes to bet. And by the way, I'm buying lunch. I hope you like seafood. That's most of what we get these days."

"Seafood is fine. It's new for me. We didn't have it where I grew up."

"Where was that?"

She avoided giving a specific answer as we maneuvered through a crowd of rowdy off-duty soldiers jamming the sidewalk in search of prostitutes. "Pennsylvania."

"That's pretty far inland."

I didn't press for details. To direct attention away from herself, she asked, "Where are you from?"

"Eddie and I are from Boston. We're not new to seafood. Plenty of it there. Practically lived right on the ocean. We got married while he was going to Harvard. His father wants him to become a lawyer. Eddie hasn't made up his mind about that, but he was drafted before he could graduate. He had one more year to go before starting law school."

"How did you meet each other?"

"A blind date."

"What a coincidence. That's how Bob and I met."

"I was in my senior year at Wellesley."

"You went to college. How lucky you are. That's what I want to do after the war, go to college. What was it like?"

"Wellesley is a snooty all woman's school. I didn't like the snooty part," I said, "but I liked my classes. I was majoring in Journalism and English literature."

"Journalism?"

"I want to become a news writer," I said. "After Eddie goes overseas, I'm applying for a job."

"In Boston?"

"Here in Miami, at the Signal."

"Do they hire women news writers?"

"They're going to hire me," I said with greater confidence than I felt.

We stopped and waited at a street corner for a twelve military truck convoy of Negroes to pass by.

"Negroes. I didn't know they could be soldiers," said Mary. "Where do they come from?"

"You're in the South," I said. "They're everywhere."

Other than the convoy, Negroes were nowhere to be seen on the streets. "They don't come into the city. They have their own places in

139

Color Town. You won't see them on white beaches either. They're banned."

Eventually, I learned the Depression and the war effort had created a level playing field eliminating the perceived barrier of a social and economic class for white military personnel, but not for Negroes, now called African Americans. All soldiers' lives were at equal risk going into battle, but, with the exception of officer candidates, Negroes underwent training separately at Camp Blanding to become engineering regiments building living quarters, landing fields, and roads through mountain jungles. They were banned from commingling socially with white soldiers and the white civilian population of Miami.

As for white soldiers and civilians, the high spirits and good times in the city provided an interlude impregnated with the logistics and realities of aerial, land, and sea combat training.

"Here we are," I said. "I haven't tried this place yet." I pushed open the door to *El Cubana* and we entered, joining the noisy lunch crowd.

Chapter 14

Mary Wenger

I had brought my beach bag stuffed with my swimming suit and towels.

After lunch, we shopped for a swimming suit and sunglasses for Mary. Using the women's restroom at the Biltmore Hotel officers' club, we changed, then wandered out onto the soft white sand. I spread straw mats for each of us. We slathered our exposed backs and limbs with lotion and succumbed to the sun's rays. The warmth and the repetitious roll and cascade of surf lulled Mary.

"So, what do you think?" I asked. "Nice?"

"It's so beautiful here. I've never seen the ocean before. It's so blue."

"And warm. We can take a dip after we digest."

"I don't know how to swim and I'm afraid of the waves."

"You can just stand in the shallows and let the waves splash you a little. You don't have to go out. They aren't big here and there's no undertow."

"What's that?"

"It's the current the waves create when the tide pulls them back. This is a sheltered beach. It's safe for swimming and there's a lifeguard in each one of those towers."

"I'll have to think about it."

I smiled. "I'll even hold your hand when we go in."

"That won't be necessary. I can wade. If my older sister were here, she'd dive right in. She's not afraid of anything."

"Sounds like my older sister, Tess. Do you have other brothers and sisters?"

"One brother and two sisters."

"Are you close?"

142

"We're best friends. We always looked out for each other when we were growing up. We all left home together."

"Was that before you moved to Rockford?" I began to delicately coax her story out of her. Since she valued education so highly, I started with that. "You must have enjoyed school. Did you do well?"

"Yes, but even though I had straight 'A's in English, Science, and Math, and I graduated at the top of my class, there was no college in my future. I always considered school my second home. More than anything, I loved to read and study and participate in classes that dealt with concepts and ideas. I liked to use my brain. I was the first to raise my hand in class. Any question on any subject, I had the answer ready. I read and studied ahead in the regular curriculum and made up questions I thought the teachers would ask.

"During my senior year, I had to take accounting, shorthand, and typing classes to prepare me for the working world. But since the country was sunk in the middle of an economic depression, work was hard to find. My primary textbooks were Gregg Shorthand and an Underwood typing manual."

"What about friends at school?"

"I had only one, Violet Karpinsky. We only saw each other in class and during lunch period. Since Violet lived in Wilkes-Barre and I lived in Colver, we didn't see each other outside of school."

"What was Colver like?" I noticed her stiffen slightly. I didn't want her to feel trapped into talking about the town, since she had said Rockford was her home, but she had unintentionally mentioned Colver.

"It's a mining town in the Alleghany Mountains. My dad was a coal miner. I love my mum and dad. They did the best they could for us. We lived in hard times."

"Did you keep in touch with Violet?"

"No, we lost track of each other when I left Colver. She once wanted to introduce me to her older brother who played on the high school

143

football team, but if he would ask me out on a date I would have to turn him down. My sisters and I weren't allowed to date. I would have never let him come to my house to pick me up anyway.

My older Sister, Ruth, was a flirt. My little sister, Nina, had boys constantly ogling her. Your husband talks about being sexy. Nina had an over-abundance of natural sex appeal. Mum criticized how she swayed her hips whenever she saw her walk down the street. She would shout at her to 'walk straight. Boys will think you are bad girl!' Mum had old country opinions, because she was not educated and her father and brothers treated her like a slave. She was as much a victim of her times as we were. When she was sixteen, she left her mountain village home in Austria-Hungary to escape an arranged marriage. She traveled across Europe and came to America on a freighter. She was a strong woman. We had no future in Colver. None of us did. I loved my family, but I hated living there."

"It's hot," I said, shielding my eyes from the sun. "Let's go in the water."

I helped Mary to her feet and we walked in. She squealed as the first wave splashed against her legs. She watched me dive in and swim out a short distance.

An hour later, we changed our clothes and rode back to Mr. Chelton's on the bus.

***

A kind of awkwardness came over Mary when I introduced her to my loud vociferous husband. She was unresponsive at his attempts to joke with her and say what he thought were clever sexual references that made her blush with discomfort.

Bob didn't interfere. He just looked at Eddie with his good-natured, unabashed silence. He tolerated Eddie, as he seemed to get along with most people.

144

I mentioned it to Eddie when we were alone. "It's okay to say things like 'You look sexy' to me. But Mary doesn't know how to take it."

"Hey, she's a big girl. I don't mean anything. Anyway, she's too uptight. I'm just having some harmless fun."

"She isn't uptight. She's different. She comes from a different background than us. She told me she grew up poor in a coal mining town. I think she feels inferior and it makes her shy."

"Inferior? Don't bust my balls. She's beautiful. Why would she feel inferior?"

"Not about her looks. She never went to college. Her parents couldn't afford to send her."

"College is not all it's cracked up to be."

"She's very bright. Education is important to her."

I sensed Mary disliked seeing Bob being influenced by Eddie to bet even a few dollars, but I didn't say anything to discourage his youthful enthusiasm. Hialeah was part of the Miami tour he had promised Mary, who would just as soon have foregone a visit to the famous racetrack.

Wearing sleeveless summer dresses and straw sun hats, we withered in the broiling heat and humidity. The stale odor of sweating bodies, cigar smoke, beer, and crushing bodies of uniformed men nauseated even me. She covered her ears at the deafening roar of the crowd, shouting and cheering encouragement to the horses and jockeys on which the men had placed money at the long line of betting windows.

A close second to the maneuvers of aerial combat, the contagious thrill of gambling pulled at Eddie like a magnet. He discussed the racing form with Bob as though it contained the secret of how the races would be run and their outcome.

I sipped a beer and ignored my husband's heated discussion about the quality and bloodlines of the thoroughbreds and their racing history. I jokingly said, "I think Eddie identifies with the horses, because he was a championship runner in college."

I could not deny Eddie's dark good looks and swaggering charisma. His restless hazel eyes reflected an intense competitive spirit. His certitude about any topic dominated our conversations. Mary followed Bob's example and just listened politely as Eddie expounded on his feats of flying a P-51 fighter. I didn't know why he was so fixated on that topic. I tolerated his bragging, until his brash statement, "There's always a chance I'll go down in flames over the Pacific, but I'll take thirty Jap zeroes with me."

"I really wish you wouldn't say things like that, Eddie," I said.

"Oh, it's okay," he teased me. "It doesn't mean anything. Nothing's gonna happen to me. I can outfly anything and anyone up there."

After completing the twelve weeks Officer Candidate School training commissioned as second lieutenants, Bob and Eddie received their orders to report for duty at transport. This time, Mary would be allowed to make the five day train ride with Bob to Sacramento. He would undergo training as a supply officer at Mather Field.

That evening, we went out to dinner at an open air waterfront restaurant. Tossing back rum punches, Eddie suddenly grew agitated at Mary's reluctance to order a cocktail. "All I've seen you drink all since we met is Coca-Cola. I've noticed how you watch me. You don't approve of me, do you, Mary? You're uptight. Go on. Have a drink. Bob, you need to teach her how to loosen up. Enjoy herself."

"I'm fine. I don't drink," she said. "I don't like how it makes me feel."

"I get it. You don't want to lose your edge. I'm sober as a saint when I'm flying, but off-duty, it's my time. Is it a religious thing with you?"

"No, everything in my life is not a religious thing."

"She's fine, Eddie," said Bob in a friendly tone to defuse him. "I love her just the way she is."

"Well, Mary doesn't seem to be merry."

"Eddie, that's enough," I warned. "This is our last night together for a while. Be pleasant. "I'm hungry. Let's order."

146

"I'm sorry, Mary. I apologize. I was out of line. Bob, you're too nice. You should have punched me in the nose."

Bob grinned and shook his head. "Mary can handle herself."

Later at Norma's house, Eddie had gone to bed and I was in the kitchen getting a glass of water. A symphony of crickets came in the open window. I overheard Bob and Mary talking quietly on their balcony overlooking the backyard fruit trees and gardens bathed in moonlight.

"Eddie can certainly be obnoxious," said Mary.

"Oh, he's not so bad, Honey. Pilots have it rough. Aerial combat is one of the most dangerous, more than infantry. He just likes to unwind when he's off duty. I told you he's a character."

"I hope all of your Army buddies aren't like him."

"We need each other. We have to look out for each other."

"I hope you never have to carry a gun and shoot somebody."

"I'll be a supply officer, behind the front lines. Because I'm an officer, I'll have a handgun. But there are a lot of unknowns out there."

"Where are they going to send you next?"

"Supply officers go to Mather Field in Sacramento, California. I'll be there for a short time, then ship out to Australia."

"Can I go with you to Sacramento?"

"It will be another long train ride, clear across the country. As an officer, I think I can arrange for you to travel with me, actually have your own seat. We might have to share a sleeping berth. Sleep in two shifts."

"You're kidding."

"I'm kidding. You can have the berth. I can sleep fine on the seat."

I was envious that they could be together for a while longer. Eddie would be flying on a troop transport to California. This night would be our last until he returned from the war.

For my earlier comment to be pleasant, he took out his anger at me by first refusing to have sex, then nearly assaulting and raping me. I understood his rage. Despite his show of bravado, he was afraid.

The next morning, I rode the bus with him to the air transport terminal on the base. We held one another for a long, tearful goodbye.

Chapter 15

Paper Dolls

The controlled chaos of the newsroom overwhelmed my senses as I navigated the sea of desks occupied by mostly men and three women bent over clattering Underwood typewriters and answering ringing phones. I focused on the editor's glass-walled office at the far side and a heavy-set, silver-haired man wearing a white shirt with sleeves rolled up his forearms and a loosened green tie. The name Roger Bolton, Editor was imprinted on the office door. He peered intently through black-frame bifocals at a page of copy clutched in his left hand while his right held a red pencil poised and moving like a pendulum a few inches above the print. Even though the door stood open, afraid of disturbing his concentration I didn't knock or say anything. So when he spoke without looking up, I was surprised he knew I was even standing there.

"What have you got for me?"

When I didn't respond, he glanced up. "Who the hell are you?"

I stepped forward and extended my hand. "Good morning, Mr. Bolton. I'm Gwen Gebhardt. I came to apply for a job as a news writer." I hoped my two piece tweed black and tan tweed business suit created a professional appearance. I had decided against wearing a hat.

"Is that a roundabout way of saying you're applying for a job as a news writer?"

"Roundabout?"

"I can see you came here. You don't have to tell me that."

"I apologize. That was a slight oversight."

"And I don't accept apologies. I only accept well-written copy. Once I mark it up, you bring it back as it should be."

"Of course, sir. Does that mean I'm hired?"

"Did you hear me offer you a job?"

"No, sir. I inferred from your comment."

"No one infers here. We deal with verified facts from proven sources."

"Did you read my resume' then?"

"Look at what's on my desk. What makes you think I have time to read your resume?"

"Your secretary gave me an appointment for an interview."

"She did, did she? Well, she didn't tell me."

"I'm sorry to waste your time." I turned to go.

"Good reporters don't waste people's time. They steal their time. They own their time. I don't think you have what it takes to be a good reporter. You're not tough."

"Try me out. I might surprise you."

"Only men make real reporters. You're just another one of those." He gestured with the page out at the newsroom. "A paper doll. Nice looking broad, but no guts and no brains."

"Graduating from Wellesley requires a high level of intelligence and academic achievement. If you read my resume, you'll see that."

He dropped his pencil and smacked his forehead with the palm of his empty hand. "My God, I must be blind. How could I not see that the moment you walked in here. How could I not surmise that you inferred that just by showing up. I see you're a Wellesley graduate. That means you come from high society. So if I do hire you, you can write soft news. You should be good at society columns, since all you upper crust ladies stand around drinking champagne at posh parties and chitchat. Am I right?"

"I can write any assignment you give me, sir."

"Think you're that good, huh?"

"I do."

"For no experience in the real world of news, you have an outsized ego, Gebhardt. I read your samples from your Wellesley days. It's Pablum, apple sauce, hearts and flowers. You have a lot to learn. You have to pay your dues."

"I can do that."

"Journalism is an honorable profession."

"I couldn't agree more."

"Our purpose is publishing the news and meeting the expectations of public interest."

"I understand."

"There's an empty desk out there. Introduce yourself to the other ladies. Marge Ogilvy is the section lead. She edits the society page. She'll give you your assignments."

"Thank you, Mr. Bolton. I really appreciate this opportunity. My husband was just sent overseas. He's a fighter pilot."

"A man to be honored and admired. Maybe someday you can write about him."

"So, you want me to start right away?"

"You asking for a day off?"

"No, sir."

"Don't you want to know how much you're getting paid?"

"The human resources manager told me, a dollar twenty an hour."

"Go knock 'em dead, Gebhardt."

"Yes, sir." I quickly left the office before he changed his mind. I waded through the others to the vacant desk. As I sat in the wooden chair and pulled open a drawer to deposit my purse, the woman at the desk next to mine stopped typing and looked at me.

"Did The Bolt hire you?"

"You mean Mister Bolton?"

"We call him The Bolt, not to his face, of course. He allows us to use his first name. If you made it this far, he hired you."

"I don't think I should call him Roger at least not until he gets to know me, know my work and I definitely would not refer to him as The Bolt."

"All that gruff stuff is just a front to intimidate the staff. He's really a pussy cat."

"I don't think I'd want him in my lap."

The large woman chuckled and extended her hand. "Welcome to the paper dolls. I'm Marge Ogilvy."

I smiled and relaxed slightly. "It's nice to meet you, Marge. I'm Gwen Gebhardt. I look forward to working with you. What do you mean by paper dolls?"

"That's what Roger calls us, dolls who write for the paper."

"Oh, I guess that explains it. I played with paper doll cutouts when I was a little girl."

"Not that any of us look glamorous, except Celine, the pretty one with the blue hat."

"Should I wear a hat?"

"Only if you want to. Gives us a kind of ladylike professional look when we go out on interviews. There's paper in the lower drawer. Typewriter ribbons just above that. Pencils and paper clips in the center drawer. Get yourself set up and I'll give you some copy to start."

"Okay, thank you." I pulled a stack of blank paper from the drawer, inserted a sheet between the typewriter rollers, and waited for Marge to finish sorting through her rough drafts. She scooted her chair over next to mine. Her fleshy upper arms quivered as she placed three pages on my desk. Probing brown eyes and a kind expression overshadowed the early age wrinkles and sagging folds of her neck. Layered waves of graying hair swept back from her seasoned face.

"We don't get to write about the most interesting events. Society columns on family, food, fashion, and furnishings don't make for exciting headlines, but the people are always interesting. I've lived in Florida for the past fifteen years. I've come to know a lot of them."

"Here in Miami?"

"Mostly."

"Do you happen to know Norma Chelton?"

"Norma and I go way back. We're old friends. Why?"

"My husband and I rented a room from her and I'm staying on while he's overseas."

"Norma's a wonderful person, a gem. She and her family have a long history in Southern Florida. By the way, this is Joan Novotny and Celine Comeau. Joan's husband is in the Army overseas. Celine is single. My man is too old. He runs a fishing trawler, but we have two sons in the Navy."

The two plainly dressed women glanced up at me with a brief nod and continued their rapid typing. Joan leaned back in her chair and surveyed the lines as they appeared like a live creature that insisted on crawling across the page each time she reached out and smacked it away with the carriage return. She wore a tilt-topper hat at a jaunty angle on her brunette, Hepburn style locks that gave her the appearance of a vaudeville actress.

The light veil of Celine's blue chapeau against her auburn hair brought attention to her soulful brown eyes and delicate French features.

"You'll all be working independently on different stories. Now that there are four of us, I want to expand our coverage of women in the workplace doing men's jobs now that they're off fighting in the war. I've proposed a column to Roger titled Call To Duty. At first he wanted to give it to one of the men to write, but when the hack discovered he would be interviewing and writing about women, he declined. So the assignment came back to me, to us."

"It sounds interesting. I definitely want to do that."

"There's so much to cover, it'll take all four of us. Plus, we still have to write the society page."

"Well, I'm familiar with that. I wrote about social events at Wellesley for four years. I was on the news team."

"Wellesley. Back in the Twenties, Roger's wife attended Wellesley."

"How about you?"

"High school education and two years of college, Florida State. Dropped out to get married and raise my two boys. After they graduated, I started working at the Signal as a typist. As a matter of fact, all three of us started in the typing pool and worked our way up, thanks to Roger. None of the men would write society news. Can hardly blame 'em. They get to do the heavy stuff, sports, politics, crime, finance, the war. We better get to work. Roger doesn't like to see us chatting when we're on deadline."

"Gotcha." I read the marked-up copy about a local society wedding and began to type.

They appeared seemingly out of nowhere like an explosion of Mother Earth pouring them forth from an invisible realm where their existence was taken for granted. What had been the spheres of male dominance were transformed by armies of women. In a national War Production Board campaign to support the material and massive food needs of the military, owners and politicians and thousands of posters, news articles, advertisements, and billboards appealed to women's patriotic duty and the chance to earn good wages as glamorous heroines of commerce. From all walks of life, they invaded factories, local government offices, farms, hospitals, logging camps, construction sites, shipyards, and defense plants. Society as we had known it erupted in the turmoil of war. Millions of married and single women signed up for jobs to replace the millions of men who had been drafted and sent to fight overseas.

Women who did not respond to the call were publicly accused of being idol slackers who endangered the lives of fighting men by not upholding their side of the war effort.

The sudden shift in the employment status of women awakened me to the insidious, underlying discrimination and ambiguity against us and our prescribed roles as girlfriends, wives and mothers and prostitutes encouraged by the Government to be friendly to the boys in uniform to support their morale, but with the duplicitous decree blaming, arresting and incarcerating them as enemies for infecting troops with venereal disease. The ruling left men as victims with no responsibility but to indulge in sex. However, they were warned to be aware that "even the girl next door" could be a carrier of the disease. Health department propaganda injected the suspicion and fear factor of "Is your gal really everybody's pal?"

With so many women and different occupations, Marge deliberated over assignment decisions for Celine and Joan and me and ultimately gave us a choice of what stories we would like to cover.

"This one's big," she said holding up an official looking printed announcement. "The Emergency Farm Labor Program is recruiting a land army to keep the farms producing food for soldiers and everybody else. The Government is funding twenty-six million dollars. Posters are everywhere and women are joining up all over the country. They're out there planting and harvesting crops, mowing and baling hay, picking fruit, and milking cows--according to recruitment information, about two-hundred fifty thousand. Women can earn twenty-five to sixty-six cents an hour. We can get local stories. Who wants it?"

In a surprising contrast to her delicate appearance and demeanor, Celine took farm workers. She had been born and raised on a Midwest dairy farm in Wisconsin and had migrated to Florida following graduation from Northwestern University in Chicago.

Since her sons were in the Navy, Joan took the WAVES, Women Appointed for Voluntary Emergency Service.

"Here's another story," said Marge. She showed us an announcement in the Washington Post that the National War Labor Board had ordered the shift to granting women equal pay for performing men's jobs.

"This is revolutionary," she said. "Go out and interview a cross-section of women working in factories and see what they think of this. Get their opinions."

Because I was somewhat familiar with the manufacturing process from my father's textile mills, I would interview women who worked in shipyards and aircraft defense factories.

"I'm on it," I said and stuffed a clean notepad and freshly sharpened pencils into my leather satchel.

I went down the elevator and walked out of the news building to a corner bus stop. I waited for one whose destination sign said Embry Field.

The door suctioned open. I mounted the corrugated steps and dropped my token into the changer next to the female driver wearing a prim brown uniform and official cap.

As the door closed behind me, I walked unsteadily down the aisle of the bus crowded with women dressed for work wearing steel-toed boots and men's heavy coveralls. My rayon dress, flats, and makeup made me feel conspicuous and out-of-place.

With a grinding of shifting gears, the bus lurched forward releasing a blast of diesel fumes floating through the open windows. I took an empty seat near the rear next to a woman whose clothes gave off an odor of engine oil.

The paved palm-lined streets transitioned to cane fields bordering a country road cratered with potholes caused by heavy autumn rains. Each shudder of the bus sent a spine-jarring jolt along the chassis that bounced the passengers in their seats. The worn shocks and coils in the undercarriage would not be replaced due to the lack of available parts.

We came to an aircraft defense plant several miles from the city. The bus approached through a glistening sea of tightly-parked cars patrolled by roving armed security guards. Rubber was such a crucial commodity for the manufacture of aircraft tires, that, along with rationed fuel, car tires were prized targets for thieves.

I stepped off with the women. An armed coast guard at the entry gate kiosk window asked the nature of my business and to see my identification before allowing me to enter and walk across the compound to a reception office where another security guard with a thin mustache and short-cropped hair confronted me. The name tag Cranston was sewn over his right pocket.

I showed him my laminated press pass. "I'm Gwen Gebhardt from the Miami Signal. I'm doing a story on women working in defense jobs. I'd like to interview some of them."

"Sorry, Ma'am, only employees can enter the factory." The young guardsman's stern expression discouraged her. "You can't be interrupting them while they work. In the first place, you can't go out onto the factory floor. You're not dressed for it and it's not safe."

"You must have steel-toed boots and coveralls and hardhats for visitors, dignitaries from Washington and others."

"Sorry, Lady, you just can't go in. Those are my orders."

I noticed he dropped the respectful Ma'am for the derogatory Lady. "How about a guided tour then? Don't you give tours?"

"This is a top secret facility. We don't give public tours."

"I'm a reporter, not a spy."

"Don't matter, Lady. You can't go in there, even with a guide."

"May I at least speak with the foreman?"

"He's out on the floor. He's busy. And I can't leave my post."

"What about the plant manager."

"Lady, I don't want to have to throw you out, but you're gettin' under my skin."

"My husband's a fighter pilot. He's in the South Pacific. He flies planes like these. What are they, Mustangs, Corsairs, Avengers?"

"How do you know about them?"

"My husband flies all of them. He told me about them."

"He's got guts."

"Yeah, he's got guts. He's up there risking his life, not sitting at a desk."

A sudden flush invaded the guardsman's face. He looked away."

"I'm in the Coast Guard, Lady. I'm a Navy man. I'd rather be out patrolling for U-boats, but this is my duty assignment. I'm tryin' to get assigned to a cutter or a frigate. I want to be in the fight, not sittin' at this goddamn desk. One of my brothers is on a subchaser and I have a cousin on a destroyer escort in the Pacific."

"What's your brother's name?"

"Jeb Cranston."

"Are you from Miami?"

"Born and raised here."

"Do you happen to know any of the Ogilvy family? Mr. Ogilvy and his sons are all in the Navy."

"I know 'em. We went to school together."

"I work for their mother at the Signal, Marge Ogilvy."

"Mrs. Ogilvy? No shit. Sorry, language."

"Doesn't bother me. It's just a word. I've heard it all from my husband."

"Mrs. Ogilvy and my mom are friends."

"Then you know how dedicated they are with all their boys fighting for their country."

"Yeah, they're the best."

"I'm doing my part telling about you and them, the women, the sacrifices all of you are making."

"From what I can see, the ladies who come in here every day don't have it easy and they do a hell of a job."

I whipped out my pad and pencil. "Can I quote you on that?"

"Ah, yeah, I guess so. But I don't want you writing about me, a desk jockey."

"How about if I don't identify you as the source of the quote?"

"I guess that would be okay. Just don't use my name."

"I promise. Obviously, you respect and admire what these women are doing."

"Yeah, yeah, I gotta hand it to 'em. They're doin' a man's job."

"Lots of men's jobs, all kinds of men's jobs, since the men are gone."

"Yeah, I've noticed. Why you writing about them?"

"I'm glad you asked that, Seaman Cranston. To recognize them for how they've stepped up to the tasks vacated by the men out of necessity. Women are the home front. They're making the ships and airplanes and growing the food to support all of you men so you can fight. Some women are even flying airplanes."

"Flying? In combat?"

"No, the finished aircraft to the bases."

"Ladies flying."

"They're called ferry pilots."

"So even some of them are doin' more than me."

"Every job's important."

"Except mine."

"You've got that wrong. Security is important. You said it's top secret. You're protecting what goes on in that plant. I apologize for my earlier comment."

"Don't take a man. A dame could do this."

"Don't underestimate yourself, Seaman."

"I don't. I'll get on a cutter yet or a frigate."

"I can put in a good word for you with Mrs. Ogilvy. Her husband is a Naval commander."

He stared at me. "You would do that?"

"Sure, you're a man who should not be overlooked."

"Thanks, nice of you to say. What's your name again?"

"Gwen, Gwen Gebhardt."

"Okay, Gwen, I can't promise, but let me see what I can do." He picked up his phone and called the guard at the gate. Jones, have to step into the plant for a few." He listened to the acknowledgement and stood from his desk. "I'll ask the floor manager."

"Thank you, Seaman. I'm grateful to you and I will speak to Mrs. Ogilvy."

Cranston nodded and disappeared through the door at the rear of the reception room. Ten minutes later, he returned accompanied by a stout blonde woman wearing brown boots, coveralls, and a hairnet. Her piercing blue eyes looked me up and down.

"This is Shirley Heckler," said Seaman Cranston. "She said she'll give you a tour."

Shirley extended her hand. "Your story going to be about this operation?"

"It's one of them. I'm Gwen Gebhardt. My editor is publishing a series."

"You been in an aircraft plant before?"

"This is my first time. My husband is a fighter pilot though. He has taught me a lot."

"What we do here we do for him and the other pilots. We do good work, the best. The women on the line are pros."

"That's what I want to talk about in my article."

"We have to get you fitted out first and you need to know a few safety rules. Come with me."

She led me to a locker room and fit me with steel-toed boots, coveralls, safety goggles, and a green hardhat. "You can store your shoes and dress in my office." She handed me a pair of wax earplugs. "You'll need these. It's loud out there." Ten minutes later, I was walking shoulder to shoulder with her through the machine shop.

All the women wore hairnets and scarves to prevent their hair from catching in tools and moving gears churning and grinding out metal parts. My body thrummed at the concussive pounding of giant presses to shape and form sheet metal and perforate them with holes that corresponded to engineering drawings spread on work benches.

Shirley didn't try to shout over the volume of noise but pointed at activities.

The searing, acrid odor of scorched metal rose from behind protective dark plastic curtains in the welding area. Women wearing elbow-length protective gloves, full length leather aprons, and welding masks leaned into explosive showers of sparks as they created precision seams and joints from reels of solder.

I watched workers assembling electrical wire harnesses on diagram boards.

Further along the cavernous hangar, the screaming whine of high speed drills jammed with the rattling cacophony of rivet guns wielded by women on scaffolds fastening sheet metal over pipes and tubing to build the fuselages of hundreds of planes.

At the end of the line, with the assistance of an overhead crane, teams of women positioned and attached engines and propellers.

Avoiding forklifts moving palletized parts, we exited through an opening in the hangar wall. Shirley removed her earplugs and motioned for me to do the same. "We can talk now."

"It's like a different world in there," I said. "All those women are impressive."

"They're the greatest," said Shirley. "Not a shirker among 'em. They earn every cent they make."

"How long have you worked here?"

"Since the war started. My husband, Bill, was a machinist. I took his place when he was drafted. I had a knack for it and moved up to supervisor."

"Do you have children?"

"Five – three boys and two girls. They're the oldest. They take care of the house, cook and clean. The boys are in school, but they do scrap drives to support the effort."

"All of these women working here can't be single."

"Most of 'em are married and have kids. The plant has childcare service for preschoolers. Costs a little, but it's worth it. These women would rather work than stay at home. It's the first time most of 'em have had a paying job."

Walking out of the plant through the security gate with a mob of workers going home after a ten hour day, I introduced myself to the woman next to me and asked if I could interview her.

"Not now, honey. My carpool's waiting." She continued with the surging crowd toward the parking lot.

I stuck with her. "We can talk while we walk. Anything you'd like to say is fine."

"Maybe some other time, not now. Sorry."

We arrived at her car where three other women, including the driver, were climbing in. Filling the air with exhaust fumes, engines were starting up all around us.

"Who's the dame?" shouted one.

"A reporter from the Signal. She's writing about us."

"Say some good things," shouted another.

"I will. I promise." I waved and had to dodge to avoid being hit by cars maneuvering along the open gravel aisleway.

I saw a city bus arriving at the pickup stop and hurried to join the line of women waiting to board. This time, all the seats were taken, so I had to stand for the ride back into the city.

The defense plant was my first exposure to the cataclysmic social changes forced by the war and resisted by those who were waging it.

Chapter 16

Cheesecake

After he read my article, Roger Bolt said, "There's something missing here. Something important. We need to see these women you're describing at their jobs. We need photographs. We need captions, and commentary that glamorizes these women in defense plants doing men's work, but we want to show they haven't lost their feminine appeal and charm. Even though women are working in factories, we have a tradition to uphold."

"You mean they still have to be sexy," I said.

"Goddam right they have to be sexy. Just because they put on work clothes doesn't make them men. Underneath they're women and men want it that way."

"Since Gwen has a connection at the plant, I'll have a photographer go out with her."

"I want photos of everything you're covering."

"We'll get photos." Marge glanced at me. I nodded.

As we left Roger's office and returned to our desks, Marge said, "I'll line up the photographer. Rick Wexler does a good job. I don't know how much longer we'll have him. He's talking about enlisting to become a military photographer. After this, I know Roger's going to want photos of the land girls and lumber Jills. Don't know about the WAVES. They don't look glamorous in a uniform. They aren't thought well of either."

"Why's that?"

"The cheesecake propaganda the Government puts out. Soldiers resent that WAVES are taking away clerical jobs and civilians think they're being recruited as Government prostitutes. To discourage lesbianism, the military brass has issued harsh rules and regulations against the women being masculine and fraternizing. Of course, it's all scandal and prejudice

164

and lies. The Navy's take on it is their women are feminine and patriotic. Interesting that the naysayers don't worry about men in uniform in close contact being homosexuals. It all sounds pretty silly."

"Not for the women, I guess."

"Not for the women."

The next morning, the photographer, Ray Wexler, rode with me on the bus filled with female defense workers to the aircraft plant. Other than being introduced to me by Marge, he didn't say much, but just occasionally nodded during my attempts at a one-sided conversation.

Because of the oppressive Florida heat and humidity, he didn't wear a suitcoat. A tight belt snugged pleated brown trousers at his waist. A wide green tie barely concealed a small coffee stain on his white shirt. He cuffed his sleeves at the elbows to free his arms.

His observant brown eyes peering out from under his Fedora were in constant motion, scanning and noticing details of people and activity and behavior. Later, watching him work, his Graphix speed camera became an extension of his vision that framed and recorded what he saw.

As we left the bus and were walking to the gate at the defense plant, his lowered voice at my shoulder surprised me. "They ain't dames, are they? Not like real dames."

I glanced sharply at his smug expression. "What do you mean?"

"Except for the hairnets, they all look like men."

"What do you expect? They're wearing men's clothes."

"I guess so."

"They're still women," I insisted.

"I know. I know. I'm just trying to figure out how to get the kind of photo's the boss wants for the paper."

"Are you married, Ray?"

"Not married."

"Have a girl?"

"From time to time."

"What does that mean?"

"Dates. I have dates. What's with the questions? You ain't doin' a story on me."

"No, just being friendly."

"So mainly you're lookin' for a cute face," he said.

"Mainly."

At the kiosk, we checked through and walked directly to the reception office. This time, Seaman Cranston didn't even ask to see my ID. I explained Rick's purpose and he showed his press pass.

"Ours news editors would like to publish some photos of the women," I said.

"Cameras aren't allowed in the plant."

"I won't take any pictures of the factory," said Ray. "I just need a few close shots of women with rivet guns."

"Shirley can show us what's okay and what isn't," I said. "And by the way, I talked with my supervisor and she's putting in a good word for you with her husband."

"Thanks, Ma'am. I'm grateful. I'll get Shirley." Cranston left his desk and walked back into the factory. Returning with Shirley a few minutes later, he reminded us that she would decide what photos could be taken.

"You tryin' for cheesecake?" she asked Ray.

"No, this ain't for a magazine and they ain't models. We just want to show some pretty faces of women doing men's work."

"We have hundreds," said Shirley, "and most of 'em good lookin', even with no makeup. Even some real beauties. Could be on magazine covers. Follow me."

After pulling on coveralls and fitted with steel-toed boots, we accompanied Shirley out onto the plant floor. The high noise level of drills, saws, and rivet guns limited conversation. So Shirley relied on touching Ray's arm and pointing to certain employees she would pull aside and gesture to us and Ray would hold up his camera. Intuiting what he wanted, coyly smiling subjects struck naturally provocative and suggestive poses. One even removed her hairnet and flounced her brunette waves about her shoulders.

The camera flashbulbs popped with reflective explosions of light off adjacent aircraft metal.

When Ray indicated he had enough photos, we waved to the girls and returned to the locker room. We removed our boots and coveralls and thanked Shirley. As we left the plant, Ray said, "This beats my last shoot. Good lookin' dames are much more interesting, even if they're wearing men's work clothes. Kinda sexy."

"What was your last shoot?"

"Beautiful young girl, dead. Her face slashed and her throat cut. Blood everywhere. Cops cleared everybody out. Shut down the hotel. Place was a dive. Mostly whores and their johns. You see today's paper?"

"No."

"Story's on the front page. Shock and gore. Cops and Government dicks want to scare the girls away. Run 'em outta town. Fat chance with all the soldiers lookin' for nooky."

When we returned to the news office, the first thing I did was grab a copy of the morning paper.

***

Joan met with a shock when Roger Bolt rejected her story on colored Army nurses restricted to attending only colored soldiers in war zones. She had interviewed Ina Roberts, who had been medically discharged and returned home suffering from malaria and a skin disease resistant to available treatment.

Ina told stories of how the colored soldiers weren't allowed to carry guns and fight the Japanese in Burma. They had been sent there to build a road through the jungle and relied on white soldiers to protect them when they came under attack.

In addition to nursing wounded men, she described how they had to avoid lethal poisonous snakes and patch up soldiers mauled by tigers.

Roger said he refused to print her column because they presented an unpatriotic negative image and undermined the war effort by discouraging colored women from volunteering.

"We don't publish stories about colored people anyway," he said to all of us. They aren't worthy of being in the news. Joan, stick to writing about the patriotic white women and their dedicated work in the WAACS and the WAVES. Those are the women our readers want to hear about."

At every turn, I kept encountering a paradox.

Chapter 17

Home Front

Except for the home front stories that Celine, Marge, and I were covering, the descriptions of the overseas campaigns that appeared in daily front page bulletins gave the impression the war was unreal, being fought far away in distant lands and only remotely touched our lives due to the absence of men.

The death toll numbers had the effect of game score tallies: 620,000 in North Africa, 60,000 in Italy, 120,000 in France, 7500 Guadalcanal, 3500 Saipan, 12,510 Okinawa in the Pacific theater.

The invasions and counter-invasions reminded us of the spreading global plague by the presence of German prisoners of war incarcerated at Camp Blanding and its extensions to other locations throughout the state.

While covering the land girls story, Ray and Celine had come into contact with German soldiers working as citrus fruit pickers and harvesting melons, peanuts, sugar cane, and truck gardening. Celine showed me the photographs Ray had taken of agricultural land girls and POWS working side by side in the orchards and fields.

They also brought back photos of strong-looking women working in a sawmill, wearing breeches, high laced boots, caulks, and web belt harnesses climbing and felling pine trees for the pulpwood industry. Roger ran a feature story captioning the physical prowess of these lumber Jills, who reminded me of my sister.

The caption read *Lumber Jills Topple Timber. Samantha Platt wields her axe like a pro.*

The razor sharp edge of her long-handled axe cut a deep wedge low into the pine trunk. A thick vanilla chip flipped back like a spent rifle cartridge. A balanced stance in high-top laced boots provided a sturdy foundation and a bloused green forester's shirt and brown breeches gave

170

her freedom of movement. The left corner of her thin mouth upturned in a tight grimace as she concentrated on aiming the trajectory of her swing and powerful downward thrust. A long dark braid hanging down her back from her white hardhat bounced with each impact.

Gwen figured Roger had selected Samantha's photo because of her impish, brown-eyed sex appeal. Celine had captured the young woman's patriotic spirit in an engaging profile of her life as the only daughter among three brothers who had worked as loggers with their father until they had all enlisted.

Demonstrating similar upper body and shoulder strength of her brothers, she had volunteered to work on a lumber crew felling trees for pulpwood and Kraft paper mills. An experienced logger, not only did she take down trees, she drove a flatbed truck stacked with chained, trimmed logs from the forests to the mills.

She was paid $31.21 a week.

"POWs work right alongside the land girls," said Celine. "There are some real handsome lookers, and friendly too. They're watched by armed military guards, but they laugh and flirt with the land girls just like our own boys. I did interview one who spoke English and is fluent in French. He graduated from the University of Frankfurt in languages. He said he had been recruited as an interpreter with the Afrika Korps. He's a nice young guy. Incredible blue eyes and a smile that melted my heart. If he wasn't a prisoner, I could see getting to know him."

"Celine," said Marge, "do you hear what you're saying? He's the enemy. He killed our boys. You don't fall head over heels in love with the enemy."

"He told me he wasn't like the others and he didn't support Hitler. He's an anti-Nazi."

"And you believe him? The Afrika Korps are Hitler's elite soldiers."

"He said he didn't have a choice. He was drafted."

"Celine, you need to clear your head. Wait for our own boys to come home."

""I couldn't have a relationship with him even if I wanted to, which I don't. He's a prisoner."

"Just don't lose your journalistic objectivity when you're out there."

"Come on, Marge. Not a chance. I'm just telling you what he told me. I can learn more by being open to conversations. He said he was anti-Nazi. A lot of the prisoners are, but it causes trouble in the camps."

"What kind of trouble?"

"If someone says that Germany is losing the war, they get beaten. Gunther said he keeps a low profile. He witnessed a beating happen to one of his friends who had to be treated at the camp infirmary. He said the hardcore Nazis want the others to refuse to work and not to cooperate, but he said he likes the work. It gives him something useful to do."

Shipped with two thousand other prisoners from North Africa, the Atlantic crossing had been a gut-wrenching ordeal. Plagued with sea sicknesses, Gunther and many of the troops couldn't keep food down and arrived weak and undernourished at Newport News, Virginia. They were then transferred by train under guard to Opelika, Alabama and, weeks later, on to Camp Blanding, Florida.

Within a short period, he was surprised and relieved to discover how well-fed and reasonably they were treated as prisoners. Their assimilation and acceptance as members of organized work teams led by German officers further eased their fears and anxiety.

Gunther Graf had gone from driving Panzer tanks and burying landmines in North Africa to digging up potatoes in rural Florida. For a short time, he had worked on a sugar cane cutting crew in snake-infested fields until he was assigned to another site.

He preferred picking oranges and grapefruits in the citrus groves and working in a fruit packing plant, but he and two-hundred fellow prisoners had been transported on military buses from Camp Blanding to the potato fields early that morning.

The taste of scrambled eggs, bacon and biscuits with gravy, fried potatoes, orange juice and black coffee lingered on his tongue. He did not miss the canned rations given to the Afrika Korps. Unlike many of his comrades, he did not complain when General Rommel ordered the retreat and surrender in Tunisia. He and his tank crew joined the troops quick-marching along the scarred coastal road from El Alameine to Medenine from where they had advanced only weeks before.

He had visions of the bloody carnage of desert battles, men's body's torn apart, faces obliterated, arms and legs blown away. Encrusted with flies, ropey entrails spilled out onto the sand.

Here, he felt he had been delivered into a tropical paradise. Warm sunshine and the honey sweet aroma of orange blossoms wafted over him from the vast forests of friendly green groves and momentarily dispelled his memories of dust and violent sandstorms, smeared goggles covering his bloodshot eyes and the need to wear a scarf wrapped around his head and face so he could breathe.

He listened to the cricket ticking sound of a distant tractor as opposed to the metallic clanking of the turret in which he and two fellow soldiers crouched crammed together stinking of diesel fuel and gun oil.

Here, clean sweat stained his shirt and the pith helmet he wore deflected only the intense sunlight, not bullets.

Sea breezes and tropical bird calls replaced the percussive booming of cannons and rattling artillery fire and the grind of halftrack treads crunching over miles of shifting sand and gravel. A feeling of sanctuary and well-being replaced the pitched anxiety of painful explosive death.

Paper Dolls

Dirt encrusted under his fingernails and the loamy smell rising from leafy long rows of the potato fields reminded him of his youth. As a boy, he had spent many pleasant summers on his aunt and uncle's dairy farm in Normandy. In addition to family evenings with six cousins around the dinner table, driving a tractor during the corn and hay harvest and picking and pressing apples to be made into Calvados cider were among his fondest memories.

His throat constricted with an emotion of kinship, during the interview, when Celine Comeau shared she came from a French family and had grown up on a dairy farm in Wisconsin.

While on a wine buying trip to Paris, Gunther's German father, Herman Graf, had met and married his French wife, Viviane, during the early 1920s. Herman owned and managed a restaurant on Potsdamer Platz in Berlin's Tiergarten district. As partner and hostess, Viviane introduced French cuisine to the traditional German menu, which further attracted Government and business patrons.

During the war years, she had to suppress her distaste for Nazi officials who complimented the French cuisine on the one hand, but were the most frequent, vociferous, demanding, and often demeaning customers.

Before his redeployment to North Africa with Field Marshall Rommel's Panzer division, the irony of invading the small French towns of Normandy did not escape Gunther. The farmers and villagers reminded him of his Aunt and Uncle. He was relieved that they did not resist and that soldiers of the Panzer divisions did not fire on them.

On occasions when the convoy bivouacked blocking the narrow cobblestone streets and seized food and wine from the half-timbered homes of residents, he spoke in French and assured the frightened occupants that as long as they cooperated, they would not be harmed. Other soldiers threatened inhabitants and ransacked their homes for food *and valuables. Any men who resisted were led away, forced to their knees, and executed with a single shot to the head.*

Gunther took a long drink, emptying the canteen strapped to his belt. He watched the sun fading to the west. A cool evening breeze touched his tan sweat-soaked shirt with the letters PW stenciled on the back. He removed his helmet and rubbed loose his damp blonde hair. The group leader called an end to the workday and Gunther joined the other two-hundred prisoners trudging out of the potato fields to the line of military buses waiting along the road. His full bladder ached, but he would wait until he returned to the barracks to relieve himself.

Through his window, Gunther could see Negro soldiers practicing marching drills, as the bus caravan route skirted the boundary of the segregated Camp Blanding Negro section. He had learned from guards that Negroes were trained and housed apart from white soldiers and prohibited from social comingling and military maneuvers. They were given only noncombatant duty as janitors, truck drivers, stevedores, and serving white officers meals and cleaning their rooms.

The image recalled the one protestant church service he had attended at the multi-denominational chapel available to the prisoners. When the chaplain made a reference that Christ would condemn the inhuman treatment of Jews by the Nazis, a fellow prisoner interrupted him with a counter-accusation as to how Negroes were treated in America. Unable to justify prejudice and white supremacy, he watched the small congregation of fifty German soldiers stand up from the pews and walk out of the chapel.

Within the barbed wire confines of the internment camp, Gunther and the other field workers poured out of the buses and shuffled past the guard towers to a city of multiple rows of barracks that housed five thousand prisoners.

Paper Dolls

When he arrived at the shack that accommodated twenty of his comrades and served as their living quarters, he paused at the entrance to inspect the small flower garden plot they maintained to brighten and beautify the otherwise drab board cabin structure. Similar gardens had proliferated to decorate the front of most of the barracks giving the compound the appearance of an extensive flower nursery.

The multitude of colors reminded him of the flower boxes in the windows of houses lining the narrow streets of villages in France. He didn't know why nostalgic boyhood memories of France leapt to the forefront of his thoughts, perhaps his encounter with Celine.

He entered the barracks and sat on his single mattress cot among several head to foot along one wall lined with a collage of photographs of female movie stars clipped from magazines.

He and his comrades talked incessantly about girls back in Germany and ogled American girls through the windows when the prison bus passed through town. He knew of only one occasion when a German soldier managed to have sex with a willing female worker in the citrus packing plant. Otherwise, masturbation in the barracks latrine was a poor substitute.

Chapter 18

The Death of A Victory Girl

The murder of Evelyn Blaine reinforced the specter of how surreal and absurd the war had become at home.

I stared horrified at the black and white police photo of the young woman sprawled on the floor of a hotel room with her face disfigured and her throat slashed. The photo and accompanying story garnered the front page headline as news and as a warning to the legions of prostitutes and, especially, unprofessional victory girls who frequented the streets, taverns, dance halls, bars, and hotels of towns and cities attached to military bases. How these "victory girls" and "good time Charlottes" were treated became a turning point in my life.

I was busy at my desk when I first saw the disturbed woman carrying a battered suitcase enter the newsroom. Her hand trembled about her sallow face as she reacted to the reporter who confronted her. Asking her to wait, he walked quickly to Roger Bolt's open office door. After a brief exchange, Roger stood up from his desk, looked across the newsroom at the woman, and came out to Marge. I stopped typing so I could listen.

"That woman there is the mother of the girl who was murdered. She says the police can't tell her anything. She saw the photo in the paper and came here. She wants us to help her."

"That poor woman. She looks so distraught."

"She has a suitcase," said the reporter. "She's from out-of-town."

"What does she think we can do for her?" asked Marge.

"Talk to her," said Roger. "Explain we just published the story. The crime desk doesn't have any more from the police than that."

"I'll talk to her," I said. "There's more to tell behind the photo. The fact she's here tells us she cared about her daughter."

"Could be a story," said Marge.

"I'll leave it up to you two," said Roger and returned to his office.

"She doesn't look comfortable," I said and grabbed my purse. "I'll take her for a cup of coffee."

Her confused milky blue eyes watched me approach through the field of desks manned by reporters and clacking typewriters. An ill-fitting dress did not conceal her thin bony frame. A faded cloche hat concealed her unwashed brown hair as an attempt at respectability.

"Mrs. Blaine?" I said in a conciliatory tone.

"Yes, I'm Naiomi Blaine."

"I'm Gwen Gebhardt. I'm very sorry about your daughter."

"Did you know her? Evelyn was a good kind girl. She would never harm a creature or anybody. How could someone do this to her. Who would do such a horrible thing? We are good Christians. We go to church and we pray. How could God let this happen?"

"I'm sorry, Mrs. Blaine. I did not know your daughter and God did not let this happen. She was killed by an American soldier."

"But her picture was in your newspaper. God should have protected her."

"Yes, I saw the photo, but I didn't know her."

"The police didn't even tell me. A neighbor showed me her picture in the newspaper. Evelyn and me sewed uniforms for the troops. We was doing our part to support the soldiers. I can't believe that's her in the photo."

"Would you like to have a cup of coffee and something to eat and you can tell me about her?"

"I haven't eaten for two days since I saw the picture."

"Let's go get something. Can I help you with your suitcase?" I reached for the handle.

"My husband's somewhere. I don't know where. He's in the Army. I write him letters. I got one back. I don't want to tell him about Evelyne."

I took her suitcase, looped my other arm through hers, and escorted her out the door.

The soldiers and women moving along the sidewalk mesmerized her as though she were sleep-walking. Avoiding a large restaurant filled with boisterous patrons, I urged her forward to a small uncrowded café where we could easily hear one another.

When we were seated and I had ordered pancakes, two fried eggs, and sausages for her and a coffee and Danish for me, I asked, "Do you have any pictures of Evelyn when she was a child or even taken more recently?" I asked.

"We didn't own a camera, but my sister and her husband did. They took family pictures."

"Did you bring any with you to identify your daughter?"

She slipped the leather strap off her shoulder, rummaged inside the oversized purse, and pulled out two black and white photographs. One showed a smiling dimple-cheeked Mrs. Blaine, her gaunt husband wearing an Army uniform and a somber expression, and their blonde eighteen-year-old daughter beaming an innocent exuberant smile. The second photo was of Evelyn as a ten-year-old.

"That's my husband, Jake," Naiomi pointed. The trembling of her hands had not subsided. I wondered if it were attributed to long hours of sewing but realized she might have a nervous disorder.

"Where do you live, Naiomi?"

"Sanford. It's a small town. Jake was a mechanic and drove a delivery truck until the war. I taught Evelyn how to sew and we both got jobs at the clothing factory to make uniforms. The money kept us going, at least to buy food. I don't know what possessed our daughter to leave without telling me. I would never have let her go. We never went to the city."

"Did she know anyone in Miami? Did she have a friend?"

180

"I'm ashamed to say it, but she and her friend said they were going to work at a dance hall to support the soldiers. I don't know where they got that idea. They came together."

"What is her friend's name?"

"Miriam Holder. Her parents are mortified. She talked my Evelyn into coming to Miami. She was always talking about boys. When the war started, she said soldiers were romantic and she was always bringing over magazines to show Evelyn with stories about supporting the troops."

"Do you know where to find her?"

Naiomi shook her head. Her small straight nose snuffled like a puppy as her steaming breakfast plate was put in front of her. The waitress poured coffee and held the pot up indicating a refill. I nodded and watched the dark liquid level in the cup rise two inches. Naiomi's chapped lips touched the edge of her cup. She hesitated at the heat, waited a few moments, then gulped thirstily.

She voraciously stabbed at the eggs so the syrup-coated pancakes absorbed the yolks. She put small bites in her mouth and chewed slowly at first. The pace of eating increased as though she were filling more than the emptiness of hunger. She choked. I reached across the table and touched the back of her hand. "You okay?" She nodded and drank from her glass of water. Ignoring her napkin, she rubbed away errant drops from thin lips with the back of her hand and continued to cram her mouth with food.

I nibbled at my Danish and thought better of asking about her daughter and Miriam Holder. She burped without apology at the conclusion of her meal. I asked, "Would you like anything more?"

She shook her head. "Can't eat nothin' more. Thank you for bein' so kind."

"I'm glad to help you, Naiomi. We can leave whenever you're ready."

"Have to pee." She rose from her chair.

"The restrooms are to the left past the counter."

She nodded and moved quickly toward the sign on the wall. I left a tip for the waitress, paid the bill at the cash register, and waited standing with Naiomi's suitcase at the end of the lunch counter.

She returned ten minutes later and I led her outside.

Waiting next to me at the bus stop, she stared at young women strolling by as though at any moment her daughter might appear among them. As the bus approached, she asked, "Where are we going?"

"To where I live. It's calm and quiet and we can talk there. My landlady has a beautiful garden."

"But what about Evelyn?"

"You can tell me more about her and her friend."

"I think Miriam talked her into coming here. She was always the bad one when they were girls. She didn't mind the rules. Got my Evelyn in trouble, even at school. Her pa took a switch to her many a time. My Evelyn would never dream of doing such a thing coming here. Miriam was the troublemaker. Miriam put her up to it."

I nudged Naiomi up the steps into the bus, dropped tokens into the changer, and guided her by the elbow along the aisle to two empty seats.

Naiomi gazed silently out the window for several blocks until I touched her arm at the Orange Avenue stop. Naiomi's uncomprehending glance caught me unaware. "This is our stop." I stood and assisted her to her feet.

We escaped the exhaust fumes of the departing bus by walking quickly for several yards in the opposite direction. Then I slowed our pace so Naiomi could take in the tall palm trees and elegant old homes nested among luxuriant foliage and oaks dripping gray bearded moss.

We stopped at the front sidewalk of Mrs. Chelton's two story colonial. A black wrought iron grill edged the balcony and white magnolia blossoms accented the orange tile roof.

"Do you live here?"

"I rent a room."

"It's beautiful. I love flowers."

"Do you have them at home?"

"Not like this. Not at a house like this. We're poor folk, but we get by."

"I think you'll enjoy meeting Mrs. Chelton. This is her home. She and her husband raised a family here." As we approached the door, I asked, "How long have you lived in Sanford?"

"Most of my life. Me and Jake moved there from Ocala a year before Evelyn was born."

"Do you have other children?"

"My second died during childbirth. We didn't have no doctor, only a midwife."

"I'm sorry. That makes losing Evelyn more difficult."

"She's lost but I know I can find her."

I pushed open the door and we stepped inside. The aroma of vegetable soup filled the house. I saw Mrs. Chelton notice us across the living room through the kitchen entry. Naiomi stared at the colorful pillows on bentwood furnishings and peered at framed family photos on tabletops and the fireplace mantel. I gently moved her along.

"Mrs. Chelton, this is Naiomi Blaine. She came down from Sanford. Her daughter's picture was in the paper."

Mrs. Chelton silently studied the despondent expression of the woman I had brought home, then rose from the kitchen table and came around to greet her with a gracious smile. She gently took both of Naiomi's trembling hands in her own, storied and wrinkled with age.

"How very nice and special to meet you, Naiomi. Her quiet voice soothed and calmed the troubled mother. "I am deeply sorry for the loss of your daughter."

"You know Evelyn? You know where she is?"

Mrs. Chelton glanced at me, then her understanding compassionate gaze returned to Naiomi. "I never met your daughter, Dear. I only saw her photograph."

Naiomi pulled her hands away and reached into her purse. "I brought pictures of her so you know what she looks like in case you might happen to see her."

"I'll be happy to look at your pictures. Come in, Dear. Let's sit at the table. Perhaps you'd like a cup of tea. I just finished brewing a pot." Her look at me said to pour cups of tea from the kettle on the stove. I set down my purse and complied with her unspoken request as she helped Naiomi to a chair at the table.

"Do you have relatives back home?" Mrs. Chelton asked.

"My sister lives the next town over," said Naiomi. "She has two daughters, older than my Evelyn. They went to work in the shipyards at Tampa. Her husband's in the Navy."

Mrs. Chelton referred to the photograph. "Evelyn looks like a very dear girl."

"Oh, she is. She is. My sister took that picture last year when Evelyn turned sixteen. I don't think the picture in the newspaper is my daughter. It's just someone who looks like her. There're are lots of girls who look like her. I need to find out and then I need to find Evelyn and bring her home."

"She needs a place to stay for a few days," I said.

"Of course, she is most welcome to stay here with us."

"She can have my room. I can sleep on the couch."

"That won't be necessary. The couple renting the other room moved out this morning. He's being sent overseas and she's going back home to Chicago."

"You are both very kind," said Naiomi. "It seems that kindness in the world has gone away."

"It's an unsettling time," said Mrs. Chelton. "At least here at home, we need to be kind to each other. Drink your tea, dear, before it gets cold. Have a cookie. They're fresh baked."

Naiomi drank a sip of tea and nibbled at an oatmeal raisin cookie from the plate at the center of the table. "These are so good," she mumbled with crumbs falling from the corners of her mouth. She swallowed the bite of cookie and washed it down with a gulp of tea. "I taught Evelyn how to bake when she was just a little girl. We made cakes and pies and muffins. We even won blue ribbons for our cakes and pies at the county fair. And they were always favorites at church socials and picnics. Our fruit pies were the talk of the county. We baked for the café in Sanford and some cafes in other nearby towns. People wanted to know our secret, but we never told them it was love. I love my child more than anything in the world. Even if Jake don't come back from the war, I'll still have my Evelyn."

"You will always have her in your memory and in your heart."

Softened by describing her daughter's childhood relationship, Naiomi's expression suddenly hardened into an antagonistic stare. "What do you mean in my memory?"

"We all keep our children in our memories. We value our memories. I miss my children too. They've grown up and moved on. Have children of their own. My sons are in the service. I often think of them and remember when they were children."

"What if they don't come back? I read about soldiers dying."

"That is news we don't want to hear and hope it doesn't come to our door."

"But what if it does come to your door?"

"I don't have any choice but to accept that reality and I will mourn the loss of any of my children."

"But if you believe it won't happen, then they won't die."

"Your belief will help keep you strong." Mrs. Chelton held her gaze. Naiomi clutched another cookie from the plate and slowly moved it to her mouth.

"Naiomi likes flowers," I said. "Perhaps you might show her your gardens."

"Flowers are my joy," said Mrs. Chelton. "I'd love to show you. There's satisfaction in bringing plant life from the soil and nurturing it. Do you plant flowers at home?"

"Some, vegetables mostly," said Naiomi. "Flowers grow wild everywhere. Flowers and fruit trees. We just have to pick 'em."

"Nice to have such abundance," said Mrs. Chelton. "Did you and your daughter do any canning?"

Naiomi's enthusiastic nod shifted her attention. "Once a year. We always beat the frost."

From a rocker on the back porch, I watched Naiomi walk side by side with Mrs. Chelton pointing out features of her large vegetable garden. She encouraged Naiomi to help pick green beans and tomatoes and deposit them in the wicker basket she carried.

The diversion seemed to affect Naiomi in a positive way. As she and Mrs. Chelton returned to the porch, the stiffness of her face and rigidity of her body visibly lessened. I rose from the rocker and assisted Naiomi up the wooden steps to a second rocker. Mrs. Chelton carried the basket of vegetables into the kitchen. She partially opened the screen door and said she would get a towel and run a warm bath for Naiomi.

"What do you think of the garden?" I asked.

She nodded and tipped the rocker into gentle repetitive motion.

"Tomorrow, we can try the dance hall to see if your daughter's friend is still working there," I said.

"Miriam will know where to find her. She can tell us where to find her."

Following her bath, Naiomi went to her room. Mrs. Chelton and I sat out on the back porch. We didn't' talk much. There wasn't much to say.

"It will take time."

I nodded.

Later, I helped prepare dinner, then went to check on Naiomi. She was in a deep sleep. I left the door ajar hoping the aromatic seasoning of grilled fish and vegetables might wake her and draw her downstairs.

Mrs. Chelton and I ate quietly together.

The next morning after breakfast, Naiomi and I rode the bus into town. Of three social clubs, I selected the USO sponsored dance hall, which would be the most likely employer of girls like Miriam and Evelyn.

Even at mid-morning, several girls were chatting with young soldiers playing card games and helping them write letters home. Naiomi hesitated at the entrance.

"Is this where she worked?"

"I don't know for certain," I said. "We'll have to ask." I led her across the spacious wooden dance floor to the reception booth where a private from the Women's Army Corps greeted us with a smile.

"Good morning, ladies, I'm Private Flaherty. Can I be of assistance?"

Naiomi didn't know what to make of the trim uniform, Marcel-waved brown hair, and rosy face. She looked away toward the girls and soldiers seated at tables and chairs.

"This is Naiomi Blaine," I said. "She came to Miami in search of her daughter and her daughter's friend. The circumstances are unusual. You may have seen the photo of the girl in The Miami Signal."

The WAC's eyes widened.

"Don't say anything yet," I cautioned. "It's a delicate situation. I'm a writer for The Signal. She came to me seeking help."

"Is that her daughter in the photo?"

"She doesn't believe so. She doesn't want to accept it. She wants to find out more to disprove it to herself."

"Oh, I see. I'm so sorry for her."

"Did Evelyn Blaine work here?"

"She was one of our volunteers. She and her friend."

"Miriam Holder?"

"Yes, Miriam Holder. They were both good dancers, much in demand."

Naiomi turned back. "You know my daughter? You know my Evelyn?"

"Yes, Ma'am, I did know her."

"Where is she? How come I don't see her? Why isn't she here?"

I gave a brief shake of my head. Private Flaherty suddenly realized what I was dealing with. "She and her friend haven't checked in with us for several days. The girls pretty much come and go as they please. We don't keep tabs on them."

Private Flaherty found Naiomi's accusing vacuous stare a little unnerving.

"What about Miriam Holder?" I asked. "Under the circumstances, is there anything you can tell us about her."

Private Flaherty looked directly at me. "I think that is something we should discuss privately." She motioned for me to come through the side door into her spare office. "This is not a pleasant topic, but rules are rules and I have to uphold them. We don't let immoral girls work here. I got wind from one of the other girls that Evelyn and Miriam were picking up soldiers here and going off to have sex for money."

"Were Evelyn and Miriam popular?"

"Very much and well-liked by the boys."

"Are you sure this other girl wasn't just jealous of them?"

"Not that I detected. But like I said, these victory girls come and go. I don't follow their personal lives, but if they break the rules. You understand. You want my opinion? I think she gave VD to a soldier and he came back and killed her for it."

"Did you tell that to the police?"

"No, I don't want to give the USO a bad name. You won't tell them, will you?"

I hesitated. "No, I won't tell them. They probably already suspect that might be the motive. Even if I did tell them, it wouldn't bring Evelyn back and the Army would not likely investigate. They would deny any of their men would do such a thing. They're trained to kill enemy soldiers, not teenage girls. I appreciate that you told me and I won't share the information about her daughter with Mrs. Blaine."

When we returned to the reception counter, Naiomi was no longer there. I asked one of the other victory girls. "That woman who was standing there, did you see where she went?"

The girl pointed to the door. I found Naiomi outside. She looked at my face and touched my arm. "It's time for me to go home. I know that my Evelyn was here."

We returned to Mrs. Chelton's for Naiomi's suitcase. Then I took her to the bus station and bought her a ticket to Sanford.

As we parted, she said, "Thank you for your kindness. I think Evelyn will come home someday. Maybe she'll be married to one of those soldiers."

I said nothing.

"I'll tell Ethel about Miriam. She should come and see her, but she'll probably say whatever happened to Miriam she got what she deserved."

"No woman deserves this, Naiomi. No woman deserves this."

I watched her board the bus. Her face appeared at a window. She raised a hand in farewell. It did not tremble.

My mother would never have come to Miami in search of me.

I raised my hand and smiled.

Chapter 19

Quarantine

When I walked into the county jail, the scathing glare from pouchy eyes and the derogatory tone of the balding, heavy-set police sergeant did not intimidate me as he expected. I showed him my press pass.

"I'm Gwen Gebhardt from the Miami Signal."

"Who sent you over? We don't give interviews to lady reporters and nobody from here called the crime desk with a story."

"I work for the chief editor, Roger Bolton. He sent me over here."

The sergeant straightened up with indignation. "He needs to call us first. We let him know if there's anything to report."

"I'm looking for a missing person."

"We aren't investigating no missing person."

"Have you arrested a teenager named Miriam Holder? She's sixteen years old. She's a friend of the girl who was murdered, Evelyn Blaine."

"We already gave the information on the Blaine girl to your crime reporter. The photo was in your paper two weeks ago."

"What about Evelyn's body?"

"You'll have to ask the coroner."

"If you arrested Miriam Holder, where would she be now?"

"We don't have anyone by that name here."

"But if she was here even for a short time, where did you send her?"

"Where we send all the little harlots, quarantine. She's a sex delinquent."

"Can you give me an address or tell me the location?"

"No, Ma'am. You'll have to go to the Department of Public Health. Our job is to arrest them. Public Health takes 'em from there."

Without another word, I marched out of the sheriff's office and walked steadily down the street to a cluster of drab gray government buildings. A glass-enclosed listing of Federal administration officers pointed me to an elevator and up to the third floor.

I introduced myself to a frumpily-dressed secretary at the front desk and explained my purpose. She went into the closed back office of the health director and returned a few minutes later.

"Mr. Lawry is quite busy," she drawled, "but he said he can talk with you briefly."

"Thank you." I followed her into his office. She closed the door behind me. He acted preoccupied with paperwork on his desktop and did not immediately look up. I clutched my purse in front of me and stood impatiently waiting.

He wore a gray business suit minus the jacket. I focused on the precise Windsor knot of his blue tie supporting a starched white collar in an attempt to conceal his protruding Adam's apple. His pinched face and round wire-rim glasses reminded me of a predatory owl. After a full minute, without shifting focus from his documents, he said, "As you can see, I'm quite busy and I don't grant interviews. Mrs. Berry said you're searching for a Miriam Holder. I can give you limited information about her. What is it you want to know?"

"You might have seen the story in the paper about the murdered victory girl, Evelyn Blaine."

"It's unfortunate the police didn't get her off the street in time. The coroner confirmed that she was a disease carrier."

"I'm trying to find her best friend, Miriam Holder. The police told me she was arrested and turned over to the public health department."

"The best I can tell you is Miriam Holder has been quarantined and hospitalized and is being treated for venereal disease. In addition, when she recovers, she will be held in a quarantine facility and receive psychological counseling until it is determined she can be safely released without returning to her immoral activity."

"Quarantine facility? Why? She isn't a prostitute. She's just a teenage girl."

"Who is now a VD carrier that has infected some of our fighting men who cannot be sent overseas until they recover. To be blunt, most of the girls we process through here are not very bright, especially the young ones. Unless they grew up on a farm, they don't understand the biological function of their bodies. Sex is a taboo subject. It isn't even talked about in most families. So how are these girls expected to know what is happening to them?"

"So you're just going to lock them away instead."

"For one year, and in some cases longer, especially the colored prostitutes. The point is these girls are undermining the fighting effectiveness of U.S. soldiers. The military wants their men out in the front lines, not lying up in a hospital because a woman gave them a disease."

"And what about the men? Why doesn't the military educate them?"

"Oh, they do. They even have prophylaxis stations to prevent them from getting VD. If they do get it, once they're cured, they can be returned to duty."

"But you have nothing for women except to lock them up."

"It's a massive and difficult undertaking, let me tell you. There are thousands all over the country doing their patriotic duty spreading their legs for soldiers."

"And you're saying soldiers don't spread the disease."

"No, women are the carriers. They give it to the men and men are entitled to have sex. They're putting their lives on the line."

"Do you hear what you're saying? Men are not at fault?"

"That's the way we're put together, Lady."

"I would like to see Miriam and talk to her."

"That's impossible. We don't allow visitors and especially the press into our quarantine centers."

"Centers? They sound like prisons."

"That's our concern, Mrs. Gebhardt. You're looking for something sensational to write about and will distort the good work we in the public health services are doing."

"Can you tell me where they're located?"

"There's no point. You are restricted from visiting them."

"How many are there?"

"We have them all over the country where there are military bases. There aren't enough jails to hold all the girls. So they're arrested and quarantined on immorality charges.

"There are some quarantine locations in Florida then?"

"We send our patients to Georgia." He eyed me closely. "I really don't recommend you try to go there. The guards would arrest you and you would be incarcerated. It could get quite ugly."

"Excuse me. I'm an American citizen and married to an Army Airforce officer."

"Take my advice, Mrs. Gebhardt. It's the way things are."

I turned and walked out of his office, slamming the door behind me. Mrs. Berry bolted up out of her chair and asked, "Is everything all right?"

I marched past her and slammed out through the front door. The final image in my head was of her pouched dark eyes, jowly chin, and wrinkled brown dress.

The odor of formaldehyde in the coroner's office nearly brought up my breakfast. I covered my nose with my hand and followed him into the laboratory where he showed me Evelyn Blain's corpse. Even having seen her photograph in the newspaper did not prepare me for the reality of the abuse to her face and body.

That same day, I made arrangements for her funeral and hired a minister to say a few consoling phrases over her grave at the public potters field cemetery. I placed a bouquet of flowers from Mrs. Chelton's garden on a simple headstone engraved with Evelyn's name and date of her death.

I never told Naiomi Blaine that I had buried Evelyn. I thought it best not to influence her memories of her daughter.

I was not officially assigned to the police crime desk. That was for male journalists only but none of them were interested. Because of the sensationalism about sex, Roger told me to interview and write about the camp followers and Victory Girls in dance clubs.

I also spoke with prostitutes in bars and hotel lobbies. They plied their trade caught between the Government, on the one hand, wanting to boost the morale of soldiers and, on the other, identifying them as the vector carriers of venereal disease that endangered male health and undermined the capability of fighting forces. Prostitutes were branded enemies and arrested for committing acts of treason. Suspecting me of being an undercover cop, most of them wouldn't talk to me.

The May Act of July 1941 had made prostitution a Federal offense near defense plants and military reservations. But the girls came in droves anyway, in cars, on trucks and buses. The mob gathered down the road from the camp gate waiting for the soldiers and the sexual frenzy of payday.

On my first investigative effort walking along Flagler Street in downtown Miami, I wasn't able to identify who might be a prostitute from among the military wives, secretaries, and shop girls. They all wore lipstick and similar dresses and flats with socks. None wore nylons, but I noticed a few with painted seams up the backs of their sun-tanned legs.

At mid-morning, I sat in a café and ordered a cup of coffee and a Danish.

Hank Stacker coming through the door was unexpected and unwelcome. He noticed me, hesitated, then ordered coffee and a piece of apple pie at the counter. To my chagrin, he walked over to my table.

"Hello, Gwen, long time no see. Mind if I sit down?"

I gestured to take the opposite seat. "I see you're in uniform. We're told to be kind to soldiers."

"Got my bars." He pointed to the brass second lieutenant bars. "Graduated two days ago. Another ninety day wonder. Since you're here in Miami, you and Eddie must have gotten married."

"We did right out of college. He's a fighter pilot in the South Pacific."

"Guess I lucked out. I got England, communications command. Not likely to see combat, but you never know. One scar's enough." His sly grin accentuated the facial scar given to him by Tess. "How's your sister doing?"

"I don't know. We've been out of touch."

"She was some athlete. Such a waste though with that girlfriend of hers."

"What are you insinuating?"

"Nothing. She's a real babe. And you, here alone?"

"I'm a reporter. I work for the Miami Signal."

"Congratulations. Looks like being on the Wellesley News staff paid off. "

I shrugged. "It helped. I majored in literature."

"And what about your roommate, Justine?"

"She married Ronald Sarkozy. He's a Navy doctor."

"Not bad duty. He on a ship or land hospital?"

"I don't know. We haven't maintained correspondence since the beginning of the war."

"The war gets in the way of just about everything, doesn't it?"

"At least everything we'd like it to be, instead of out of kilter."

"So, you hunting down a story, writing something big?"

"I'm working on a series with three others about women on the home front."

"Oh, that's right. That's right. Women are taking over all the men's jobs until they come home, if they come home."

"The war can't be won without women."

"Strange flip flop, isn't it? Out of the kitchen onto the assembly line."

"Sounds like you read one of my articles."

"Actually, yes. I was surprised to see your name as the writer. I didn't think I'd ever be sitting here talking to you."

"Well, here we are. Small world."

"Lot of people passing through here." Hank sipped his coffee.

Through the window, we noticed a turmoil on the sidewalk. I jumped up from my table and dashed outside. "Excuse me," I asked the two police officers. "Why are you arresting her? She was just standing in front of the coffee shop."

"Ma'am, it's none of your business. Now move aside or we'll take you in for interfering with an arrest."

I pulled my press pass out of my purse. "I'm with the Miami Signal. I'm doing a story."

"Not here you're not."

"But what did she do?"

"She was loitering."

"Loitering?"

"Yeah, women can't just stand around like they're waiting for a John. She could be a prostitute and, if she is, she's probably got VD. We have orders to take prostitutes off the streets." He and his partner handcuffed and muscled her into the back seat of a police car.

I went back inside and returned to my seat.

"What was that all about?" asked Hank. "Why did you run out there?"

"I'm doing a story on Victory Girls."

"Ah, the VD thing. We get briefings on it constantly and they hand out little pamphlets that get thrown away."

"You throw yours away."

He nodded with a smirk. "A dose of the clap can keep you out of the fight, at least for a while."

"You think having VD is worth it?"

"No, we get condoms anyway to protect us."

"Obviously a lot of soldiers don't use them."

"They're a nuisance but you can't be too careful. Women are the carriers."

"I'm not so sure men aren't."

"Not likely. That what you're writing about?"

"Not specifically. More about what happens to women who are arrested."

"Ah, we hear about the cleanup in briefings."

"Cleanup?"

"Get the diseased ones off the streets. Makes it safer for the men."

I avoided his glance and looked across the room at the crowded counter. "I have to get on."

"You haven't finished your Danish."

"I have a lot of work to do." I picked up my receipt and stood.

"I'll take care of that."

"Wouldn't think of it. Good luck in England."

"I'll try my best." He spoke to my back as I moved away. "Nice talking with you, Gwen."

I did not respond and did not look at him again. I paid the cashier and walked out of the cafe.

I continued my investigation of the sexual underworld of home front women. I talked with numerous girls. Some participated. Not wanting to be identified and fearing entrapment, others shunned me.

I saw from police statistics that more arrests were made of lower class white and Negro women. The attitude of politicians was that girls were just dispensable, collateral damage, especially contrasted with men who were fighting and dying overseas in defense of their country.

The girl's aversion to being interviewed did not take me long to notice. I was

suspected of being an undercover spy who would notify the police. But seeing me interviewing soldiers raised the police's suspicion about me. They suspected me of soliciting soldiers.

The day I was physically accosted and accused of being a prostitute disgusted me beyond belief. I was brought into an examination center and threatened with incarceration at a quarantine camp if I did not subject to being medically examined.

I raged at the medical examiner at what was being done to me. "You're violating my legal rights!" I screamed at him. "I'm a reporter for the Miami Signal, not a prostitute!

"You are suspected of being in contact with someone who has a defective disease."

"Like whom? My husband is fighting overseas. I haven't slept with any other man."

"Nevertheless, we are required by law to examine you for your own good."

"Excuse me, but you are completely wrong and out of line."

"Do not purport to tell me how to conduct my business, Ma'am. Please fill out the information on the examination form. All you have to do is cooperate. If you are not in need of medical treatment, you will be free to go."

"I'm free to go now, you charlatan! I told you I'm a news writer for the Miami Signal. Call the chief editor, Roger Bolton. He's my boss, for God's sake." I grabbed the patient form from the attending nurse, threw it to the floor, and charged to the door to get out of the examining room.

He motioned with his head and two strong orderlies, both white females, grabbed me and pinned back my arms. I struggled and kicked one in the shins. The second locked an arm around my throat so I couldn't breathe.

"Lie down and be still or we will have to strap you down," said the doctor.

"Your white lab coat and stethoscope don't impress me," I shouted. "Shouldn't you be working in a field hospital somewhere?"

I did not respond well to excessive force, so I just did his bidding and glared at his blunt nose, high forehead and slicked black hair while his latex-gloved fingers probed my vagina and up into my uterus. He suddenly backed out. "Do you know you're pregnant?"

"Yes," I lied. Since I had not kept track of my most recent period, I was as surprised as he was.

"Why didn't you say something?"

"Because it's none of your damn business. Now, I'm leaving."

"No, not until I finish my examination."

"What are you? Some kind of pervert?"

"If I determine you're not a carrier, you will be able to go. Not until."

I submitted myself to the indignity of the examination just so I could get out of there.

The repression of prostitution had become a method to control the female sexuality of all women. The social paradox and contradiction of portraying women at home as keepers of the ethical norm and of ethical respectability clashed with being encouraged to provide sexual moral support to servicemen. Single women were portrayed and perceived as being sexually aggressive and promiscuous and potentially diseased.

Government propaganda everywhere encouraged young women to become IT girls with sex appeal to attract a man. Having sexual intercourse with a soldier before he shipped out was a way to contribute to the war effort. As a carrier of venereal disease, however, a woman became a public menace.

After I was released, I went to the news office and wrote a story about how women were being treated. When she read it, Marge warned me that Roger Bolton would reject it.

"This is a well-written piece and I know you're angry at what was done to you and how all these women are being incarcerated, but you can't express your opinion about the men putting out the propaganda and the rulings. In the first place, Bolt will never accept this story for publication. You either need to rewrite it or I'll have to edit it. Your criticism will be seen as being unpatriotic and if Bolt reads this, he'll fire you."

I knew he would fire me anyway as soon as my pregnancy became visible. The only person in whom I confided was Mrs. Chelton.

I was able to hide my emerging bump for five months before Roger noticed and told me I could not work at The Signal as a pregnant woman. I had to clean out my desk and leave immediately.

While waiting to see a doctor at the Army Hospital at Camp Blanding, I noticed an advertisement in McCall's Magazine promoting beauty products featuring Millie Dietz, who now worked for a New York modeling agency. She also appeared on magazine pages showcasing dresses and knee-length skirts without pleats and ruffles. Government regulations on the use of material needed for military mobilization limited women's fashions to brown, black, or white straight cuts and slim lines, not leaving any room for style. Dye coloring was not available and we were all limited to two pairs of shoes a year.

The article was a reminder that I would soon be returning home to Boston.

Chapter 20

A New Phase

There wasn't any reason for me to stay in Miami and I didn't want to travel by train from Florida to Boston with an infant.

I parted from Mrs. Chelton with a sinking feeling and a teary embrace. She was more of a mother to me than my own mother.

As the clanking grinding iron wheels of the smoke-spewing engine pulled into the station, I staggered up from a waiting bench and walked to the nearest passenger car that came to a standstill. I boarded amid jostling soldiers rushing along the narrow, crowded aisle to claim seats.

Explaining that his own wife was pregnant with a second child, a sympathetic corporal placed my suitcase in the overhead rack and gave me his seat next to a young, fresh-faced Navy seaman, who spoke with a Florida drawl. His curious glance kept returning to my over-sized abdomen.

"You feel the kid movin' around in there?" he asked.

"It kicks once in a while."

"You hopin' for a boy or a girl?"

"No preference. Whether it's a boy or a girl, I just want a healthy baby."

"Gotcha. Don't have me a girl or I'd put one in the oven for her."

"You finish your training?"

"Yeah, destroyer engine mechanic. I ship out of Newport News, Virginia in two weeks."

"I wish you good luck. My husband is a fighter pilot."

"Gotta hand it to him. I wouldn't want to be up in the air. Long way down. So you headed home?"

"Yes."

"Where's home?"

"Boston."

"Never been that far north. You sound like a Yankee."

"I am a Yankee."

He reached across his lap to shake my hand. "Lee Weatherby, a pleasure to meet you ma'am."

"Thank you, Lee. Gwen Gebhardt."

"You're sort of like I imagined a Yankee woman to be."

"Pregnant?"

We both laughed. "No, sort of highbrow, educated. No offense meant."

"None taken. I am highbrow and educated."

We laughed again.

"You're all right, lady. Are all Yankee women like you?"

"Not all. We're just as different as your southern gals."

"But you're friendly. I didn't think Yankee women were friendly."

"Who told you that?"

"You know. Guys talk."

"About Yankee women?"

"Just women, all kinds of women."

"It's nice to be well-thought of and appreciated," I said.

"A lot of the talk ain't like that."

"I'm sure it isn't."

"But don't get me wrong. You're okay."

"Thank you, Lee. That's a nice compliment. When you meet the girl of your dreams, be sure to tell her the same."

"I will."

I dozed fitfully on and off for most of the journey. In Atlanta, I said goodbye to the corporal who had so kindly given up his seat and, later, in Virginia, to Lee Weatherby.

I stepped off the train at the Boston terminal and rode the trolley through the city to Beacon Hill. Lugging my suitcase, I trudged up a nearly deserted Pinckney Street to the Vanderveer mansion.

Expecting the house to be empty, I retrieved a key to the kitchen back door that Gladys had hidden in a small tin in a flowerpot for Tess and me when we were young girls.

The appearance of Millie at the noise of my entrance surprised me. Even wearing a caftan and slippers and not dolled up like in her magazine photos, her natural beauty was undeniable.

"Gwen, what are you doing here?"

"Millie, I was just wondering the same. I thought you were living in New York."

"I am, but I come here from time to time for a break. The work is hectic. Look at you. You're pregnant. How far along?"

"Six months."

"Well, congratulations. I thought you were in Florida with your husband."

"Eddie is in the South Pacific. He's a fighter pilot."

"It's nice that you'll have a child, in case, you know, he doesn't come back."

"I try not to think about that. He's a gambler. He's always been lucky."

"The servants are gone too. They were drafted. The chauffeur, George, he drives a bus."

"Did my parents stay here?"

"No, your father moved to North Carolina to be near the new textile mill. And Astrid won't stay here, because there aren't servants and a cook and housekeeper."

"Did you ever find out what became of Gladys?"

"She sent me a letter. It was delivered here. I'll let you read it."

"Is she all right?"

"She's a prisoner in a concentration camp in Texas. What she described is pretty horrible. But she's adapting to the conditions."

"Did you tell my mother about her?"

"I did and offered her the letter to read, but she refused. She said the details would be too unpleasant and there was enough unpleasantness in her life."

"She said that?"

"Yes."

"Your mother made a sacrifice for you or you'd be there with her."

"I'm grateful to your mother for everything she's done to help me."

"You turned your back on Gladys. Don't you have any feelings for her?"

Tears suddenly brimmed Millie's eyes. "Of course I do. I love her, but your mother has been kind to me. I'm indebted to her."

"And do you love my mother?"

She hesitated. "Not what you would call a mother daughter love. I respect and admire her."

"I don't. I haven't ever since she substituted you for me."

"I'm sorry."

"What do you have to be sorry about? You're her favorite daughter."

"I didn't realize that was happening."

"How could you miss it?"

"You and Tess had everything. I had nothing."

"We didn't have a mother and father who loved us."

"Your mother doesn't love me. I'm just someone she tried to make like herself."

"She succeeded."

A blush of embarrassment rose in Millie's face. "Not entirely. In social tastes and manners and in fashion, yes. But I'm not selfish and self-centered like your mother."

"Really?"

"I was when I was younger, but I've outgrown it."

"Do you live at her apartment in New York?"

"No, I have my own."

"Do you live alone?"

"Yes."

"Any boyfriend?"

"I've dated, but never a serious relationship."

"Men from my mother's circle?"

"A few. She introduced me as her niece."

I smiled. "That's become a convenient family relationship for you. She didn't throw a cotillion for you?"

"Yes, but I'm not a Wellesley graduate or Sarah Lawrence or any of them."

"At least you're beautiful. Most men would overlook your lack of a college education."

"Your mother taught me what I need to know to get along socially. And I am knowledgeable about art and music and theater."

"I'm sure you've seen everything Broadway has to offer."

"She took me to a lot of concerts, plays, musicals, and art galleries. Lots of art galleries."

"Did you happen to see anything by Dove Delaney?"

"Dove, your sister's friend?"

"That's the one."

"I had no idea she was an artist."

"Actually, she's very good. Maybe not good enough to be exhibited in a museum, but I've seen some of her work. Tess was her patron when they were teenagers."

"I never knew that."

"There are some nice things about Tess and some not so nice."

"How is she?"

"I haven't seen or heard from her for the past three years. She and Dove disappeared right after Tess's graduation."

"They're together?"

"Partners, I assume. I work with people like them. Men too until they were drafted. Women do the photography for the magazines now."

"Do you have any food?" I asked. "I'm starving."

"There's milk and Oleo and cheese in the refrigerator. Day old bread in the cupboard. An onion, a few carrots and potatoes. Most of a head of lettuce is gone. If you're going to shop for groceries, you'll find better pickings in the Italian sector. A lot of those families have farms upstate. You'll have to go down to the harbor to buy fish. All the Italian fishermen had their boats taken away from them. Scandinavians and Irish still have boats."

"Why is that?"

"The same thing happened to the Italians that happened to my mother. The employees talk about it at the Schiaparelli fashion house where I work. Men who belong to the Italian Brotherhood are suspected of being spies and are loyal to Mussolini. A lot of Italian men enlisted in the Army to prove their loyalty against Hitler and Mussolini, but thousands more in violation of the Alien Registration Act were sent to internment camps. Federal agents raided homes and tore them apart looking for ham radios, cameras, binoculars, explosives, and any propaganda about Mussolini. They took the boats away from Italian fishermen so they couldn't earn a living. The Coast Guard uses the boats for shore patrol."

"How long are you staying?" I asked.

"I'm going back to New York tomorrow. What did you do in Miami?"

"After Eddie went overseas, I worked as a news reporter."

"That must have been exciting."

"Not so much exciting as eye opening. Speaking of, I've seen your picture in ads in McCalls Magazine."

"I've been lucky. They made me one of their regulars."

"Well, congratulations. You made the big time."

"I don't think of it that way. A model can be there one day and gone the next. It's not a stable career unless you have what they want."

"You have your parents to thank for giving you such a beautiful face."

"Thank you, Gwen. That's a nice compliment."

"An accident of birth can work both ways, good or bad."

"I suppose. I'll stop talking and let you eat. I'm going to bed. I have to leave early in the morning. So if I don't see you, I'll say goodbye and wish you and your baby the best. Shall I tell your mother?"

"Sure, do that. Learning she's a grandmother should upset her. She hated the thought of growing old."

"Well, goodnight."

"Goodnight."

With a swish of her caftan, she vanished down the hall.

I opened the refrigerator and grabbed a bottle of milk, a package of cheese, and a small tub of butter. I snatched a half loaf of white bread sitting on the counter and a plate from the overhead cupboard and slapped together a sandwich. My yearning for lettuce and a green vegetable could not be assuaged, since there were none.

I wondered what Millie lived on when she stayed here, but she was a professional model and used to starving herself. I, on the other hand, was carrying a child and my nutritional demands would not settle for less than substantial food. I would shop at an Italian market the next morning.

After eating two sandwiches and gulping down two glasses of milk that emptied what was left of the bottle, I carried my suitcase down the hall from the kitchen, through the living room. The carpeted staircase muffled the cavernous echo of my footsteps on the wooden floor. I took the letter up to my room. The envelope was addressed to Millie Vanderveer, not Millie Dietz. Even in a concentration camp, Gladys was protecting her daughter's identity.

Too tired to even take a bath, I kicked off my shoes, threw off my dress, and, with memories of Gladys, crawled into my childhood bed. I propped myself up with pillows and forced my heavy eyelids to stay open as I read her simple words.

Dear Millie,

Since letters censored, I hope you receive this.

I am in Texas, a place called Crystal City. In desert. Very hot.

Twenty women in shed with me. We sleep on cots. Tarantulas everywhere.

Watch for rattlesnakes. High barbed wire fence keep us in. Guards in towers with machine guns. Guards watch us all day and all night.

Guards call our names three times every day to see no one missing.

German and Japanese prisoners are together.

Japanese grow crops on farms. Prisoners pick fruit in orchards. Children get cow's milk every day.

I good cook. Boss give me job in bakery and mess hall. I am paid for work and have money to buy clothes.

Mexicans come into prison to work. Go home at night.

Some Germans here are Nazis from American bund. They try to make trouble.

Guards put them in jail and send to other camps.

I am friends with other women. Some have children. Live in other sheds and huts. German children go to German school. Some families will go to Germany in exchange for American prisoners.

Many sheds in camp have flowers.

There is hospital. Sick prisoners see doctor.

I don't know where my husband is. No one will tell me.

Liebst Du.

Gladys

When I came downstairs the next morning, Millie was gone. Even though we had our differences, her absence emphasized the emptiness of the house. The pale light of deserted rooms conveyed the feeling of a ghost mansion.

Ever since living in Florida, I was familiar with food rationing. The nearest food stamp center to my house was a public school. I walked down Beacon Hill to the school for coupon rationing books, blue for canned goods and red for meat. I then continued to a corner grocery in the Italian sector.

Pushing through to the counter was difficult. Seeing that I was pregnant, the mothers, housewives, and grandmothers bargaining with the grocer in Italian, which I didn't speak or understand, accommodated me. I purchased two large bags of produce, canned fruit, oleo, flour, limited sugar, milk, and bread. The long climb back up the hill to my house left me short of breath.

Given the shortage of meat, the cost of nine points per pound out of an allowable fifty points per month for all food was a hardship. Fortunately, coupons were not required for baked goods and fresh vegetables. I deposited my groceries at home and walked down to the harbor fish market. I bought cod caught off the local coast and clams that I would combine with potatoes, milk and flour to make a pot of chowder.

Chapter 21

Connections

The Gebhardt mansion was within a short walking distance. I took it slowly so I wouldn't strain or exhaust myself. Although I couldn't count on much, if any assistance, from Phobe Gebhardt, having at least one family connection nearby who knew I was pregnant was important to me.

Phobe Gebhardt's rouged florid features, and ebullient voice belied her sophisticated trappings of wealth. She wore jewels and pearls for their gaudy effect and loved to crown her marcel-waved dark hair with a diamond tiara. Her commanding blue eyes and dominating manner reminded me more of a stage actress than a Beacon Hill matron.

When I tapped the large brass knocker and waited, knocking again, the door swung inward and her ample girth filled the opening.

"Why, hello, Gwen. When did you come home?"

"A few days ago."

"You stayed on in Miami after Eddie went overseas."

"For six months. I was working as a news reporter."

"Really? How interesting. What did you write about?"

"The war at home. Women who are doing men's jobs."

"Remarkable, aren't they? I read about women working in the shipyards here in Boston. Come in, Dear. Come in."

"Thank you. It's nice to see you, Phoebe." I stepped into the spacious entry hall.

"Are you planning to stay awhile?"

"Until I have my baby and Eddie comes home."

"Well, you are pregnant, aren't you? Everything going okay?"

"So far. Little nausea is all, but that's passed."

"Where do you plan to have the baby?"

"The Naval hospital in Chelsea."

"Convenient that it's close by."

"I'm going to see a doctor soon for a preliminary exam."

"Well, come in. Sit down. My cook is off for the day and my servants are in the Army. But I'll be glad to brew us a pot of tea."

"That would be delightful."

"Why don't we go into the kitchen so we can talk."

"Of course," I followed her through the expansive living room and dining room dominated by a large cut glass chandelier. We entered the enormous kitchen bordered by three stoves, stoneware counters, wooden pantry and glass cupboards, two massive sinks, and two refrigerators tucked into a side alcove.

She put a kettle on to boil and a platter of shortbread cookies on the table. I sat and waited politely until the tea was ready to serve. Then I consumed two in rapid succession.

As she poured the tea, Phoebe asked, "Have you heard from Eddie?"

"He never answered my letters unless he never received them. The military censors everything."

"That could be typical of Eddie. He was always a willful, independent sort. Then again, I'm not making excuses for him, but maybe he doesn't have time to write."

"As long as he gets my letters, that's what counts. I do worry about him."

"He's a winner, Gwen. He'll be all right. He can't stand to lose."

"Running track and betting on horses and aerial combat are not the same."

"Oh, I understand. The stakes are much higher. But everything's a game to him. He thinks life is a game or he makes a game out of it."

"I think his feelings run deeper than that," I said.

"I don't mean he doesn't have strong feelings. Even as a boy, he was competitive about everything. He wasn't a bully about it. He was good at everything. He was looked up to and respected by his friends at school. He was quite social. He had many friends."

"His childhood was certainly different than mine. I didn't have any friends until I was in college. Working on the school paper put me in touch with a lot of people. And I had a wonderful roommate. We're still friends to this day. We actually write letters to each other."

"Did you let your mother know you're having a baby?"

I shook my head. "She wouldn't be interested. She was never interested in me or my sister."

"That's strange. You were both high achievers as I remember."

"I was just ordinary to her and Tess was a rebel. She even refused to come home her last three years of high school."

"What is she doing now?"

"I have no idea. I lost contact with her when she graduated from Wellesley. She refused to let our parents, particularly mother, mold her. She was always her own person."

"Strong-minded. Actually, I admire her for that. I was raised to become what I am today, fat, traditional, conforming, and rich. Funny isn't it? As different as we are, your mother and I have always been friends socially. We're not close by any means. I think I amuse her. She's cool and pristine and fashionable. Despite my efforts at fashion and beautification, admittedly, I'm rather slovenly at it. A part of me doesn't care. I have friends because I have a sense of humor. I don't take myself seriously and I don't take their pretensions seriously." She paused. "You look surprised."

"I guess Eddie never really told me about you."

"Oh, he wouldn't dare." She flashed a wicked smile. "Except for the good things. I was a kind and loving mother. I spoiled him but it didn't do me any good. All boys grow away from their mothers, but they try to find her again in a wife. The little boy in Eddie is still there. You don't have to confide in me, but I would guess he likes you to mother him."

"I am wearing your wedding ring."

"I noticed. What did I tell you?"

"I never really thanked you."

"I thank you for being his wife."

"I never thought of our relationship in a motherly way, but I do worry about him and will do my best to take care of him. I think of it more that I love him." Aspiring to be a caring loving person was a goal I hoped to achieve.

She reached across the table and lightly patted my hand. "You be sure to let me know when you're going to have your baby. The early days can be a trial. I can be helpful."

"Thank you. I'm pleased to hear you say that. You're very kind."

"Kindness is not one of my obvious traits, but once in a while, it emerges. Your tea is getting cold. Let me freshen that." She took my porcelain cup and saucer and poured what remained of the tea into the sink. She returned to the table, poured a new cup and placed it in front of me. "Would you like to stay and have dinner with me? I never grew accustomed to dining alone. Usually, I go see friends or they come here."

"I'd like very much to have dinner with you. When I was growing up, Gladys Dietz taught me how to cook. At least she let me help her. I can be your sous chef."

"Your mother told me what happened to Gladys. The FBI came and arrested her and her husband because they were from Germany."

"She's being held at an internment prison in Texas. They took her husband somewhere else. I read a letter she sent her daughter."

"That's awful."

"She's been in America for thirty years and she's a U.S. citizen. I went to the FBI office when it happened. They told me she was a security risk. A cook and housekeeper a security risk."

"I'm sorry for her."

"I do wish she were here. I miss her terribly. She was more of a mother to me than my real mother."

"I'll keep that confidence between us."

"She already knows. She's always known and it never bothered her. I think she was actually glad because of it."

I went over to Phoebe's for dinner once a week, on an evening she didn't have a social engagement or hadn't taken the train down to New York to shop or see a Broadway show.

She talked openly about her ex-husband, Harold, a congressman, calling him a womanizer.

"He was an attractive and outgoing man, a smooth talker. He admired beautiful women and was very complimentary to them. He's always been a big business political insider. He hates President Roosevelt. Calls his tax plan a scheme to soak the rich and redistribute wealth. Thinks FDR is taking the country down the path to socialism."

"What about all the poverty?"

"He doesn't think it's Government's responsibility to do something about it."

"But the New Deal is helping the country to recover. The Depression isn't just here in America. It's world-wide. We studied the economic causes at Wellesley."

"Just because I was married to him doesn't mean I'm like him or agree with him. Frankly, I think he became an arrogant, self-absorbed plutocrat."

"From what Eddie told me, I guess he wasn't always like that."

"Things were different when we were younger. I was sexy, frivolous, fun-loving, still fun-loving, but tempered by twenty-five years, especially my weight. In my day, except for dancing the Charleston and the Lindy Hop, we didn't exercise like you young women today. You even play sports. We wouldn't think of it, except for a little golf and croquet and lawn tennis. And we didn't watch what we ate. We ate anything we wanted and drank like fish. I even wore corsets. I refuse to wear them

216

today. I always hated them. They were so tight I could barely breathe. When I changed from the ingenue he married to a middle-aged woman, Harold couldn't handle it. He couldn't handle growing older himself. So he pursued younger women, young enough to be his daughter. I hired a good lawyer. I didn't give up anything in the divorce. That's why I'm still living in this mansion."

"I don't' think Eddie is anything like his father."

"They do share an obsession, however."

"Obsession?"

"Winning."

"Winning? You mean winning at games and sports. Eddie never lost a track meet in college. But I agree, he hates to lose bets at the horse races. And he admits he likes to gamble at cards."

"Roger played cards. He often cheated to win. He was unscrupulous in election campaigns. Power and politics are a game to him, a game to be won by any means, including ruining the lives of his opponents. I didn't realize he was a pathological liar until a year after we were married. He lies about everything and does it with a straight face. It's no wonder he cleans up at poker and makes promises he doesn't keep. But he keeps getting reelected. His cronies are just like him. They pay off a lot of people."

"Well, Eddie doesn't lie to me. We don't keep secrets from each other."

"My son has many fine qualities. I'm happy the two of you are together."

"Thank you. I feel fortunate."

"Well, let's talk about dinner. Do you like lamb chops? I was able to get a pound with my ration card."

"Lamb chops sound delicious."

"I have green beans and red potatoes to go with them."

"I can make a salad," I said.

"Let's get started."

To keep myself occupied while waiting for the main event, I began making notes for the book Justine encouraged me to write. I accumulated many personal impressions in addition to the news stories I wrote for the Miami Signal. As I worked, approaching my subject as a memoir rather than as a series of nonfiction essays grew in my mind.

I also rediscovered my father's library. Although he never struck me as having literary interests, I was surprised to find titles of leather-bound classics, *The Iliad and The Odyssey*, *Don Quijote*, and *Moby Dick*.

A few books about boats and sailing clustered against books about horses and polo. A book containing photographs and drawings of boxing stances did not surprise me. There was also a book on how to play golf written by Bobby Jones, a professional golfer.

There were books about business and textile manufacturing.

Not surprising, there were no books written by women, but four novels written by male authors caught my attention: *For Whom The Bell Tolls* and *The Sun Also Rises* by Ernest Hemingway, *Look Homeward Angel* by Thomas Wolfe, and *The Great Gatsby* by F. Scott Fitzgerald.

As an English and literature major, I read these in college and recognized how conceptually and culturally different they were than the women's novels of Edith Wharton, Louisa May Alcott, Daphne Du Maurier, Willa Cather, Margaret Mitchell, and Virginia Woolf.

I had immensely enjoyed being a student at Wellesley, especially the knowledge and influence of the professors. They were all intelligent, self-confident, independent women who did not rely on men for their livelihood nor for men's political, economic, and cultural opinions. I witnessed and participated in many campus debates on these topics.

The increasing movements of the growing life within me sharpened the passage of time and raised doubts and fears as to my ability to raise a child. I worried that through my bumbling incompetence, I might injure him. Since I didn't have anyone to turn to for instruction and advice, I would have to learn by trial and error. It was the errors I wanted to avoid.

As events turned out, Phoebe was a conscientious and supportive grandmother. I considered myself fortunate to have her for my mother-in-law.

I worried what I would do if the contractions started at night, but they began at midday. I called Phoebe to let her know and told her I was leaving the house. She said she would see me at the hospital. Carrying a satchel with a change of clothes and a toothbrush, I waddled down Beacon Hill to the trolley and, hoping my water didn't break, rode through town to the Naval Hospital.

Except for my howls and screams of pain, my son, Edward Gebhardt, Jr. was born without incident.

I had sent a letter to my college friend, Justine Sarcozy, letting her know I was pregnant. She surprised me by visiting me after the delivery. I hadn't contacted her since my previous letter. She told me her husband, Ronald, Doctor Sarcozy, who was stationed at the hospital, had noticed my name on a patient roster. When he came to look in on me, I was already in prep and he was about to go into surgery. He called Justine, who had taken the train up from New York.

I woke from a shallow doze to find her sitting next to my bed. "Justine, how did you know I was here? How long have you been here? You look blurry. I feel groggy."

"Hi, new mom. I saw your baby boy in the nursery."

"Isn't he beautiful? I mean he really is beautiful."

"He's a beautiful boy."

"A nurse brought him in for a feeding. Then I fell asleep. How did you know?"

"Ron called me."

"Who's Ron? I'm sorry. My brain is fuzzy."

"My husband, Dr. Sarcozy. He's a Navy doctor."

"Here? In this hospital?"

"He was lucky to be assigned here."

"How about you? Are you planning to have children?"

"Absolutely, but since Ron is stateside, we don't have to be in a hurry. We're going to wait two years so I can pursue my career in publishing. Which is why, by the way, I want to talk to you about writing your book."

"I don't think I'll have much time for a while, but I have been making notes."

"Wonderful." She smiled. "You know I'm going to harass you until you have a manuscript for me."

"I expect that you will."

A nurse brought in my swaddled baby. "Feeding time."

Justine started to rise. "I can wait in the lobby."

"That's okay," I said, "you can stay."

"I thought you might like some privacy. I'll grab a cup of coffee." She touched my infant's head. "Such a beautiful boy."

"Thanks, Justine."

"I'll be back." She left the room.

A few months earlier in a letter, she had suggested I continue what I started as a reporter with the Miami Signal and develop the book, which was the farthest thing from my mind. I had not been truthful about the notes I was making. For the time being, I was focused on being a mother.

Holding Eddie Jr.'s vulnerable little body and nursing him gave me a new perspective I never anticipated. With a frantic hunger, he attacked my swollen nipples, raking across my flesh like a shark, his toothless mouth rasping back and forth seeking a firm latch point.

My love for him overshadowed the rejection of me by my parents. I would ensure my son would never experience the same. He was now the center of my life and being a caring and devoted mother was my sole purpose. As he grew, I wanted him to feel welcome and accepted into the world.

From my hospital window, I had a view across the Mystic River of the Naval shipyards. I could see hundreds of women wearing workpants and lumberjack shirts, arriving on the train and on buses. They carried lunch pails and their hair was tied up with bandanas topped with a hardhat. They welded sheet metal and steel frames to manufacture the ships and landing craft used throughout the war.

The women welders and shipbuilding process and my writing about women working on the home front planted the seed for Justine's book idea, to describe what she called a social revolution.

Chapter 22

A New Beginning

Phoebe came to visit me twice in the hospital after Eddie Jr. was born. She was there when the doctor told me I would be able to go home in two days. She came to my room and walked with me being pushed in a wheelchair by a female orderly.

"I have a taxi waiting," she said and chuckled. "I didn't think you wanted to take the trolley again."

She helped me into the back seat of the taxi and handed me my baby, being careful to support his head as the nurse had instructed. I cradled the blanketed bundle in my arms.

Phoebe took the seat next to me, gave the taxi driver directions and we set off for home. I was grateful and indebted to her for her selfless assistance.

When we arrived, she carried my overnight bag and helped me to the living room couch where I nursed Little Eddie. The nurse had instructed me that, given his stomach was only the size of a marble, he would require feeding every two hours. He let me know he was hungry by crying, by making sucking motions with his tiny flower petal lips, and by just opening and closing his mouth. His nose was slightly flattened to allow for latching onto my nipple.

She taught me how to swaddle him so he felt warm and secure similar to when he was in my womb.

I had been in labor for twelve hours. Some minor tearing of my uterus requiring a few stitches had occurred as Little Eddie's cone-shaped head squeezed out of me into the world and his high-pitched wail filled the delivery room. The doctor had told me I would experience pain and discomfort for a few weeks and that it would fade.

I desperately needed to sleep. Phoebe ran me a warm bath and I soaked briefly while my infant son slept in a bassinet, also provided by my benefactor.

My life was no longer my own. It belonged to Little Eddie. His demands came in the form of different cries that I quickly learned to interpret for hunger, diaper changes, comfort cuddles, and sleep.

Physical exhaustion and sleep deprivation altered my ability to think clearly and stay focused on tasks. My mind wandered and I had to catch myself from falling into a doze while nursing.

Phoebe had purchased a stack of cloth diapers and guided me through my first diaper change, cautioning me not to prick Little Eddie's bottom with a safety pin.

We had taken to calling him Little Eddie to distinguish him from his father we referred to as Big Eddie

"I appreciate all that you're doing for me, but I'm interrupting your life," I told her.

"My life? You mean my social calendar? You're my daughter-in-law and Little Eddie's my grandson. You are life, the both of you. Card games and teas and cocktails are meaningless compared to you. I'm happy that I can be helping you. It gives me a purpose I thought I would never have again. It gives me a sense of revisiting motherhood. Also, I have something that I know you'll find useful. I was digging around in a storage room and found the stroller I used when Big Eddie was an infant. I cleaned it up. It's in the living room."

As the weeks and months progressed, Phoebe practically moved in with me. Helping with diaper changes, bathing Eddie, sterilizing bottles, doing the laundry, grocery shopping, and cooking meals, gave me time for occasional naps. I didn't remember having a full night of uninterrupted sleep for ten months.

When Little Eddie was a few months old, she brought him toys that his father had as a toddler and small child.

Paper Dolls

Millie occasionally came up from New York on weekends. Little Eddie was the attraction. We took him on walks with the stroller and she shared gossip about her modeling world.

At eight months, Little Eddie began crawling. Thrusting with his knees and pulling with his arms, blonde head bobbing from side to side with each effort, his wide smile revealing two new top and bottom baby teeth, blue eyes sparking, he was life coming at me.

When Little Eddie began climbing the staircase, Phoebe hired a handyman to construct and install gates at the top and the bottom to prevent my intrepid toddler from falling.

Phoebe brought me a stack of children's story books and taught me lullabies. We observed Little Eddie learn about objects by placing them in his mouth, including his toes. His hand and finger dexterity amazed me. He transitioned from bottle feedings to solid food and grew quickly. Before I realized the time passage, he was two years old and speaking recognizable words.

I heard the about the end of the war from Phoebe. The Germans had surrendered on May 8, 1945, followed by the unconditional surrender of Japan on September 2. On both occasions, she came to my house and showed me the news headlines. We turned on the radio and listened to a broadcast of the celebration happening in the streets of New York. Two million people filled Times Square.

American troops were returning on ships to ports on both the Atlantic and Pacific Coasts.

I didn't know how long I would have to wait for Eddie to arrive. I had written him many times about our son and that I had moved back to Beacon Hill. I could only hope he had received my letters.

One month after the announcement of the armistice, I heard a knock at the front door. Holding our son in my arms, I opened the door and choked on a sudden rush of tears.

"Eddie, Eddie, it's so good to see you. You're home. You're home."

Unshaven, wearing a wrinkled brown and tan uniform, he dropped his duffle bag on the porch, tore the officer's cap from his head and tossed it inside. He leaned in to exchange a greeting kiss. I smelled the odor of travel on his clothes and whiskey and cigarettes on his breath, which surprised me. As an athlete, he had never smoked before going overseas.

"And who is this?" he grinned and tousled our son's hair.

"Eddie, Jr., meet your Daddy," I said. I stepped back. "Come in. Come in. Oh, my goodness, just come in."

He picked up his duffle and dropped it in the foyer.

I leaned in for Eddie to get a clear look at his cherubic face, his wonderous blue eyes, rosy cheeks, and dimpled chin. "He's your Daddy, Eddie. Your Daddy has come home. Here, would you like to hold him?"

"Not now. After that long train ride from San Francisco, I'm beat. I stink and I need a beer. I need two beers." He turned away and stomped off into the kitchen.

"I'm sorry, Eddie. There isn't any. I never got food ration stamps to buy alcohol."

"The war's over, goddamit! We don't need food stamps to buy anything. I'll go down the hill and get some."

"Don't you want to take a bath and shave, relax a little?"

"Fuck no! I want to drink a cold beer! I'll be back in a few hours."

"But you just got home."

"This isn't my home. It's your parents'."

"They don't live here anymore."

"Isn't that convenient. I have to get out of this monkey suit." He tore off his Army blouse and shirt revealing savage scars across his chest and abdomen."

"Eddie, Eddie, what happened to you?"

He brushed away my hand. "I took some shrapnel when our ship was hit. But not one goddam nip ever got my plane." He bent over to rummage around in his duffle and pulled out a Hawaiian shirt patterned with red flowers. Then I saw his back crisscrossed with stitches. I didn't dare ask how he got those wounds.

"Were you in Hawaii?" I asked.

"On my way to the fight." He quickly shrugged on his shirt and lunged out through the front door.

Notwithstanding what Eddie had gone through for the past four years, my shock at his reaction floored me. The joy of seeing him did not stop the hollow emptiness that sank to the pit of my stomach. I wiped at tears with the back of my hand and lowered Little Eddie to the floor. He promptly wandered off to play with his toys. Despite photos of Eddie I had shown him, the strange man who had come to the door meant nothing to him. He had no concept of a daddy.

I hoped Phoebe would not suddenly show up and I would have to explain Eddie's behavior. But Phoebe was not the next person to come to the door. An hour later, I heard a timid knock and went to answer. Gladys's haggard smiling face lifted my spirits and brought more tears.

"Gladys, oh, Gladys, I am so glad to see you. I'm so glad you came home."

She dropped her suitcase. Her tears gushed forth as we embraced. "I thought I never see you again."

"Come inside. Come inside. You're here now and you'll never have to leave again."

"I don't know where Ekkehardt is."

"He'll come back. The war's over. I know he'll come back." I heard Little Eddie's footsteps approach us from behind. Gladys noticed him past my shoulder and released me.

"You have a son, a darling beautiful son." She didn't immediately reach for him. She knew letting him eventually come to her would be better. "What is his name?"

"Eddie, like his father. Eddie Junior. I've been calling him Little Eddie."

"Hello, Eddie."

"Eddie," I said, "this is Gladys. She has come to live with us."

His momentary interest faded from his eyes and he returned to his toys in the living room.

"Millie showed me your letter."

"Oh, I am so glad she received it. I didn't know."

"Gladys, what a horrible experience."

"I survive."

"I'm sorry. They should never have done that to you."

"But they did. *Ich bin Deutsch.*"

"But you're back. You're back. I'm so glad. I need you, Gladys."

"I need you."

"Eddie's mother helped me the past three years."

"Mrs. Gebhardt?"

"Yes, she was here every day."

"*Sie ist eine guten Frau.*"

"She will probably come over to see Eddie, Big Eddie."

"He come back? He is home?"

I hesitated. "He'll be home tonight."

Gladys glanced at Eddie's duffle bag. "He has been here?"

"Yes, but he had to go out." I looked away. "He's changed, Gladys. Something happened to him. He's different. He was wounded. He has wounds all over his body."

"He is same husband. He will get over the war. *Mein Fater* was strange after first war. He became okay."

"Your room is just as it always has been. Settle in. Take your time. I'll make dinner tonight and we can talk more. I'd like to hear about what happened to you."

"It is gone. It is past. Don't want to talk about."

"Of course, of course, how thoughtless of me."

"I want to know your son. That more important. This is new time, new beginning."

"Yes, a new beginning."

"I'm going to have bath and sleep now. Train ride long and dirty."

"Eddie said the same. I'll wake you when dinner is ready," I said.

"I should cook for you."

"There will be many more opportunities."

"Where is your Mutter?"

"She doesn't live here anymore. She moved permanently to New York and father lives in North Carolina. That's where the mill is now. Tess and I inherited the house in our trust. At least we have money and a place to live."

"Where is Tess?"

"I don't know. I've tried to find her but I don't have any information. Millie comes to visit once in a while on weekends. She hasn't heard anything about Tess either."

"I hope Millie comes to see me. I not go to New York."

"I'll send her a letter and tell her you're here."

"*Danke, meine Liebe.*"

"Go take your bath. Have a nice nap."

"I am so glad to be home. *Gemuetlichkeit.*"

"*Gemuetlichkeit.*" I shooed her off and watched her dear old figure limp down the hall to her room. I recognized the same plain long dress and long brown coat she had been wearing when the FBI agents arrested her.

Eddie came home late that night. I heard the thudding of the brass knocker and steady pounding on the front door. I climbed out of bed. Looking down from the top of the stairs, I saw Gladys wearing her nightgown, robe, and slippers admitting him in. He pushed past her, staggered across the living room and collapsed onto the couch. His loud spasmodic snores filled the air.

I gave Gladys a hug. "I'm so sorry you have to see him like this."

"It's okay, *Leibchen*. He is suffering much."

"Thank you for letting him in."

"You go back to bed. I will have strong coffee and strudel for him in the morning."

I went through the baby gate and up the stairs to sleep in my bedroom.

I woke the next morning to the sound of wood splintering and crashing down the hall. Eddie was breaking apart the baby gates and hurling them across the living room. His trouser legs were stained with urine.

"What the fuck are these doing here?"

"They're to protect Little Eddie from falling down the stairs."

"Fuck the kid! They're gonna make me fall down the stairs!" He stared at his wet trousers. "Fuckin' Christ! I pissed myself. I never even did that in combat. Fuckin' Christ!"

Gladys came out of the kitchen and watched from the dining room. "You need *kaffee*, Eddie. I have *kaffee* and apple *strudel* for you. Come and sit. *Kaffee* will clear your head."

"I do smell it but these gates have to go."

I guided him by the arm to the dining room table and eased him onto a chair. He stared at the plateful of oven warm *strudel* and inhaled the steaming aroma of strong black coffee. I have one hell of a hangover. Got any aspirin?"

"Yes," said Gladys. "I'll get it." She hurried away to the kitchen while I watched Eddie sip his coffee. He picked up a square of *strudel* and, chomping vigorously, stuffed it into his mouth.

I sat opposite him and served myself *strudel* from a platter and poured coffee from a sterling silver pitcher. I pushed my long blonde hair

229

at the sides of my head. I wanted to make myself attractive and presentable to Eddie, but the morning had started off on an unexpected footing.

Gladys returned with the aspirin and placed it on the table. Eddie popped the lid off, tipped the bottle to his lips, and shook several tablets into his mouth. His teeth ground them to a pulp which he washed down with two swallows of coffee. Eddie stopped eating and glanced up at Gladys standing nearby.

"You're a good cook, Gladys. You gonna feed us like this every day?"

"You have my promise. But you have to be good."

"Don't know if I can promise that." He grimaced. "But I'll have my moments."

"We understand. You've had a rough time of it," I said.

"I can't believe it's over."

"It's over, Eddie. It's finally over."

"I was really drunk last night."

"We know. We'll all get past it."

"Just keep some cold beer for me in the frig. If I want hard stuff, I'll go down to the pub."

"Once you start your new life as a daddy, you won't want hard stuff."

"Sorry what I said about the kid."

"His name is Eddie."

"Gates on the stairs is a good idea. Safety always came first on the carrier."

We heard Eddie Jr.'s voice calling, "Mommy, Mommy."

I leaped up and ran into the next room. Little Eddie was standing at the top of the stairs. "Mommy's here, Eddie. Stay right where you are. Don't come down. I'm coming up to get you." Hoisting my nightgown, I raced to the landing.

My grip on his arm lowered to his hand. "Okay, hold the banister and we'll go down one step at a time. We made a slow foot-wobbling descent.

I continued to hold his hand as we walked into the dining room. He stopped at the sight of his father sitting at the table. Eddie turned to look at his son.

"Hello, Junior, maybe not right away, but we'll get to know each other."

Little Eddie hugged my leg and hid his face in my nightgown.

"I don't blame you. I wouldn't want to get any closer to me either. Can't even stand myself. I look and smell like a bum. Time to get cleaned up."

Little Eddie peeked out and watched him stand and approach us, then pressed his face harder against my leg. Big Eddie tousled his hair as he went past to get his duffle.

"Where do I sleep? What room am I in?"

"In our room," I said. "The master bedroom."

"Sounds right, now that the master's home." He hooked the duffle strap over his shoulder and, trailing a roguish laugh, trudged up the stairs.

Little Eddie looked up at my face. "Ready for breakfast?" I asked. He nodded. "Gladys made some nice pastries, but you might like milk and cereal." He nodded again. "Let's go sit at the table," I said.

Gladys was already moving toward the kitchen to bring milk and cereal.

Chapter 23

The Curse of Winning

After breakfast, Little Eddie wanted to stay dressed in his pajamas and play with his toys in the family room. I helped him go potty and asked Gladys to keep an eye on him while I ran upstairs to change out of my nightgown.

Eddie's duffle lay at the center of the floor. I saw him soaking in the bathroom tub. With an encouraging smile, I stepped to the door. "How's the water?"

He glared at me. "Shut the goddam door!"

I stepped back and quickly closed the door. Since I couldn't get into the master bathroom, I went to my childhood room to wash my face and brush my teeth. I returned to the master bedroom and selected a plain skirt and blouse and flats from the closet. I gave my hair a cursory brushing at the powder table and pinned it back with a clip. Lipstick and cosmetics weren't yet available in department stores, but my complexion was presentable without it.

Wearing a long sleeve civilian shirt and trousers, whiskers shaved and hair slicked back, Eddie came downstairs to where I was watching Little Eddie play with his toys. We had just finished reading a picture book with colorful drawings of farm animals.

"What's that crib doing in our bedroom?" his accusing tone aggravated me.

"Little Eddie slept in it for the past two years."

"Why in there?"

"For the first six months, I had to wake up and feed him and change his diapers during the night. I didn't get much sleep. Taking care of an infant is not easy. Without Phoebe, I don't know how I could have made it."

"Phoebe?"

"Your mother. She was here almost every day helping me."

"You're joking."

"I'm not. She's a lovely woman."

"Couldn't prove it by me."

"I'm indebted to her. She treated me like a daughter. I learned so much from her. She's a caring giving person."

"Ha! Sure had me fooled."

"Maybe you didn't realize it when you were growing up."

"Yep, that's it all right. I grew up in residential private schools."

"She thinks very highly of you."

"Then that's where I am, high up in her head."

"You might want to go over and see her."

"And why might I want to do that?"

"As a courtesy."

He laughed.

"I'm sure she would be happy to come over here."

"Go ahead and ask her."

"I will. Is today okay with you?"

"Yeah, yeah."

"But when she's here, please be polite."

"Don't' know how that feels anymore."

"At least try. She knows you've been through a lot."

"Unless you've done it yourself, nobody knows."

"But we sympathize."

"And what good is that?"

"It means we love you."

Eddie's lips spluttered. "You know what? I can use a real breakfast. Tell Gladys to rustle me up six fried eggs, bacon, sausage, and toast."

"Of course. Eddie," I spoke to our son. "Would you like to show Daddy your toys?"

"Yeah, Junior, show me your toys."

"I'll be right back." I hurried off to talk to Gladys in the kitchen.

"Eddie's all cleaned up and asked to have a big breakfast, six fried eggs, bacon, sausage, and toast, and, of course, more coffee."

"I'll have it in ten minutes. How is he this morning?"

"Cranky and grumpy. A good breakfast should bring him around."

"He liked the *strudel* and I make good *kaffee*."

"You make good everything, Gladys. Maybe the way to his heart is through his stomach."

"What do you think he will want for supper?"

"Probably a steak. I'll ask him."

"Be sure to ask how well done."

"Probably rare. I remember from when we were in Miami. Actually, he liked his bloody."

"Men always like steak rare. My Ekkehardt liked his rare. I think there is some animal hunter in men."

"With Eddie, I can believe it. He ran track like a panther. He told me he liked aerial combat. He said he liked shooting down and killing enemy pilots."

"That was his job. That was what he was trained to do," Gladys cracked six eggs in succession into a cast iron skillet of sizzling bacon. "*Mein Fater* was not a killer. He was a kind and loving man. The Kaiser's army trained him to kill."

"When he was training in Miami, Eddie told me they forced him to see things differently. They were told the enemies were not human. They called Germans krauts and the Japanese nips. The enemy pilots were just target practice to Eddie. They didn't have lives."

"It is hard for men to come home from war. They think they have to still be soldiers." Gladys dropped two slices of bread into the toaster.

234

I walked back to the family room. To my surprise, Eddie lay stretched out on the floor and was waving a plastic toy plane overhead accompanied by noises of the plane flying and climbing and diving. Little Eddie watched him mesmerized.

"This is a great way to get to know him and for him to get to know you," I said smiling. "He loves toys and music. When I play the piano, he comes over and bangs on the keys with me."

"After breakfast, I'll take him for a walk."

"That would be wonderful. I'll go with you."

"No – No, this is just between him and me."

"You have to hold his hand and walk slowly. He's still not all that steady. Or you can take him in the stroller."

"You might as well chuck the stroller. He won't need it anymore."

"There are times when it's very handy."

"You'll never catch me pushing him in it."

"Where will you take him?"

"Down the hill to the park. If he gets tired, I'll carry him."

"He'll like that. He wants me to pick him up from time to time."

"How's that breakfast coming along? I can smell the bacon."

"Almost ready. Gladys will bring it to the table in a few more minutes."

"Okay, Junior, have to fuel up." Avoiding stepping on the scattered toys, Eddie untangled his legs and, ignoring my offered hand, rose to a standing position. He stepped around me and went into the dining room.

I got down on my knees among Little Eddie's toys and gave him a hug. I watched him pushing a truck around the floor, but he kept looking at the plastic airplane his father had been swooping over him. Eventually, he left the truck and picked up the toy airplane. He raised it and moved it around with motions that copied what Eddie had shown him. He did not attempt to make the propeller engine noises.

About twenty minutes later, Eddie finished his breakfast and thanked and complimented Gladys, which I was glad to hear. I saw him trot up the stairs, presumably to use the bathroom. He returned and joined us.

"Okay, Junior, like to go for a walk?"

Little Eddie looked up, which was his usual response to a question.

"Let's go." Eddie hoisted him into his arms and headed for the front door.

I followed and held the door open for them, then watched as Eddie set our boy down on the sidewalk and took his hand. They did not progress far with Little Eddie's small steps. His father picked him up again and they set off down the hill.

That Little Eddie, not me, was the key to healing his father suddenly occurred to me. I would encourage Big Eddie to spend more time with him.

I closed the door and went to the office to work on notes for the book I began to feel motivated to write.

They returned two hours later. Little Eddie was sleeping with his nose buried against Big Eddie's neck and shoulder.

"I was pushing him on the kids' swing and he dozed off," said Eddie. "I'll take him to his room."

"He might need a diaper change."

"I thought you were potty training him," said Eddie.

"We're only halfway there. The diapers are in case of an accident."

"I don't do diapers. Wait until he wakes up."

"Okay. How was the park?"

"Mostly, he liked playing in the sand."

"He likes the texture."

"The park hasn't changed much."

"What's to change?"

"Nothing, I guess. I'll take him up."

"Should I give your mother a call? She'll want to know you're home."

"No, I'm not ready to see her. Don't meddle. When I am, I'll go over there."

"What about your father?"

"I'm going to meet him for lunch on Saturday."

"You didn't tell me. I didn't hear you call him."

"I haven't yet. But I will. And will you get off my back? You're not my secretary."

"I'm sorry. I thought you would like me to know."

"It's not necessary that you know everything I do. I don't pry into your affairs."

"I'm happy to share anything I'm doing."

"I don't need to hear it, at least not right now. I need time and distance."

"You've been on the other side of the world for the past three years. How much more time and distance do you need?"

"Enough. Do you want to take him?"

"No, please do. Let me know if he wakes up. I'll potty him."

"Just don't ever ask or expect me to do that."

"Only if you'd like to learn," I grinned.

"Don't be stupid. That's a woman's job." Eddie continued up the stairs.

I went back into the library to add this latest comment from my husband to my notes. A few minutes later, I heard him coming down the stairs. I quickly covered my notes and beginning manuscript pages and shoved them into the desk drawer. I did not want him to read what I was writing.

The front door slammed shut, so I knew he had gone out. Curious, I decided not to concern myself as to where and for what reason. His homecoming that I had envisioned was beginning to feel like an encroachment or an emotional invasion with which I had to cope and adapt. Unanticipated stress took up residence in my mind and knotted my stomach.

Gladys appeared at the library door. "We are low on groceries. I have to go to the store. Is there anything special you need?"

"Not that I can think of. At least we don't have to use ration stamps anymore."

"Eddie went out."

"I heard the door."

"Did he say anything to you?" I immediately regretted asking. Inquiring after him showed my insecurity.

"He has to do something for himself."

"I don't want to push him."

"You also don't want him to push you."

"I can handle it. He needs me to be accepting and understanding."

"You are a good wife."

"Thank you. I'm trying my best."

"Little Eddie is asleep?"

"Yes, I'm listening for him."

"What about baby gates?"

"Eddie said he would replace them."

"*Gut*, but needs to be soon."

"I'll remind him when he comes back. Do you need cash?"

"Take food money from drawer. I'll be gone for two hours. Take cart."

"Thank you, Gladys. You're a lifesaver."

"I cook steak tonight."

"Eddie will love that."

"You writing on book?"

"Yes, but I don't want Eddie to see what I'm writing."

"It about him?"

"Parts of it. Mostly other topics."

"Maybe he go look for job."

"It's too soon to tell."

"Work be good for him. Take his mind off troubles."

I nodded and took my notes out of the drawer. Several minutes later, I heard Gladys leave by the kitchen back door.

While scribbling my notes, I kept one ear tuned for Little Eddie's voice should he call from the top of the stairs.

I dwelt on Gladys' comment not to let Eddie push me. I was tough and always had been, to put up with how my parents and older sister had treated me. That didn't mean they hadn't hurt me. Deep emotional pain had festered within me during those years. Somehow I had accepted it as my lot in life and was grateful for the crumbs and particles of recognition and inclusion scattered my way. But I had never had enough. I had been starved for a love and acceptance that I never experienced until I met Eddie at Wellesley. Now that he had returned from the war, his love and acceptance seemed to be short-lived. I did not want to lose it and would fight for it. I could endure verbal and behavioral abuse by blunting its impact. I could rise above disappointment and overcome it with kindness and a smile.

Eddie returned with a newspaper and sat in the living room to read.

"What the fuck is the matter with the world? We finish one war and are getting ready for another. They call it the cold war, but it's still a fucking war."

I asked, "What's in the news?"

He cast the paper aside. "Read it for yourself. Time for lunch." He headed to the kitchen. "Gladys, what's for lunch?"

"She went to the grocery store," I called after him.

"I'll find something," he called back.

I picked up the scattered sheets and scanned the headlines.

Truman Pledges To Aid Nations Threatened By Soviet Expansion

Announces Global Containment Strategy

Berlin Airlift Carries Food, Fuel, and Supplies To People Caught In
Soviet Blockade.

House Unamerican Activities Proceeds Against Hollywood Ten

President Harry Truman Ends Racial Segregation In The Military

Margaret Sanger Founds International Planned Parenthood
Federation

That one particularly caught my attention since the topic was related to women's rights in the face of political subjugation.

I was in the middle of reading the obituaries for Babe Ruth, Orville Wright, and D.W. Griffth when there was a knock at the front door. "I'll get it," I shouted to Eddie, set aside the newspaper, and went to the door.

"Is he home yet?" Phoebe's anxious face softened at my nod.

"Come in. He's here. Not like you remember him, but he's here."

I stepped aside for her to enter. "What do you mean?"

"I can't explain, but he was seriously wounded. He's not like the same person who left."

"At least he's alive."

We moved into the living room. "He was going to come and see you."

"I beat him to it. So where is he?"

"In the kitchen."

"If he's cooking, then he did come back different."

"Gladys went to the grocery store. He's making lunch. This way." I led her through the dining room to the kitchen.

Seated at the table, he looked up from chewing a peanut butter and jelly sandwich. His milk mustache expanded into a grin of embarrassment that disappeared with a backward swipe of his hand.

"Hello, Eddie, it's so good to see you home." Phoebe started around the table to give him a motherly hug. He dropped the remains of his sandwich and stood up with the chair between them.

"Hi, Mother."

She leaned over the chair and held his face between her hands. Surprisingly, he didn't pull away. He gently took her hands and planted a kiss on them.

"So, how's our war hero?"

"Back in one piece."

"Gwen said you were wounded."

"I'm okay. Not worth talking about."

"You look wonderful. You could be in the movies."

"Sure, with John Wayne. You know those pretty boys were never in the service. John Wayne only shot blanks. I hated those fake war movies. We had war all day and all night. Once in a while, we'd get to see a comedy. Not much that was funny out there."

"I know. I'm sorry."

He released her hands. "Why are you sorry? You had nothing to do with it."

"I'm sorry you suffered."

"Don't be."

"Don't be? You don't tell your mother how she should feel."

"Gwen told me you came over almost every day after Junior was born."

"Yes, it was the least I could do for my grandson."

"Where was her mother?" asked Eddie.

"My mother wasn't interested," I said. "She doesn't care for anyone but herself. She never did."

"Enough of this talk," said Phoebe. "We should be happy. I have a son and a grandson. I'm happy. Have you talked to your father? He should know you're back."

"I'll meet him for lunch in a few days."

"He will be glad to see you."

"Will he?"

"Of course, he bragged about you to the Boston Herald, that you were an ace shooting down Jap zeroes in the South Pacific."

"Who told him that?"

"He has connections in the Pentagon. He closely followed the war."

"He probably had a way to profit from it."

"What makes you say that?"

"I know my old man. A wartime economy doesn't have to stop at the end of the war. Defense is big business."

"With your wartime record, you can have any job you want."

"Haven't given it any thought."

"I haven't told your Father about Eddie Jr. I figured you might like to do that, an additional nice thing to your coming home."

"I didn't know you still talked to each other."

"Generally, we avoid each other socially. He has his friends. I have mine."

Eddie flashed a sardonic grin. "Share the same enemies."

Phoebe looked askance.

"Politically speaking," said Eddie.

"I don't disagree with what FDR did for the country and I vote democratic," said Phoebe.

"What turned you around?"

"A disagreement with your father. Women should be on an equal footing with men in the workplace and in government."

"You never had to work a day in your life," said Eddie, "and what do you care about government?"

"To my regret. I think I've missed out on a lot. But at least now I can make charitable contributions to the women's causes and social reform."

"Why bother? Things will go back to the way they were before the war."

"Nothing will be the same. The war changed everything."

Eddie shook his head. "We didn't fight to come back and find everything change. We liked things the way they were."

"Things will only get better, not worse."

"That depends on who you are and what you want. Life is all about conflict and winning. When you're a thousand feet over the ocean trying to kill each other, that's all that matters."

"Social conflicts are different and not of that magnitude," I interjected. "We're not trying to kill each other. We're trying to create the political and economic conditions for better lives. That's what you fought for."

"What the fuck do you know about it? You running for office?"

"No, but I've been studying these topics at Wellesley and ever since, especially when I was working as a reporter at the Miami Signal."

"You were a reporter?"

"Yes, I guess you didn't see my letters about that."

"No idea. I knew you were smart, but not that smart."

"Meaning?"

"Reporting the news is a man's job."

"There were four of us in the newsroom. Women were doing men's jobs all over the country. Without them, men would never have won the war."

"Like hell."

"Not like hell. It was hell for us too."

Phoebe interrupted. "I think this is a discussion best left for another time."

"It's a discussion we're never going to have again," Eddie snarled.

Phoebe moved back to my side of the table. "I know you two need some time to yourselves to get reacquainted. I'd like to have you both over for dinner next week," she said. "Gladys could sit with Eddie Junior for a few hours."

"That would be lovely," I said. "Let us know when it would be convenient."

"Better that you let me know," said Phoebe. "I'll show myself out." She left the kitchen. I heard her exit by way of the front door.

"You didn't have to be rude to your mother."

"I wasn't being rude. I was being honest."

"Not what I call honesty. Just plain rudeness."

"I say what I believe."

"So do others."

"I don't have to agree."

"You can at least disagree politely."

"There's nothing polite about winning. You do what it takes."

"Your mother and I are not the enemy."

"That's good to know, Gwen. I'm just trying to get back to the way things were before."

I grinned. "Guess I'll have to cut you some slack."

"Horse shit."

"No, Dear, slack."

"Don't you belittle me."

"I'm not belittling you. I'm teasing you. Lighten up, Eddie."

"There's nothing funny."

"Gladys said she's making steaks for dinner."

"Tell her to make mine bloody rare."

My inward grin was to avoid him noticing and from going off on another tangent. We heard Little Eddie calling from the top of the stairs, "Mommy, Mommy."

"Doesn't he know any other words?" asked Eddie.

"Hungry, milk, potty, toy."

"When will he say Daddy?"

"When he's ready." Calling to Little Eddie, I rushed out of the kitchen to the stairs. "Stay right there, Eddie! Mommy's coming! Don't try to come down the stairs by yourself!"

"How the hell else is he going to learn," Big Eddie grumbled after me. "I know. When he's ready."

Chapter 24

The Crib

After reading Little Eddie a picture book story and tucking him into bed that night, I decided I deserved a relaxing hot soak in the tub.

Big Eddie was downstairs listening to the radio. The strains of big band swing music drifted up the stairs through our open bedroom door. I thought that his listening to entertaining popular music was an auspicious sign. When we were back in college, he had especially liked Benny Goodman playing the clarinet and the double bass and the dynamic percussion of Gene Krupa on drums.

I was a great fan of swing music. Before the war, Eddie and I had been jitterbug fanatics. I was thinking music might help reunite us. As angry and depressed as he was, he might reject a suggestion to go out dancing, but it was worth a try.

Adding hot water as necessary, I stayed in the tub for about an hour. When I heard Eddie in the bedroom, I stepped out of the tub. Giving him a full view of me naked through the open bathroom door, I toweled dry. I wasn't sure he even noticed, or if he did, he didn't let on.

Exposing the full arresting length of my bare legs, I rested each foot on the edge of the tub to dry between my toes. I saw his figure pass across the doorway. He had changed and was now wearing pajamas. I quickly finished toweling my breasts and torso, snatched my nightgown from the wall hook, and slipped it on over my head. I brushed my teeth, rinsed, and inspected them in the mirror. I practiced an alluring expression but didn't impress myself.

I did not find his having a tumbler of whiskey on the bedside table encouraging. But if he needed that kind of fortification, I could accept it. I folded back the sheet and blankets and eased onto my side of the bed. I flounced my hair and lay on the pillow. Then the conversation started.

246

"Why did you name him Eddie?"

"What?"

"Our son, why did you give him my name?"

"I wanted him to have your name."

"Why? In case I didn't come back?"

"You're Eddie Gebhardt. I never doubted you would come back."

"That's comforting. What if he turns out to be a loser?"

"Why would you even think that? It's not possible. You're his father. He'll grow up to love and admire you. He'll want to be like you."

"I'm a loser."

I cranked my head sharply to look at him. "I can't believe you just said that. You're not a loser now and you never have been."

"I'm a sham. I didn't shoot down thirty Jap zeroes."

"How many then?"

He waited as though unable to speak.

"How many?"

"Ten."

"What's wrong with that?"

"I made a bet with another pilot that I'd shoot down thirty before he did."

"And?"

"I lost the bet, because I was wounded."

"Did he make thirty?"

"Yeah, but he never collected. Another Jap pilot shot him down."

"You lived. You came home. That's what's important."

As I reached over to caress him and put my arms around him, he pushed me away with a firm, but quiet, no. He wouldn't let me touch him.

"Would you like to talk about what happened?"

"No, I can't tell you. You wouldn't understand."

"How terrible it was?"

After a long silence, he said, "I liked it. Every time I went up and every time I fought and outmaneuvered one of them and sent them down in flames, it was the best feeling of winning I've ever known. I was flushed with triumph and couldn't wait for the next time. I wanted to kill them all."

"But from your wounds. . ."

"Up there, they couldn't touch me. These are not wounds from fighting. They're from collateral damage. A kamikaze tried to take out our carrier. He didn't make it. Don't ask me to tell you anymore."

After a long silence, I asked, "What do you plan to do?"

"I just got back from the war. Nothing. Take life easy."

"That's okay," I said. "You need time. You earned it." I paused. "I love you. I will do anything to help you."

"What the hell are you talking about? I don't need help. I can take care of myself."

"I want to be a good wife to you, Eddie."

"Just don't ask too much of me."

"I'm not asking anything of you."

"I need to get reoriented."

"You have your law degree."

"Why are you bringing that up? That was four years ago. It's worthless to me. I don't remember any of it."

"It will come back when you go to work. Law is something you learn in the process of doing it."

"And what makes you an expert? You don't know shit about law."

"Please don't talk to me like that. You don't have to use that kind of language. You're a civilian now. You're home with your family. We love you and care about you."

"Then you shouldn't question how I talk or what I do."

"We're together, Eddie. We're together. Remember how we used to be when we were together."

"I was listening to swing band music before I came up."

"I heard."

"It didn't bring back anything."

"Maybe if we go out some time and dance to a real live band. We were fantastic on the dance floor."

"We can't go back."

"Why not?"

"We're here now."

The next morning, Eddie complained about having the crib in the master bedroom. I ignored him and went about my business, including a trip to the pediatrician with Little Eddie, who had a slight fever.

When we returned, I discovered the crib was gone.

Eddie was just coming out of the bathroom. "What happened to Little Eddie's crib?" I asked.

"He sleeps in a bed. He doesn't need it anymore."

"But what did you do with it?"

"It's in the back to be picked up with the trash."

"Eddie! We'll need it when we have another child."

"There won't be another kid. One's enough."

"Why? What makes you say that?"

"It doesn't matter why. One is enough."

"But I love children."

"I don't."

"How can you say that?"

"Stop asking me that. If I say it, that's enough."

"I don't mean to make you angry."

"Then don't ask me again."

I went out into the back courtyard and retrieved the crib and the mattress. Gladys saw me through the kitchen window and came outside to help. I told her what Eddie had said. We covered the parts with a blanket and stored them in the garage where Eddie wouldn't find them.

When we went back inside, I heard two male voices in the living room, Eddie's and someone's who was vaguely familiar. "Who's that?" Gladys shook her head. I walked down the hall. Ron Sarkozy looked up from conversing with Eddie, whose back was facing me, and nudged his arm. Eddie turned in his chair.

"Look what the cat dragged in."

I didn't know if he were referring to me or to his former college roommate.

An impulse of hope and excitement, "Doctor Sarkozy, how wonderful to see you."

"Hi, Gwen." He stood up from his chair. "Your hubby is home." His smile filled the room and belied the seriousness around his eyes from emergency hours in surgery. A vestige of early grayness fringed his dark hair and gave him an aspect of maturity that added to his attractive features and calm demeanor.

I walked over to his embrace.

"How's your little guy?"

"Taking a nap."

"Bet the war hero is having fun getting to know him."

"Don't call me that," said Eddie. "I don't even want him to know that about me."

"Of course, of course, he should never see a war in his lifetime. I thought Eddie would be home by now, so thought I'd just pop in and surprise you. We have a lot to catch up on. Justine's coming from New York this weekend and we'd like to take you both to dinner. Italian. How about it?"

I looked at Eddie. "Eddie, what do you think? It would do us good to get out."

Ron's blue eyes crinkled with curiosity that I was deferring to Eddie.

Eddie nodded with a good-natured grimace. "Yeah, haven't had real Italian in a long time, years."

"It will be a real treat." My emotional exuberance caught Ron's eye again.

"I'm still at Chelsea Hospital," he said. "Different patient load than during the war. I'll tell you about it."

"We'll go to dinner, but no talk about the war," said Eddie.

"I couldn't agree more," said Ron. "Fun times, happy times, lots to look forward to. You're a father now. You have a family."

"When Justine came to visit me in the hospital when our son was born, I asked when you plan to have children."

"Probably within the next year or two. We agreed to wait until after the war."

"That's what she said."

"We should have waited," said Eddie, "then we wouldn't have to worry about it."

"Luck of the draw," said Ron. "Those little cells sometimes have a say in the matter over what we think we want."

"Should have used condoms," said Eddie. "The Army and Navy were handing them out."

"Had quite an epidemic of VD going regardless," said Ron.

"When I was working as a news reporter, I wrote about some of the women who suffered as victims of male discrimination," I said.

"Ah, you and Justine have been talking," said Ron.

"Talking about what?" Eddie bristled.

"Nothing. What was happening here during wartime."

Ron detected I didn't want to pursue the topic.

"You mean the whores," said Eddie. "In Hawaii, soldiers lined up at cat houses like they were going to chow."

"I wasn't talking about prostitutes," I said. "There were a lot of innocent girls who got VD from soldiers."

251

"You mean the soldiers got VD from them," said Eddie.

"From a medical perspective, there was some political distortion blaming women for being carriers of the disease. Although the fact didn't want to be acknowledged, men also were carriers."

"We all knew whores could give us the clap."

If Eddie had been in one of those lines, I didn't want to know. He had come home with enough problems to deal with. To my relief, the discussion did not continue.

"Justine and I will come by to pick you up Saturday at six. I'll make our reservation for six-thirty."

"You have a car?" asked Eddie.

"Plymouth Special Deluxe, parked out front. No more gas rationing."

"Have to get me a car," said Eddie. Can't ride the trolley everywhere. Not my style," he laughed.

"Do you have a sitter?" asked Ron.

"Gladys," I said. "She's our cook and housekeeper."

"Swell," Ron started toward the front door. "Have to get back to the hospital. Saturday, six o'clock then."

I followed him for a few steps. "Thank you so much for coming by. I miss you and Justine. You're my best friends."

"Now that Eddie's back, we can see each other more often."

"Bye, Ron," Eddie called out from his chair. I thought it rude that he did not escort Ron to the door.

"Bye, Eddie. Welcome home."

"Yeah."

I closed the door after Ron.

"A Plymouth Special Deluxe. Must be takin' out a lot of gall bladders and appendix. What's our financial situation?"

"We're living on money from my trust. I'll have to get a job myself in a few years when Little Eddie is old enough to go to school."

"I don't want you working."

"I beg your pardon, Eddie. I have been working."

"I'm the one who brings home the bacon. I don't want people thinking I don't earn enough to pay the bills and I have to send my wife out to work."

"I don't have to work. I want to work. I like working. Besides, I thought you said you wanted to wait a while."

"Nah, can't let Sarkozy outdo me with his Plymouth Special Deluxe. Cocksucker."

I tried to hide my reaction of shock at the obscenity, but then I remembered Eddie and Ron had often called each other disgusting names back in college. Insulting each other was a male form of mutual admiration and friendship. "What are you going to do?"

"My old man has connections with law firms. He can get me in."

"I'm pleased that you'll be looking for a job."

"Your place is here at home except when I'll need you to go with me on social occasions, like my mother did with my old man until they divorced."

"I'm more than an arm decoration," I said.

"I just came back from the war. This is my life. You need to do what I say."

Hoping that time and events would gloss over how he saw me, I swallowed my pride and said nothing. Even though he didn't want to talk about the war, consciously or unconsciously, he was using it as an excuse for how he related to me.

Chapter 25

Undercut

Dining out with Ron and Justine did little for my morale when I observed how fun-loving and companionable they were with one another. Was I envious, yes. My initial spirit of forced levity escaped me as I sat eating lasagna next to my sullen husband and his plate of linguine and *tutti de mare*. Four glasses of *sangiovese* did not alter my disappointment. We shared three bottles of wine during dinner.

Whiskey with beer chasers did little to soften Eddie's abusive language. I noticed Ron listening and studying him as Eddie ranted rather than conversed.

Before dessert was served, Justine motioned for me to follow her to the women's restroom. When we were out of earshot from the table, she asked, "How are you holding up?"

"Not well."

"Ron told me about how different Eddie is. A lot of Ron's patients now are veterans suffering from shell shock."

"Shell shock? Eddie read something in the paper about that."

"Ron says Eddie has experienced severe trauma from being in battle."

We entered the crowded restroom and waited for commodes to become available.

"If Eddie is willing, Ron can talk to him and refer him to a psychologist on the hospital staff."

"Psychologist?"

"Ron says he thinks Eddie needs professional counseling."

"He'll never do it. He was outraged at the news story. He thinks only weak and cowardly soldiers do that."

"That's not so according to Ron. You could suggest it to Eddie."

"Are you kidding? You saw him at dinner. I can barely get him to be civil to me. He has me walking on eggshells."

"This should be something you write about in your book."

"If he ever saw that, he'd beat me to an inch of my life and divorce me."

"Does he beat you?"

"No, he ignores me. This is not the place to be talking about this."

"I know. I'm sorry. That one's opening. You take it."

I entered the commode and locked the door. A moment later, another commode was vacated.

Actually, I was a little furious with Justine for mentioning the topic. Even though she was the publishing editor, I would decide what went into my book. We didn't even have a contract, only the germ of an idea. I wasn't sure what I was thinking was the same as what she was thinking. Except for the exchange of a few letters, we hadn't talked about the development of the book in any detail. I was just discovering what I would write about in bits and pieces, most of it unexpected. The changes in Eddie's personality had thrown me a real curve.

Justine and I emerged from our commodes at the same time and washed and dried our hands. I avoided looking at her in the mirror. She must have detected that I was miffed. She touched my arm as we left the restroom and returned to the table. Eddie was gone.

"He had to process some liquid," said Ron. "Does he drink like that at home?"

"He drinks too much," I said sitting down.

"I told her about your recommendation," said Justine.

"I can't ask him to do that," I said. "I won't. Being with him from day to day is hard enough."

"That's why I think it's important he get help," said Ron.

"You know. You are good friends and a lovely couple. I know you care about us and I understand what you're trying to do, but you need to let us work this out in our own way."

Ron smiled. "In other words, you want us to butt out."

"Yes, seriously, you need to butt out."

"Understood. Your point is taken," said Ron. "I've seen some extreme cases, including life-threatening situations, not just to wives, but to the patients themselves. Two of them committed suicide."

"I don't think Eddie is that extreme. I just have to let him lead the way out of this. He has to rediscover himself."

"He might try reinventing himself to cope," said Ron.

"How could he do that?"

"It's how the brain works. I can give you a book if you'd like to read it."

I glanced up. "Not now. He's coming back."

Eddie returned to the table and slid onto his chair. "So, what were you talking about while I pissed a few gallons, me? You were talking about me. I can see it in your faces."

"Actually, we were talking about what to have for dessert," said Ron and passed him the dessert menu. "The tiramisu is exceptional. We've had it before."

"I think I'll have that," I said.

Eddie scanned the menu. "I'll have chocolate cake and cognac."

"Coffee for me and tiramisu," said Justine.

"Me too," I said.

"Coffee and tiramisu," said Ron.

"See," said Eddie, "you all ordered the same thing. You were talking about me."

I gently placed my hand over his. "We can't fool you, Eddie. Yes, we were talking about you. We tried to guess what dessert you would select."

"Put any money on it?"

"No, just conjecture," I said.

"Pussies."

I glanced at Ron and shook my head.

Paranoia was one of several topics I read about in the book Doctor Sarkozy loaned me. Since Eddie's condition had become the center point of our relationship, I was now thinking of Ron more as a doctor than an old college friend.

For a while, I thought Eddie and I would never have sexual intercourse again. One night when he didn't know I was awake, he went into the bathroom and neglected to close the door. I slipped out of bed and saw him masturbating into the open toilet. I walked in, which was a mistake, and said, "Why don't you let me do that for you?"

His savage expression unnerved me. "What the hell! Are you some kind of whore?"

"No, I'm your wife. We can have sex. We can love each other."

"Don't ever walk in on me again. You got that?" Still holding his tumescent penis, he shoved me out and slammed the door.

I didn't even want to get back in the same bed with him again. I grabbed my robe and slippers and went down the hall to sleep in Tess's old room.

A few days later, it dawned on Eddie that I wasn't sleeping in the master bedroom and that I had moved my toiletries to Tess's bathroom. At first, he didn't say anything to me. Then one morning, he stopped at Tess's door and looked in at me.

"You don't have to do this," he said. "I apologize. I'm sorry I said those things. You can come back to our bedroom." I slowly sat up against the pillows and stared at him. "It's going to take more than an apology, Eddie. I'm trying my best to cope with your – problem. But you're not trying at all."

"I'll bet you want me to spill my guts to Sarkozy. He's not a shrink. He's a surgeon. He should stick to taking out body parts."

"Ron only suggested you talk to the psychologist who knows about shell shock. He's done research. He's seen hundreds of patients who came home broken from the war. He's written a book about it. Ron cares about you. He wants to help you."

"Well, I don't want his help. I'll deal with this in my own way."

"I'll come back to our bedroom on one condition."

"What's that."

"We have to make love at least once a week. And if you don't want me to see your wounds, wear your pajama tops or an undershirt. The area of interest is between our legs."

He grinned. "I think I can agree to that."

"And you can wear a condom. We don't have to have another child."

Eddie nodded. "Okay, deal. I'm going down to have breakfast. I have a job interview today."

"That's progress. That's great news. Who with?"

"Law firm. My old man put in a good word for me."

"What time?"

"Over lunch at the Algonquin."

"Wow, fancy."

"Once I'm hired, I'll become a member. We can go there sometimes. They have great food and dance bands."

I smiled and nodded. "I'm looking forward to it."

A week later, he pulled a Cadillac into the courtyard behind the house and came in through the kitchen door. I was sitting at the table guiding Little Eddie in the use of his drawing crayons. Gladys was staring out the window.

"Beauty, isn't it?" he crowed.

I glanced up.

"Come on out. Take a look."

"Did you buy a car?"

"Oh, yeah. Top of the line."

"Come on," I said to Little Eddie. "Let's go see Daddy's new car."

Eddie continued to make lines and squiggles with his crayons. I went to the door Eddie was holding open and looked outside. The polished brass and purple sheen and sweeping long lines were impressive. What was more impressive to me was that Eddie had been with the law firm for only three months and now he had his dream car.

Because of his military record as a fighter pilot, he had found a niche in defense contract law with a team representing a major aircraft company to the Government Purchasing Office and Department of Defense.

His enthusiasm and sudden shift in his behavior caught me off guard and made me wary at first that his success might just be a temporary high and that he would emotionally crash like I had seen him do before. His sharing information about his work and his colleagues was new and refreshing. In light of my wartime experience as a news writer, the topic caught my attention.

As Ron Sarcozy had put it, Eddie attempted to reinvent himself. Despite his professional success, he continued to struggle with a kind of periodic darkness and relapsed back to his abusive behavior at unexpected moments that left me wondering to whom I was married.

When we tried to make love, no matter what I did to stimulate him, he couldn't achieve and maintain an erection. The second time, he shouted at me to stop. Infused with rage at his impotence, he blamed me as the cause of his problem. I stopped trying.

In all my years as a Boston resident, I had never been inside the exclusive Algonquin Club. My father had been a member when only men were allowed. The night Eddie took me, he wore a black tie, tuxedo, and cummerbund and I wore a blue and pearl evening gown selected for me by Millie from Filene's.

Parking along Commonweal Avenue was limited. Eddie dropped me off at the four story gray stone building with a layered colonnade edifice and went to find a space large enough to accommodate the length of his car. The polite doorman wearing a burgundy uniform escorted me into the foyer where I admired the polished hand-carved mahogany furnishings, Italian marble fireplace, and earth-tone walls and waited for Eddie to return.

We were escorted up the carpeted stairs to a white linen-covered table by the impeccably dressed maître de' and served by white-gloved waiters wearing white tie and tails. The choreographed rhythm of two waiters removing and putting down China plates and relocating silverware as the meal progressed entranced me.

Beginning the meal with sturgeon caviar and *foie gras pate*, Eddie ordered fresh crab and filet mignon and arugula salad for both of us. We had not eaten such high quality beef since before the war.

Our conversation was limited to commenting on the elegant décor, the presentation and taste of the food, and the professional service. We concluded our repast with a variety of cheeses and Portuguese port followed by cognac and coffee, and a Cuban cigar for Eddie.

What began as a beautiful evening disintegrated shortly after we walked out the front door of the Algonquin. We had planned to go dancing at the Copacabana. I waited at the curb while Eddie went to get his car. After fifteen minutes, he had not returned. Looking up and down the street, I decided he had left me standing there. I asked the doorman to call me a taxi.

When I arrived home, I let myself in the front door and saw Eddie seated at the dining room table. He turned to look at me.

"I took a taxi," I said. "What happened to you?"

"Oh, there you are. I expected to find you home," he said.

I thought he was losing his mind. "Do you remember we had dinner at the Algonquin?"

"Yes, it was a fantastic meal. But then afterwards, you disappeared."

"I didn't disappear. I was waiting for you to bring the car around. We were supposed to go to the Copacabana. You left me standing at the curb."

A look of confusion flooded his face. "I'm sorry. I don't remember. I forgot you were waiting."

"You forgot? How could you forget? We just had dinner together."

"This happens to me once in a while. I have blackouts."

"Blackouts? How come you never told me? You need to get medical help."

"Naah, they don't last long. More like a short nap."

"I'm serious, Eddie. You need help."

"I'm okay. I tell you, I'm okay. I can handle it."

"I just want what's best for you."

"What's best is that you don't keep harping at me. This happened. That's war. It happened. I'll deal with it in my own way."

But he didn't deal with it. It dealt with him.

Two nights later, he woke up screaming. Flinging himself out of bed, he scrambled about on the floor on his hands and knees, leaped to his feet and ran to the window. At the point he tried to open the window to jump out, I wrapped my arms around him from behind and kept shouting at him, "Eddie! Eddie! Wake up! It's only a bad dream. You're having a nightmare!" Shuddering and trembling, he dropped to his knees.

"It was coming right at me. We were firing at each other. We were going to crash. I had to bail out. I was afraid my chute wouldn't open."

I got down on the floor and held him until his trembling subsided. Then I helped him back to bed and held him in my arms until he fell asleep. He never realized I cradled his face against my breasts. The next morning before he woke, I gently extracted myself and moved aside.

At first, I thought he was just impatient with everything and everybody but watching him even reading a book or a newspaper or working on legal briefs in the library after dinner, his level of irritation would peak. He would curse and lunge out of the desk chair and pace the room. He inevitably poured himself a tumbler of Scotch to settle his nerves, but the alcohol also made him drowsy. He drank more of it and more often. The empty bottles piled up in the trash.

He developed a ritual of putting himself in a trance-like state and gazing at his bare torso in our full length bedroom mirror and attempting to swipe away the image of his scars against the glass. The three times I saw him performing this ritual, he didn't know I was watching him. I did not linger in the doorway on the chance he would notice me and fly into one of his rages. He hated for me to see him exhibit any form of weakness.

In addition to drinking too much, he flaunted his self-destructive behavior by driving too fast and aggressively honking at and dangerously passing other drivers.

Once or twice a week, he would drive down the hill into the Italian sector to gamble at one of the clubs. He repeatedly came home drunk, complaining he was jinxed and had lost his luck.

"I never used to lose at gambling," he shouted, as he stomped around the house. "I never used to lose."

He attempted to seduce Little Eddie's affection by teaching him to call me derogatory names. I was appalled the first time Little Eddie said, "Mommy, you're ugly."

"Did Daddy tell you to say that?"

He nodded.

"Well, I'm not ugly. I'm pretty and I love you. Your Daddy should not be telling you to say such things."

I didn't bring up the issue with Eddie. I thought it better to ignore such infantile and immature efforts to compete with me. After his second attempt, "Mommy, you stink," and a third, "Mommy, you don't love me," none of which brought me to the point of confrontation, Eddie stopped.

I wondered how I was going to endure his abuse for the rest of my married life and realized that at some point, my married life would have to come to an end. Instead, I continued to endure. I did not want to give up my son.

Chapter 26

Losing

"He keeps trying to hurt me in little ways," I confided to Gladys. "I can't fight him or get him to talk about it. I can't change him."

Gladys was a sympathetic listener. She said, "I wish I could do something for you, *Liebchen*, but I don't have the answer."

Upon the release of her husband, Ekkehardt, from an internment camp, he stayed at the house as a recluse in the room over the garage for one week before Eddie accidentally discovered him and threatened to call the police. With Gladys and Ekkehardt standing together in the courtyard, I begged Eddie not to and that the poor man had just returned from being incarcerated.

"He's getting a job working at the shipyards," I said. "He was an engine mechanic in the merchant marine before the war. He and Gladys have been apart for the entire war."

"I don't want a kraut living on the property."

"He's Gladys's husband. He's an American citizen just like Gladys. Just like you and me. Why can't he live here?"

"Next to Italy and Japan, Germany was our biggest enemy."

"Eddie, the war is over. Germany lost. There are millions of people just like you and me. They want to get back to normal. Ekkehardt and Gladys are innocent and both of them spent three years in concentration camps. We have more than enough room in this monstrosity. They have a right to live here. I gave them that right. Gladys was here before I was even born."

"I can accept Gladys."

"Why just her? Because she can cook and clean? If Ekkehardt polishes your car and shines your shoes, will that be acceptable? Even though he's not a servant. For Christ's sake, Eddie, you have German ancestry yourself a few generations back. Do you call yourself a kraut? You're living on the property."

His face turned red and he silently fumed for a full minute. "All right, I'll think about it. But if he does stay, he doesn't get to eat with us. He's not one of the family."

"I don't think he could stand being at the same table with you anyway, let alone the same room. Gladys has her meals separately in the kitchen. Her husband can eat with her."

"I don't like the way things are going here."

"What do you mean?"

"I'm in charge, not you."

"You're in charge of yourself and you're not doing a very good job of that. You are not in charge of me." I turned to the old couple. "Gladys, Ekkehardt, let's go in the kitchen. We can talk more about the arrangements."

I urged them ahead of me through the back door.

In reading listings of local citizens who had died overseas, I learned that our house servants, Harmon and Ivo Nevens, had been killed during the D Day landing on the Normandy Beach in France. I told Ekkehardt he and Gladys could have any of their former rooms, but they were happy with Gladys's room. In moving in with us, Ekkehardt took pains not to cross paths with Eddie. He signed on for night shift work at the shipyards so he would be home during the day when Eddie was at work. On weekends, he would go stay with friends he had known when he was in the Merchant Marine or work on fishing boats.

He told me he enjoyed being out on the water. He asked me about wall photos of my father's sailing yacht which had been in dry dock since the beginning of the war. At his request, I gave him permission to work on repairs and relaunch the boat. He proved to be an avid sailor and took me and Little Eddie on brief outings around the bay, which thrilled the boy and fed his sense of adventure.

Since Eddie's return, Phoebe stopped coming to visit as often, although she enjoyed watching her grandson grow into a young boy. She said I was fortunate to have Gladys back again.

Somehow, I managed to get through the next several years without losing my mind. Little Eddie and Gladys were my mainstays and kept me sane.

When Little Eddie turned six, I enrolled him in a local elementary day school where I could take him in the morning and pick him up in the afternoon. Those free hours gave me the time to work intensely on my book without interruption.

Since I didn't own a car and wouldn't dream of asking Big Eddie to buy me one, Little Eddie and I rode the trolley. He enjoyed the noisy crowds and crush of passengers, the clang of the bell and the passing traffic and buildings seen through the windows.

From the books he liked to read and the drawings he brought home from school, his fascination with fantasy and adventure were clear to me.

He also talked about friends he had made but there was no mention of wanting to get together and play outside of school hours. Had he asked, I would have found a way, even if just mothers and children meeting each other at the park or having a picnic at the beach. Oddly, we didn't interact much, largely because of the children's young age and the mother's lack of interest in socializing.

Two years later, another of Eddie's threats raised its ugly head. He had always been mildly critical of how I related to our son. "You're raising him to be a momma's boy," he said. "It's time to place him in a private residential school."

I fought him on this. "I refuse. I will not do that to him. He's a little boy, for God's sake."

"Yeah, Little Eddie the little boy. He needs to start learning how to become a man."

"At eight years old?"

"That's when it begins. My parents put me in private residential schools from the time I was eight."

"We don't have to repeat that. He doesn't have to be raised like that."

"When he turns eight, he goes to a private residential school."

"I won't do that. I won't let you do that to him. He'd be devastated."

"No he won't. After the first day with new friends, he'll get over it. He'll outgrow you by then anyway."

"He will need me. He will need his mother."

"Bullshit, Gwen. Who told you that?"

"Little Eddie and I have a loving caring relationship, something you obviously don't understand and didn't have."

"You're mollycoddling him. Life is about winning. You'll turn him into a loser."

"You just think that because you're a loser."

"What? You fucking bitch," he screamed. "What the fuck are you talking about?"

"I want to protect him from you. You want to destroy him just like you're destroying yourself. You're addicted to winning. It's like a drug for you. And when you lose, you can't handle it. And even if you do win, you're never satisfied. You have a wife who loves you and a son who adores you. You have a high paying job. Why isn't that enough?"

"You're a negative influence. You just want to turn Junior against me."

"I'm not turning him against you. You're pushing him away. You're pushing us both away. You can't stop me from raising my own son as I see fit."

"Yes, I can and I will."

"How?"

"A restraining order."

"Based on what? If anything, a restraining order should be brought against you."

"You don't know what you're talking about. You don't know how to raise a boy."

"I know more than you, Eddie."

"All right, Let's let him decide."

We ended up taking our son to visit the school. To my chagrin, he liked it. Eddie enrolled him the following year.

My writing became both my escape and the cause of our divorce.

Chapter 27

A Freak of Nature

I guess in one way Tess's role in life was to be a social reformer. I had known nothing about her during the war years. Now, she suddenly emerged from anonymity, appearing in news reels and on magazine covers as a star athlete in track and field competition.

I was particularly taken by what the newsreel commentator said.

"Seeming to come out of nowhere, track star, Tess Vanderveer, has broken every record for the pentathlon set by male competitors. She runs the mile like a gazelle in well under four minutes. Blessed with an extraordinary body and almost superhuman strength, she sails over hurdles and the high jump as though defying gravity. She throws the javelin and shotput and hurls the discus farther than any man. She pole vaults over the highest bar with inches to spare.

The crowds are in awe of this woman. You can hear the admiration in their roar and applause during every event. And you can see their support at the box office in every city hosting a track meet. Ticket sales are beyond what you would imagine. After all, a track meet is not a baseball game."

Tess even played baseball in the women's league during the war. Spectators love her. But not everybody does. There is a hue and cry from some male competitors and sports patrons that she should be banned from competition. One sportswriter described her as a freak of nature and her coach a traitor to all men. He just laughs at that. 'She works as hard and harder than any man and is a gifted athlete. She's not out there trying to show them up. The naysayers are just threatened by such a woman.'

"Tess Vanderveer's popularity is not going away. She is scheduled as the front running athlete in a dozen major cities during the coming year. She's a star, all right, not a movie star, but a different kind of star, and she's beautiful to boot. She's the closest thing we have in the sports world to an ancient Greek goddess."

Other derogatory and critical comments appeared in written news articles about her. One reporter characterized her as *"masculine. What Tess Vanderveer does is demeaning to the feminine sex. Track and field events and long distance running are not suitable activities for women. Tess Vanderveer creates the false impression that any woman can rise above the prescribed standards of acceptable feminine behavior. She is a threat to the values of our society and should be prohibited from continuing."*

Even religious officialdom piled on with their dogma regarding the role of women. What I read made me cringe.

"Tess Vanderveer is anathema to the sanctity, modesty, and virtue of all women. She is to be castigated, not set up on a pedestal to admire as a false god."

To my surprise, Eddie commented on her performance. "I saw her in an exhibition track meet in New York City a week ago."

"Did you talk to her?"

"I didn't have any reason to. Besides, the crowds are so heavy you can't get near her. I did buy one of her photos from a vendor though." He pulled it out of his briefcase. "It's for you. I thought you might like to have it. It cost a dollar."

"How thoughtful. Thank you, Eddie." I stared at the 10 by 12 glossy black and white action shot of Tess taking a hurdle in full stride. The photo captured the thrust of her muscled legs and lean body. Her streaming strawberry blonde hair gave the impression she was flying.

"She's good, really good, even better than I was," said Eddie.

"Do you know where she's going to be next?"

"Can't say. You'll have to read the sports news."

I wanted desperately to see her again and talk with her but had difficulty finding and gaining access to her until I learned the identity of her coach and manager, Joe Walsh, a stocky Irishman named in one of the magazine articles. Getting her unlisted address was impossible. The only way I would be able to meet her was to attend her next exhibition track meet where she was competing in another men's pentathlon, the only woman to ever do so. I also had to find some way to navigate or circumvent the crowds.

I decided to try Justine and see if she knew someone at the New York Times. With her help contacting an editor friend at the Times, I was able to get an address in Greenwich Village.

Upon leaving the subway, eyed by toughs, thieves, and panhandlers, I scurried along the forbidding inner city streets through impoverished neighborhoods. A ruffian gang of children surrounded me begging for money. I clutched my vulnerable purse and burst through them with determined strides as one tried to snatch it away from me.

Intimidated by three shoddy characters sitting on the steps of Tess's walkup flat, I maneuvered around them, shoved my way into the entry, and quick-stepped up three flights of rickety stairs. Not knowing whether or not she would be home, I knocked on the door.

"It's open!" I heard her shout from inside.

I decided waiting for her to answer would be more appropriate than my barging in.

"I said the fucking door is open! What's the matter with you?"

After another minute, I heard her angry footsteps coming to the door. Her piercing blue eyes widened in surprise but did nothing to soften her scowl. "What the fuck?"

"Tess. It's so good to see you."

She glared at me. "How did you find me?"

"My friend, Justin Sarkozy."

"Your college roommate?"

"She's a publisher here in New York. She's a friend of the news editor who worked on your story."

"What story? I don't read the newspaper."

"You had a big feature in the sports section of the New York Times."

"It's the promoter who puts out shit like that."

"I even saw you in a newsreel at the movies."

"I hate that shit. They're just commercializing women's sports to make money. I sure as hell don't see any of it. They're just pimps, except for my coach. He's an okay guy. But the rest of them are just white racist misogynist bags of shit. You were always writing for the school paper back in college. Is that why Justine told you where to find me? You here to pry into my life and write about it?"

"No, you're my sister. I care about you. Why didn't you ever get in touch with me?" I asked.

"No reason to. When I left after Wellesley, I never looked back. I didn't want anything more to do with our parents' life. Actually, I'm sorry you found me. I never wanted to see any of you again."

"Where did you go? What did you do for the past eight years?"

"Whatever I wanted."

"Hey, I'm a mother. I have an eight year old son, Eddie Jr."

"So you married that loudmouth track star. I should feel complimented, but I don't. Did he make it back from the war?"

"Yes, but in a bad way. He's physically and mentally damaged."

"Shell shock."

"You know what that is?"

"I've heard about it. Dove and I have friends who came back with it."

"Is Dove here?"

"Not at the moment. She has an art exhibit down in The Village."

"So she's been painting all these years?"

"And sculpting. She branched out."

"Can I come in? Can we talk a little?"

"I have a workout in about one hour. So you have to make it quick."

"Thank you. I am so grateful."

"For what? All our family stuff is in the past. It doesn't matter anymore."

I followed her into the apartment décor of casual neglect. Canvases were stacked against one wall where two of Dove's paintings were in progress on an easel. Unwashed dishes and pots and pans littered the sink of a small kitchen alcove. Earth tone cushions scattered about the wooden floor filled in for furniture.

Getting Tess to open up to me was difficult. Talking with her had never been easy, even when we were children. And after Dove had latched on to her, I had been excluded entirely. I guess I shouldn't have expected anything different, but I did. I thought adult maturity might make a difference.

"Where are you staying?"

"Nowhere yet. I thought I'd check into a hotel."

"Nothing but flop houses in this part of town. You can stay here. You'll have to sleep on floor pillows."

"Floor pillows are fine. Dove won't mind?"

"Why would she?"

"She never liked me when we were kids."

Tess burst out laughing. "Hey, she's a grown woman. You never got over that, did you?"

"I don't want to impose on you."

"You won't. We've had all kinds of villagers crash here. That's how we live. Just don't bring up our childhood."

"I won't even mention Eddie Jr."

"You're a grown woman. If you want to tell her about your son, do it. So you have a kid. She won't give a shit."

"It's just I don't want to intrude."

"What did I just tell you. We've had drug addicts stay here. You can go with us tonight. We're going to hear Allen Ginsberg read his poems and a jazz band."

"I don't know who he is."

"After tonight, you will. Bebop is a whole new style of music. You heard of Charlie Parker, Sonny Rawlins, Thelonious Monk?"

"The names."

"They won't be there, but there are others. And you can't go dressed like that. You look like a secretary. You'll embarrass the shit out of us. I'll loan you some clothes. This is all the time I can give you. I have to be at the track. Coach makes us run extra laps for every minute we're late to practice. A stopwatch is permanently attached to his hand."

"Thanks, Tess, I really appreciate you putting up with me."

"Nada. I'm gone. Dove might have a shit fit when she finds you here. Just tell her to fuck off and that your big sister said it's okay. She'll love that." She slammed out.

I was washing the dirty pots and pans and dishes when Tess walked in carrying a canvas under one arm.

"Who? What the fuck are you doin' here?"

"I came to see Tess."

Her irascible glance raked the room. "Who the hell let you in?"

"Tess. She had to go to track practice."

"Then you saw her. So you can move on. Get the hell outta here."

"She invited me to stay the night."

"You've got to be shittin' me!"

"No shit, Dove. I'm going with you and Tess to see Allen Ginsberg and folk singers."

"Well, fuck me."

"It's nice to see you too, Dove. You haven't changed a bit."

She approached me with a menacing squint. "Normally, I'd take that as an insult. But your sister might be a little tweaked if she comes home and finds you with your face all bloody."

"Hey, Dove, I'm a mother. I have an eight year old son, Eddie Jr."

"Well, ain't you the cat's meow? Miss Goody Two Shoes has a kid. You married? Of course, you'd be married. You're just like all the other squares."

"Actually, I'm not a square. I don't wear dresses and high heels to clean house and put on makeup to be beautiful waiting for my husband to come home from work."

"I don't believe that. You're just the type."

"Hardly, I put up with a lot, but I'm not a stereotype."

"So what are you, a paper doll? Change your costume to fit the occasion?"

"No, I'm a journalist."

"Oh, now I know why you're here. You think you have a special relationship with Tess so you can write a story about her."

"That's not why I'm here."

"The only one who has a relationship with Tess is me."

"I know."

"She told you."

"I'm glad for both of you. I don't have that with my husband."

"Men are worthless bags of shit."

I changed the subject. "Tess said you've become a famous artist."

Dove's lips spluttered. She shrugged off her black Russian Lenin hat and tousled her curly dark hair. It hadn't changed since she was a girl. She wore a black leather jacket over a black turtleneck sweater and black jeans tucked into combat boots.

"I sell a few here and there," she said. "Tourists slumming in the village. I don't paint traditional stuff. I break all the rules. Picasso and Matisse are my gods. I do best with expressionist art."

276

"I was noticing some of your work."

"Want to buy a piece?"

"I will when I leave."

Her raucous laugh grated on my nerves, but at least it was a reaction. "You're rich. You can be my patron."

"I'm not rich. I worked as a news writer in Miami after the war. But since then, I depended on my inheritance trust."

"Doesn't your husband work?"

"Yes, he's an attorney."

"Oh for shits sake. I knew it. He's that asshole you dated from Ha Ha Hawvard."

"The war caused him a lot of problems."

"Know a few of those, dopers in the village."

"Tess mentioned that."

"She tapped into her trust when she graduated and over the years, but only a little. Finding work was easy. What used to be men's jobs went begging during the war."

"I wrote about them in Florida. What kind of jobs?"

"I worked in a post office and Tess drove a delivery truck."

"Here, in New York?"

"Delaware and Jersey. Lots of jobs in shipyards and defense plants. Listen, I don't have time to stand around jawing with you. Have to finish this canvas," she referred to the one she had carried into the flat.

"That's okay. Please take care of whatever you have to. I'll find something to keep me occupied."

"Just don't try to clean up the place. I have a certain order of things." I nodded.

She walked over to a work bench covered with colorful tubes of oil paint, brushes, and a pallet. "You said you never heard of Ginsberg?"

"No."

"You know anything about beats? Not likely."

"I really don't."

"It would help prepare you, especially for where we're taking you tonight. Do you know where the name comes from?"

I shook my head.

"It's what we call thieves, con-artists, addicts, bums, the dregs of society. I've painted dozens of 'em. How about Kerouac? There's a book he wrote there on the coffee table. He's a genius."

I kneeled on a large brown floor pillow next to the coffee table and picked up the book. The title, *On The Road*, didn't mean anything to me. It invoked the image of an empty highway leading to an existential unknown horizon.

The two main fictional characters of the autobiography depicted Kerouac as Sal Paradise and Dean Moriarity as his friend, Neal Cassady in their odyssey around the country. The people they encountered influenced their quest to escape social conformity. The spontaneous prose style created a sense of movement derived from the beat of improvisational jazz and clarified for me the meaning of beat.

I had been reading for about two hours when Tess returned.

"You're still here. I thought Dove would've kicked you out."

"You said to tell her my big sister gave me permission to stay."

"Then she really would have kicked you out." Tess and Dove laughed.

"Where do you practice?" I asked.

"New York University. They have a track and field stadium. We get to use the showers."

"How about I take you both to dinner? Then I won't have to wash your dishes again."

"You're on," said Tess. "First, let me get you some decent clothes."

She rummaged in a closet and came out with a pair of jeans that were too tight. "I can't wear these," I said. "I can't get them buttoned."

"That's what you get for being a fat housewife."

"I'm not fat. I could stand to lose a few pounds, but I'm not fat."

"Denial is nine tenths of reality."

"Is that a beatnik thing?"

"No, it's a Tess thing. Here, try these on. She tossed me a pair of men's trousers.

"Men's trousers?"

"He stayed here once and forgot to take his pants when he left. He's about your size."

"Did he have cooties?" I slipped into the pants legs and tugged up the waist.

"Looks okay," said Tess. "They'll get you in the door. Here, take off your blouse and put this on."

I pulled the black turtleneck sweater over my head. "Don't you wear any color but black?"

"Black is not a color," Dove shouted from the living room.

"And clomp around in these." Tess handed me a pair of scuffed work boots.

"This is not my idea of dressing up to go out on the town."

"The Village is not going out on the town. We live in the town. Here, this should fit."

I stuck my arms through the khaki sleeves of a military jacket.

"And the *piece de resistance*." She plunked a Lenin cap on my head. "There, now you look like one of us. Wipe that smirk off your face."

Chapter 28

Beat

The rising aroma of beef and vegetable and chicken noodle soups, heavily seasoned pork, fried fish, mashed potatoes, gravy, and sauerkraut greeted us at an all-night cafeteria. We distanced ourselves at a corner table from hustlers, pimps, and drug addicts. While we ate corn beef, Swiss, and rye sandwiches, coleslaw, potato salad, and dill pickles, Tess continued her story of how she became a track star.

"I was competing in a national track meet. He came to me afterwards and introduced himself. I knew of him from sports circles. Athletes talk about coaches. Joe Walsh was considered among the best. He came from a background of coaching male athletes. He said he recognized the attraction and following of female athletes. With the advent of female teams during the war, he saw the opportunity for female athletes to enter the big time and compete nationally. Although he didn't mention the commercial profit of merging sport and sexuality, that motive was always there. At least he didn't talk to us about any of that or try to force it down our throats like with the baseball and basketball leagues.

"Officials in sports organizations accused me of being mannish and that I had no place in a man's sport. I was told the strain of competition would ruin my menstrual cycle and that my uterus couldn't take the punishing strain and that I wouldn't be able to bear children." She laughed. "As if men knew anything about my uterus. What gives them the right to think they're in charge of any woman's uterus? I wasn't even interested in having children."

"You don't want to get married and have children someday?"

"I am married. Dove and I are partners. We don't need men and we don't want to have children."

"I remember that happened a lot at Wellesley between some of the women who were resident professors and instructors."

"Yeah, it was called the Wellesley marriage," said Tess.

"How did you end up on a national track team?"

"That's a dumb fuck question. How do you end up doing anything? I worked at it. I trained and worked at it. Did some low grade meets until one day, this guy says he wants to recruit me."

"He's your coach, the one they write about?"

"Joe Walsh. He's good. He's real good. He knows his stuff and he knows how to work with us without any prejudice or old beliefs about us being women."

"How many are you?"

"Seven, that's all we need. Each of us has specialties and can cross compete in other events. He's built a team of high performance young women, including two Negro athletes, who were unbeatable in the meter sprints and hurdles and the four-hundred meter relay. One of them, Ariana Jones, could match me on the high jump. We called her Ari. And Bea Johnson logged the best time in hurdles. She also set the record in the broad jump. They were fantastic team members. I miss them. Coach had to replace them with two white girls."

"What happened to them?"

"They had to quit. A gang of white racists attacked them and tried to kill them for being on a team with white women. They escaped because they outran their attackers. They went to a Negro team. They can't compete in white track meets and the Olympic Committee has barred a Negro team.

"Bea is a mother with two kids. Now that the war is over, they don't have the same opportunities as white women. So track gave them a way to earn a living besides cleaning toilets and scrubbing floors. Only white women are considered worthy of being wives and mothers. We live in a whitewashed society. Bea had even been a nurse in the African campaign.

The Army wouldn't let her treat white soldiers. The Negro nurses had to take care of wounded Nazi prisoners. Bea finally went back to work in a Negro hospital. I don't know where Ari ended up."

"I often wondered what became of you during the war."

"Dove and I played in a women's baseball league until the owners demanded we wear tutus and makeup and have our hair done for the games and show a lot of leg. Then we found a sport that really suited us. We hired ourselves out as stringers for a women's traveling industrial basketball team.

"The games had free throw contests which were okay. That was just part of basketball, but we quit when sponsors started turning the games into beauty pageants. A lot of the girls didn't mind. Playing on a basketball team and traveling from city to city and getting paid to do it was the only chance they had in their lives to break away from farms and small towns and working in factories and textile mills."

An illicit carnival atmosphere of decay hung over The Greenwich Village streets. Licentiousness lurked behind the wall to wall brownstone flats, groceries, pawn shops, and secondhand thrift stores protected with barred windows and steel net barriers. Alluring pink and purple and red and green and gold neon signs invited curiosity seekers and patrons to honky-tonks and cellared dens of iniquity, which was where we descended, Fugazzi's Bar and Grill.

The night club was filling up fast. Dove aggressively claimed a table and we planted ourselves on stiff wooden chairs in the smoky, dimly lit atmosphere heavy with the odor of wine and beer.

An attractive lithe young woman with straight long blonde hair was sitting on a tall stool at the open mic on stage. Accompanying herself with an acoustic guitar, her melodic mezzo soprano voice warbled a dolorous folk song in a minor key. She finished to scattered applause from an audience which had come for the evening's main event.

There was no mistaking Allen Ginsberg when he took the stage greeted by a standing ovation. He nodded through his voluminous dark beard and raised his palms for people to sit and remain quiet. Three bottles of beer appeared on our table and the waitress quickly withdrew. Ginsberg waited for a full minute for all sound to fade to complete silence before he launched into the recitation of a medley of poems, from memory. A young male guitarist accompanied him during segments that he chanted. The audience hung on every word of his poetic diatribe against capitalism and conformity, themes I had just read about in Kerouac's book.

When we returned to the flat, I watched Dove smoke marijuana. She offered me the joint. I shook my head.

"Pussy."

"Tess doesn't smoke."

"She's an athlete. You're a housewife. You probably need it."

"I don't need it. It's not me."

"You don't know what's you. That's why you're down here."

I thought there was some truth in her comment, but I didn't admit it.

I finished reading Kerouac's book before falling asleep. I thought that, in their own way, Tess and Dove were wandering souls like Jack Kerouac and his friend, Neal Cassidy. Independent, steeped in counterculture protest, seeking spiritual enlightenment, they had adopted a lifestyle that rejected the post war middle class values of suburban homes, material goods, and housewifery.

And here I was, contributing to a strong healthy society through family stability. Only, my family wasn't stable. According to the propaganda and tenets of the times, I was supposed to stay home and take care of my husband and children in support of national security. I was also supposed to be a patriotic American by spending money and buying products to support capitalism against communism.

The next morning, I said goodbye and left their pad. Carrying one of Dove's paintings wrapped in butcher paper and twine under my arm, I rode the subway to Grand Central Station, and caught an early afternoon train to Boston.

Chapter 29

Unhealthy Alliance

After my foray into Greenwich Village and being called a pussy housewife by Dove, I decided I needed to do something more with my life. I related my investigative reporting experience with the Miami Signal at the beginning of the war and submitted a few freelance editorials to the Boston Herald for review before the managing editor would consider offering me a job as an investigative reporter. I did not have to look far for something to investigate.

On the strength of his popularity as the Supreme Commander of Allied Forces who had led the European campaign against Germany, Eisenhower had been elected President in 1953. By the end of his Presidency in 1961, he did an unexpected turnabout and warned the public what had been happening on the heels of war production mobilization since the war and the need to sustain our democratic society for future generations.

Driven by the postwar conflict with the Soviet Union, the New Deal reform programs to benefit American citizens had been given low priority by Congress. Political and economic forces raised the specter of defense companies collaborating with the military on weapons research, design, and production in the cold war competition with the Soviet Union for global dominance.

While reporting on social reform movements during the 1950s that circulated around my sister, Tess and her partner, Dove, I inadvertently discovered my husband, Eddie, and his father, Congressman Gebhardt, were right in the middle of partisan politics that supported the corporate and military alliance.

This political conflict gave me an opening and opportunity to restart my career as a journalist while I continued working on my book for Justine.

The managing editor acknowledged that being the daughter-in-law of Congressman Gebhardt had some cache and would lead to insider sources and newsworthy information. I didn't let on that I had no contact with my father-in-law. Other than my being Eddie's wife, he knew little or nothing about me. Whatever Eddie might have shared with him never entered our stormy disagreements until my discovery.

Gladys was the only person in my life who understood me. For a woman from a previous generation and its repressive culture, she would listen to my grievances and tirades in a nonjudgmental way. She was and always had been my closest friend.

She congratulated me on taking a job at the Herald. "It will be good for you to get out into the world. Staying cooped up writing in the library all the time is not healthy."

Against my wishes, Eddie Jr. was now enrolled in a private residential school. I would see him only on holidays. I decided not to tell Eddie about my job decision. He would show no interest anyway.

He had voiced no objection to my sleeping in my childhood bed for the past year. We rarely ate dinner at the same time at the same table. I preferred to eat in the kitchen with Gladys. Our marriage was a sham. We barely existed for each other anymore.

Looking back, I was extremely depressed that Eddie had stolen my son away from me, just as Dove had once stolen my sister, and my mother had stolen my friend, Millie.

Here I was a wife and mother at the age of thirty-six, living with a mentally disturbed estranged husband and our cook and housekeeper. I had arrived at a point in my life where it was time I stole something for myself. . . my self-respect.

Paper Dolls

Getting into a defense contractor aircraft plant as a visitor was not an easy task. Due to the technological advancements being made and suspicion that Russian communist spies might be embedded in the population, the security check I had to endure was vastly more thorough than during the war when I was in Miami. My being a news reporter did not help matters. The three guards who detained me at the gate were even more suspicious when I told them I was there to gather information.

They led me into the blockhouse, emptied the contents of my purse and conducted a pat down. Even though I now had a driver's license, they didn't trust my laminated press card. They called the human resources office at the Herald to verify my identity.

After fifteen minutes, the desk officer received a call back and nodded to one of his assistants, a solid muscular guard whose dark whiskered scowl matched his disposition. With a visitor badge pinned to my lapel, I followed him through a connecting passage to the main building and down a long hall to the barren office of the public relations manager, Lewis Nunn. His short-clipped hair, taut face, and solicitous manner as he offered me a chair left me feeling uncomfortable, more like I was being interrogated and admitted into a prison by a Government agent than about to be given a guided tour.

I watched his dry lips moving through a rehearsed speech about safety and secrecy. His predatory smile hovered above me confirming that I read and signed the nondisclosure document he placed in front of me on the table.

He closely escorted me out onto the factory floor where two lines of F-100 fighter jets were being assembled by several hundred workers. The staccato grind of rivet guns and whine of high-speed drills recalled my days sleuthing about defense plants in Miami, but for a different purpose.

Lewis knew his subject matter and clearly loved to brag about his knowledge of fighter jets. He himself had been a pilot during the war and made sure I knew that about him. Not even in the interest of making a

288

connection did I mention my husband had been a pilot. Lewis needed to feel important.

He made a point of the need for constantly improving the technical capabilities of the F-100 in design, navigational maneuverability, and delivery of payload. Most of the jargon was new to me, but I took notes.

He elaborated on rates of fire, projectile lethality, and weapons range. He stressed "pilots will no longer have to sight by naked eye. Radar is being introduced. The aerodynamic design is well in advance of our enemy. We are in the forefront of defending America against nuclear aggression by deterrence and interception."

After an hour of walking around and observing the tooling, machining, metal forming and dimensional inspections, wiring, engine building and installation, hydraulic brake system testing, and instrument panel checks, we came to the end of the line. Regulations prohibited me from witnessing startup and shutdown procedures, and takeoff and landing and flight tests.

Upon returning to Lewis's office, he asked, "Does that give you what you need? I tried to be as thorough as possible within what I'm authorized to show and tell you."

"Thank you, Lewis. The tour was educational and very comprehensive. I appreciate you taking the time and providing explanations."

"Do you have any further questions?"

"No, if I do or my editor does, we'll get back to you."

"Speaking of which, the company president and I want to review your story before it goes to press. Actually, before you submit it to your editor, we need to have a look at it to verify the accuracy and security of your information and what you are saying."

"My editor has priority in reading and approving news features. However, I will pass along your request to him."

Lewis's expression hardened in a threatening manner. "You do realize that you can be indicted and go to Federal prison for anything you say that is out-of-line."

"What I write will be validated and verified by the editor. We comply with the first amendment of The Constitution. You've given me such a wonderful tour; may I occasionally quote you in the article?"

"Absolutely not. What I have shared with you is confidential. You may not use my name."

"Duly noted. The article will be informational, only based on fact."

The hard grip of his parting handshake was intended as a warning, which I chose to ignore.

I did not go searching for the information Eddie left open and available on our library desk. He had been working late on a contract and left the documents exposed. He slept in the next morning, a Saturday. When I came downstairs and entered the library, I intended only to straighten up the desk so I could get to my own work, but certain blatant phrases caught my eye and I read on.

At the risk of Eddie seeing me in the library with his open documents on the desk, I decided I could not safely work at home that day. I had previously had breakfast and coffee and was now anxious to get out of the house before Eddie woke and came down. I drove downtown to the newsroom.

When the story broke, the reference to profiteering by industry through bribery and propaganda to increase profits and alter government regulations suddenly thrust the news edition and me into unwanted and disastrous prominence.

Eddie was outraged when he discovered I had used his confidential information as a news source. He drove from his office and stormed into the house shouting my name. "Gwen, if you're upstairs, then get the hell down here!"

I didn't respond. I knew why he was upset. I would let him come to me. I heard him racing down the hall. He paused at the kitchen and looked in at Gladys. "Where is she? Is she out?"

"She's in the library."

He swept through the door and slammed the newspaper on the desk sending my manuscript pages flying.

"What the fuck do you think you're doing? Your name's on this!"

"I'm working for the Herald. The editor put me on assignment."

"Fuck the editor! You bitch! You're deranged! You're a lunatic! You're not supposed to think or meddle in my business. You think you can get back at me by sabotaging me? What you have done could cost me my job and get me arrested by the FBI. I could be fired tomorrow, except for one important thing that you didn't know about me, but I'm telling you now. I'm a registered lobbyist. That is my saving grace. I can legally work and intercede on behalf of defense companies to promote legislation that is profitable for them. Understanding that is beyond your pea-brain mentality. Now, what you are doing and have done is all going to come to an end."

The attempted lawsuit brought against me and the newspaper was dropped in the face of the Constitutional First Amendment citing freedom of the press.

To distance himself from me, Eddie filed for divorce. The divorce coupled with Eddie's restraining order to prevent me from seeing my son motivated me to finish my book. I sent the manuscript to Justine in New York. She called me and said that as soon as she completed the edit, the book would be published and released within three months.

Six years later, when President Eisenhower's second term ended, a section of his departing speech validated what I had written about the military industrial complex.

"We can no longer risk emergency improvisation of national defense; we have been compelled to create a permanent armaments industry of vast proportions. Added to this, three and a half million men and women are directly engaged in the defense establishment. We annually spend on military security more than the net income of all United States corporations.

This conjunction of an immense military establishment and a large arms industry is new in the American experience. The total influence -- economic, political, even spiritual -- is felt in every city, every State house, every office of the Federal government. We recognize the imperative need for this development. Yet we must not fail to comprehend its grave implications. Our toil, resources and livelihood are all involved; so is the very structure of our society. . .

Only an alert and knowledgeable citizenry can compel the proper meshing of the huge industrial and military machinery of defense with our peaceful methods and goals, so that security and liberty may prosper together."

Chapter 30

Civil Disobedience

Tess suddenly dropped out of sight in the sports world news. I didn't find out why until she appeared in another kind of news.

There were thousands of men who called Tess and Dove troublemakers. Thousands of women saw them as rebels and leaders of change. I worried what would happen to them by those who hated and despised them. Letters to the editor and news announcers castigated them. They were accused of being communists and of sedition. They were called enemies and a challenge to American values. Trading on Tess's name, they organized marches and protests and strikes against unfair treatment of women and union workers which put them right into the sights of the FBI.

For the second time, Tess and I were a political embarrassment to Congressman Gebhardt. He wanted Tess and Dove arrested and locked away for violating the Taft-Hartley Act, which prohibited radical leaders and attempted to repress the labor movement by limiting labor unions' right to strike. Unions had agreed not to strike during the war but with the conclusion of the war, that promise was no longer in effect. 14.8 million workers had union contracts and they wanted better pay, benefits, and working conditions.

The National Association of Manufacturers, for which Eddie now worked as a lobbyist, wanted to crush them, or at least render them powerless.

Tess must have remembered where the back door key was hidden. Gladys heard them rummaging around in the kitchen looking for something to eat and came out with Ekkehardt to see who had broken in.

As soon as Ekkehardt turned on the light, Tess and Dove dropped to the floor.

"Turn it off," Tess shouted. "Turn it off. Leave it dark."

Ekkehardt did not question the urgency of her voice and flipped the wall switch to off. By then, I was stumbling along the hall.

"Tess, what is it?" asked Gladys. "What are you doing here? Why the secrecy?"

"I'll tell you later," said Tess. "Right now, we need to eat. We're starving."

"Go up and get Gwen," said Gladys to Ekkehardt.

"I'm in my pajamas."

"That's okay. She needs to come down."

"I'm here," I said. "I heard your voices."

Tess opened the refrigerator enough to see inside without allowing too much light to escape.

"There's a casserole," said Gladys. "I'll heat it up for you."

"Not necessary," said Tess. "We'll eat it cold." She pulled the casserole dish out of the refrigerator and set it on the table while Gladys pulled open a cupboard drawer for utensils.

"Tess, it's Gwen," I said.

"I know who you are."

"You wouldn't be here unless you were in trouble. What happened?"

"Can't talk now," she mumbled through a mouthful of sausage and cheese and noodle casserole.

"Okay, eat." I listened to them chomping away between gasping intakes of breath. "Can I at least turn on a flashlight?"

"Okay, but don't shine it up here. Keep it down low."

"How about some milk?" asked Dove. "You got any milk?"

Gladys reached into the refrigerator for a quart of milk, then shuffled over to the cupboard for glasses.

Dove popped the top of the milk bottle open. "We don't need glasses." She raised the bottle to her lips and swallowed three large gulps before handing it to Tess, who did the same.

Wiping her mouth with the back of her hand, Tess asked, "What about bread?"

Gladys tore off chunks from a loaf and placed them next to the shared casserole dish.

"God, that's good," said Dove. "You're a fantastic cook, Gladys. We'd move right in with you, except we can't stay."

"Who's after you?" I asked.

"FBI agents," said Tess.

"An informant ratted on us," said Dove. "The FBI has infiltrated any organization that is protesting how woman and union workers are unfairly treated. If I could find her, I'd beat the shit outta her. But she kept outta sight when the Feds came. We had some warning, so we could get away. My brother, Colum 'll get her though. He's a union steward."

"We've been on the run all night," said Tess. "We took the subway and changed stops three times to throw them off our trail. Except for bums and grifters, all the men started looking like they could be Federal agents. We didn't dare show our faces at Grand Central Station. They'd be watching for us."

"How did you get out of the city?" I asked.

"Fishing boat," said Dove.

"Fishing boat?"

"Yeah, we hung around the harbor and paid a fisherman to bring us up the coast to Boston Bay. He let us off at Chelsea and we walked the rest of the way through town. It's been a long fuckin' night. We can sleep in my room."

"I get the bed," said Dove. "You can have the floor."

"Fuck you," said Tess.

"Not tonight. Some other time."

"Tess," Gladys's hands flew to her mouth.

"Sorry, Gladys. They're just words, just words. We're tired and out of sorts."

"You know the FBI will come here looking for you," I said.

"That's why we can't stay long," said Tess.

"Where will you go?"

"Haven't worked that out yet. We have to leave the country. Haven't figured how."

"Canada's close."

"Not safe enough or far enough and getting there is a problem."

"You can take my car."

"Too risky and if we're caught, you'll be implicated. You shouldn't have to pay for what we're doing."

Dove stretched and yawned. "I'm going up and taking the bed."

"You can have it," said Tess. "I'll sleep down here on the couch."

"I'll get you a pillow and blankets," said Gladys.

Ekkehardt moved from where he stood listening in the doorway to let her pass. She hurriedly left the kitchen to escape hearing any more foul language.

Before I returned to bed, I joined Ekkehardt talking with Tess in the living room while she arranged the pillow and blankets on the couch.

"I've been sailing your father's yacht," he said. "It's in good shape. You can use it to leave the country."

"Why are you talking about my father's yacht? I don't know enough about sailing. And why do you even care?"

"I was incarcerated for four years in a prison camp because of my German heritage. If I can help you escape, it's the least I can do against how the Government punished me and how it is persecuting you."

"I will go with you," said Ekkehardt. "I will teach you and your friend how to sail."

"You're just going to leave Gladys? She's your wife."

297

"Only for a short time. After we reach Florida, I'll leave you and return home. By then, you and Dove will have the skills to sail and navigate in any seas."

"Florida is still in the country."

"The islands of the Caribbean are not. South America is not. You'll be expatriates wherever you go, but you will be free."

"Can we talk about this after I get some sleep? And Dove has to be in on this."

"Yes, but I have to provision the boat tomorrow. We will want to stay away from the coast as much as possible."

"Thank you, Ekkehardt. I haven't known many good men in my life. You're a good man."

"We are not so different. Sleep well."

Tess closed her eyes.

Three local FBI agents showed up at our door, flashed their badges, and asked me to let them come in. I recognized one of them, Cyrus McNab, from the time I had tried to find out what the FBI had done with Gladys when she had been arrested and interned at the beginning of the war.

"What for?" I asked. "I haven't done anything. Why are you here? What do you want?"

"We're looking for your sister and her friend. They've committed treason against the United States Government."

"I'm sorry I can't help you. I haven't seen her or heard from her for the last three years."

"Where did you see her?"

"In New York. She lived in Greenwich Village."

"We know where she lived. She's a fugitive. We suspect they came here."

"Well, they never came here and they're not here."

"We want to check the house."

"Do you have a warrant?"

"My badge is my warrant." Agent McNab's threatening voice did not intimidate me. No man was going to intimidate me again, for any reason, ever.

By the time McNab returned with a legal warrant, Tess, Dove, and Ekkehardt were sailing far south along the coast over a deep blue sea.

Chapter 31

Sand In Our Shoes

I associated palm trees and the war with the turning point of my life. When I first met Mary Wenger, we talked about the exotic environment, white sand beaches, and the tropical beauty of the house in which we stayed while our husbands underwent officer training before being sent overseas. That was when I mentioned having sand in our shoes and that the happy memories of our time in Florida would draw us back again.

My national book tour took me to Chicago and to Rockford, Illinois, where I knew Mary Wenger and her family lived. Since I didn't know her address, I hoped she might see the advance publicity about my book signing and come to see me at the Faust Hotel in downtown Rockford.

One of the main concepts in my book was that the male culture, the male mystique, defines femaleness as a desired status. During my years as a new adult woman, the cotillion of our youth and marriage were valued as the highest standards of achievement.

I had written about women who belied the stereotypes. My sister, Tess, and her partner, Dove, were the antithesis of those stereotypes. They were not soft and pliant. They were not intellectually inferior to men. They were not unstable and hysterical. They were not pure and innocent. They were strong, unique, individual, and independent.

Millie Dietz, a living paper doll, continued to find success as a fashion model. Her wide-shouldered, slim-waisted, narrow-hipped silhouette appeared in designs by some of the active fashion houses, Lanvin, Maggy Rouff, Vionnet, Schiaparelli and Chanel.

Chapter 32

The Signing

The book signing was to take place in the lobby of the Faust Hotel on a Tuesday from 1:00 to 3:00 in the afternoon. I assumed that Mary Wenger had children and they would be in school, so she would be free to stop by and see me.

I took a taxi from the airport to the fifteen story brownstone building. The penthouse tower overlooking the river rose above all others at the center of town.

Wanting to make an appropriate impression, except for earrings and a pearl necklace, I down-played a glamorous appearance, which many readers had come to expect, and dressed like a modern businesswoman. My hair was still long like when Mary and I had known one another in Miami during the war. I hoped she would easily recognize me and that I would recognize her. We had not seen each other for twelve years.

From my hotel room window, I noticed the traffic coming into town wasn't heavy at that time of day. I had arrived the evening before and met with my publicist, who had made all the arrangements and would be displaying copies of the book.

By 1:00 o'clock, the lobby was packed and had been set up with stanchions and velvet ropes for crowd control. Although I was engaged in snippets of conversation with customers, I saw Mary Wenger join the long line moving at a snail's pace up one row and down another, edging us closer by increments to the white linen-covered table stacked high with copies of the book. A seated cashier and her smiling assistant were busy at one end taking money and handing out books.

She saw me signing copies and chatting briefly with each customer. She crab stepped and edged along until she was finally in front of me. Although she wore her brownish-blonde hair cut short in a fifties style, her alert blue eyes and beautiful Czech features were unmistakable.

That she was dressed and looked like a businesswoman intrigued me. I had only thought of her becoming a housewife and mother. She wore dark low-heel shoes and a dark wool suit. A plum blouse topped with a single strand of fake pearls rounded out her image. A subtle touch of rouge, lipstick and eyeliner gave her a youthful glow.

"Mary! I was hoping you would be here. How many years has it been?"

"Hi, Gwen, congratulations on your book." She handed her purchased copy across the table to me. "I wouldn't miss seeing you. You look gorgeous as always, even more now that you're famous."

I'm sure I looked to her every inch the successful businesswoman whose professional black and white photograph dominated the back cover of the book. I did appear a little tired and older but my luxurious shoulder-length hair hadn't changed. I had added a few pounds that did not detract from my voluptuous figure, but basically, I was still Gwen.

"Oh, stop it. Give me a minute to sign this." I chattered on while she watched the brief note and slash of my signature appear on an inside cover page.

"I figured you and Bob would settle in Rockford after the war. I'm sorry we lost contact with each other. Life has a way of doing that to us. How is Bob?"

"He's fine."

"He made it through the war okay."

"Some recurring malaria."

"Eddie shot down the thirty Jap zeroes he was always talking about," I lied, not knowing why.

"I remember," she said.

"Now he's following his father's footsteps in Washington. He's a lobbyist."

"That sounds right for him."

"What about Bob? What's he doing?"

Mary hesitated. I could see she hadn't expected the question but was prepared with an answer. "He's an aerospace sales executive. Large territory to manage. He's hardly ever home."

"That happened to Eddie and me. Not being home. We're divorced. Not seeing each other. Only, I was the one hardly ever home. But the real reason is that I was writing news stories critical of the military industrial complex and he was a war hero. I was an embarrassment to him. We have a son though, Edward Eddie Jr. He goes to an elite boarding school. We only see him on Holidays. I'm sure you and Bob have children. How many?"

"Three, two boys and a girl."

"Listen. I'm here for only one night and I have to keep this line moving. Cou you and Bob join me for dinner here at the hotel this evening around seven?"

"Unfortunately, Bob's out of town on business and I wouldn't be able to fin sitter for the kids on short notice." Nudged by the next woman in line next to he Mary started to move on. "I look forward to reading your book. Congratulations on your success."

"It's wonderful to see you again, Mary. Here," she pushed a notepad across the table to me. "Write down your address and phone number. Maybe we can g together some other time." My glance shifted to the next woman now standing front of me.

Mary quickly jotted her address and phone number, raised her hand in a fir farewell, then maneuvered to the exit.

I don't know why I lied about Eddie's delusional heroics during the war. Perhaps it was a gesture acknowledging a happier time in my life. Mary Wenger had never been impressed with Eddie in the first place. I had sensed she intensely disliked him. Her calm, kind, decent husband, Bob, was the complete opposite of Eddie.

I wished now that I had met and married a Bob.

***

Not only did my son stop talking to me ten years ago, but he also wouldn't let me see my three grandchildren. I didn't think I could have done anything so drastic that he would turn against me in such a manner. He has a different view of what happened over the years, but he wasn't the only one on the receiving end. I was first in line. I didn't desert my son. He and his father deserted me.

His father's influence is behind the rift. Not just a rift, a chasm. At first, I blamed the war for his change in personality and how he treated me. In looking back, I was making an excuse, deluding myself as to how he had always been. His outer fun-loving, jokester, hail-well-met personality had masked an edginess and underlying cruelty that transferred to our son.

My attempts at being a loving, nurturing mother seemed not to matter. Eddie Junior wanted to be like his father, a swaggering, bragging hard-drinking fighter pilot, who couldn't leave the war behind once it was over. The residue of the war clung to all of us for the rest of our lives.

It was the small naturally occurring things that I didn't think about when I was growing up that mattered now. Things like a smile or a kind word. Now, except for commercial magazine ads with gleaming female teeth and glossy lips, people accosted me with scowls, especially men.

What bothered me most were the death threats, my tires slashed, and rocks heaved through my front windows. Who would have thought ideology could generate such backlash. But then, a world war had just been fought because of differences in ideology.

Of course, all the negative publicity had the unintended effect of increasing the sales of *Paper Dolls*. It also had the unintended effect of destroying my family, not a price I gladly paid. But the war had more to do with that destruction than my writing. In retrospect, thanks to my older sister, becoming who I was at the time was probably inevitable.

Unable to break free from traditional 1950s conservative ways of thinking about themselves as sexual objects and second-class citizens, there were legions of good Christian women who hated me for laying bare their subjugation and challenging them to assert themselves and change their lives.

A greater number hailed my book as "a landmark for women's equality in a male-dominated society."

Members of the clergy assailed and disparaged me in the press for attempting to "undermine the holy sanctity of marriage and motherhood in the eyes of God," and called me "Satan's mouthpiece."

Among the shifting morass of humanity, I wondered what had become of my sister, Tess, and her friend, Dove Delaney. I never heard from them again until one day I received an unmarked post card with the colorful photo of a village beach in Costa Rica.

Epilogue

Lately, not out of morbid curiosity, I've been reading obituaries. Most are lengthy mini-biographies of some very interesting people who accomplished significant achievements during their lifetimes. Most died of a terminal illness or their bodies gave out with old age, just about how I feel, but I'm on the outside like a voyeur looking into the window of their lives.

Before long, my mug shot and some words about who I was and what I did will appear in the obituary section, if there is anyone who cares or is still alive to write it. Were she alive, Justine would, but she died two years ago from uterine cancer, the ultimate repression of a woman and so senseless. By the time you're ninety, your uterus is not available for its normal function anyway. It doesn't have to be the cause of your death.

Fortunately, or unfortunately, I haven't had any of the major diseases that can kill you. A couple of minor skin cancers were not serious. My wrinkles and sagging flesh are a greater threat to my diminishing self-awareness.

I've concluded that life is a long journey, an endurance race in which we strive to reach an arbitrary unseen and unknowable finish line. It's the salvation Jack Kerouac wrote about. I have tried my best to define what that might be.

Paper Dolls

Discussion Topics

1. From the beginning, why are Tess Vanderveer and Dove Delaney so competitive? How and why do they depend on each other? Is their relationship symbiotic? What is their mutual attraction?

2. How did Tess assert dominance over her younger sister? What need did she express and from what did it arise? How did Tess's reason become clear by the end of the novel.

3. Why did Gwen admire and worship her older sister?

4. Why was the cook and housekeeper, Glady's Dietz, so important to Gwen as a child and as a young woman?

5. How did Gwen and Tess interact with the chauffeur, George Oswell, and the servants, Harmon and Ivo Nevins?

6. What is the role of resistance in the character relationships? How is resistance a motivating factor for Tess against her parents and between Gwen and Eddie later in the book? Between Dove and her parents?

7. What role does envy play in the novel? Of whom by whom?

8. The concept of prisoners and prisons of various kinds, domestic, social, and military pervade the novel. What characters see themselves as prisoners?

9. What is meant by the artifice of aristocracy? How does Tess react to it?

10. How does Gwen's college roommate, Justine Vogel, invoke and embody the image of a woman who might be considered ahead of her time?

11. What does Gwen mean when she sees Justine as her mentor, as well as a roommate.

12. What is meant by the male mystique? How does the character of Eddie Gebhardt exemplify the male mystique?

13. At the beginning of World War II, Eddie's officer candidate training takes Gwen to Miami, Florida where she and another young Army wife, Mary Wenger, become friends. Mary becomes a subject in Gwen's future book, *Paper Dolls*. From a feminist perspective, what does Mary represent in the book? *(The companion novel, The Discontent of Mary Wenger, gives the full story of her life.)*

14. The statement "We have sand in our shoes" is mentioned several times in the novel. What does it mean to Gwen and to other characters?

15. What is there about Bob Wenger that doesn't fit the male mystique?

16. What gender discrimination does Gwen encounter as a journalist at the Miami Signal?

17. How are women valued during the war as opposed to before and after the war?

18. During the war, how did men propagandize the patriotic sexual role of women as "victory girls" and create the paradox of social and moral female behavior and respectability?

19. Why are women blamed as carriers of venereal disease and not men?

20. What is meant in the novel by "social changes forced by the war and resisted by those who were waging it."

21. How does the war affect Gwen's and Eddie's marriage?

22. How does Gwen's discovery of Tess and Dove change her life?

23. In what ways does the title, Paper Dolls, apply to women in the novel?

24. How does the concept of "an accident of birth" drive the story?

Bibliographical References

Hartmann, Susan M., *The Home Front And Beyond, American Women In The 1940s*, Simon and Schuster McMillan, New York, 1995.

Wise, Nancy Baker and Wise, Christy, *A Mouthful of Rivets, Women At Work In World War II*, Jossey-Bass, Inc., San Francisco, CA, 1994.

Keil, Sally VanWagenen, *Those Wonderful Women In Their Flying Machines,* Four Directions Press, Rhinebeck, NY, 1979.

Distasi, Lawrence W., Branded, How Italian Immigrants Became 'Enemies' during World War II, Sanniti Publications, Bolinas, CA, 2016.

Whyte, William Foote, *Street Corner Society, The Social Structure of An Italian Slum*, The University of Chicago Press, Ltd. Chicago, IL 1943, Fourth Edition, 1993.

Russell, Jan Jarboe, *The Train To Crystal City*, Scribner, New York, 2016.

Hegarty, Marilyn, *Victory Girls, Khaki-Wackies, and Patriotutes, The Regulation of Female Sexuality During World War II*, New York University Press, New York, 2008.

William Gordon, Author, Volstad, Ronald, Illustrator, *Afrika Corps 1941-43*, Elite 34, Osprey Publishing, Scotland, 1991.

Billinger, Jr., Robert D., Hitler's Soldiers In *The Sunshine State, German POWs in Florida*, University Press of Florida, 2009.

Monahan, Evelyn and Neidel-Greenlee, Rosemary, *And If I Perish, Frontline U.S. Army Nurses In World War II*, Anchor Books, New York, 2004.

Steinem, Gloria, *Revolution From Within, A Book of Self-Esteem*, Open Road, Little Brown and Company, New York, 1993.

Cahn, Susan K., *Coming On Strong, Gender and Sexuality In Twentieth-Century Women's Sport*, Harvard University Press, Cambridge, MA, 1995.

Wellesley College News Publications, Archives, 1930s, 1940s.

Leake, Albert H., *The Vocational Education of Girls and Women*, The MacMillan Company, 1918.

Woolf, Virginia, *A Room of One's Own*, Houghton Mifflin Harcourt Publishing, 1929.

Farell, James T., *Studs Lonigan*, The Modern Library, New York, 1938.

Real, Terrence, *I Don't Want To Talk About It, Overcoming The Secret Legacy of Male Depression*, Scribner, New York 1998.

Kardiner, MD, Abram, *Traumatic Neuroses of War*, Mansfield Publishing, Mansfield Centre, CT, 1998.

Ware, Susan, *Partner and I, Molly Dewson, Feminism, and New Deal Politics*, Yale University Press, New Haven, CT 1987.

Kerouac, Jack, *On The Road*, Penguin Books, New York 1957.

Ginsberg, Allen, Edited by Michael Schumacher, *The Essential Ginsberg*, Harper Perennial, New York 2015.

Ledbetter, James, *Unwarranted Influence*, Yale University Press, 2011.

Ellmann, Mary, *Thinking About Women*, Palgrave Macmillan; 1st ed. 1968.

Robert Tucker

Author and retired business and management consultant in a wide range of industries throughout the country, Rob resides with his wife in Southern California.

He is a graduate of the University of California, Santa Barbara and of the University of California, Los Angeles with Bachelor's and Master of Fine Arts Degrees. He is a recipient of the Samuel Goldwyn and Donald Davis Literary Awards and has also worked in advertising, corporate communications, and media production.

An affinity for family and generations pervades his novels.

Robert Tucker

His works are literary and genre fiction that address the nature and importance of personal integrity.

Paper Dolls

***